Mack glanced at Toni and said, "If Clifford is setting you up, how close do you think he is to achieving his goal?"

If? Toni frowned. Did Mack doubt her? "According to the person he was talking to on the phone, he's almost there."

She thought for a moment. It had to be the Harper account he intended using to close the frame tightly around her. "I don't know," she answered.

Mack could tell by the look on Toni's face that she was holding out on him. What could he say to get her to open up to him? And how was he going to handle things with her once she knew his position regarding the case?

THE PERFECT FRAME

BEVERLY CLARK

Genesis Press, Inc.

Indigo

An imprint of Genesis Press, Inc.
Publishing Company

Genesis Press, Inc.
P.O. Box 101
Columbus, MS 39703

ISBN-13: 978-1-58571-240-3
ISBN-10: 1-58571-240-X
Manufactured in the United States of America

First Edition

Visit us at www.genesis-press.com
or call at 1-888-Indigo-1

DEDICATION

I want to thank my children, Catana, Alvin, Jr., Dayna, Ericca and Gloria for being there for me and always believing I could do the impossible. And my friends, Terri, Zuolga, and Lillian for their encouragement.

ACKNOWLEDGMENTS

I'd like to thank Poison Control in Atlanta, Georgia for their help and suggestions. And my friend, Registered Nurse, Doris Smith, and my daughter, Catana Clark, who helped me with the medical aspects of the murders. Also mystery writer, Paul Bishop, who encouraged me to write this book.

PROLOGUE

As Toni Carlton rode the elevator to the tower suite, she was more than a little curious to know why the president of the company had sent for her. He certainly didn't approve of her. In fact, he had made that patently clear on more than one occasion.

Toni had to smile because she was sure it irked the old die-hard chauvinist to admit that she had proven she was good enough at her job to vie for the hallowed position of director at Townsend's Stock Brokerage and Investments (TSBI). She could count on one hand the number of female directors there had been. One was Townsend's sister-in-law and the other a daughter of one of the board members. Was it possible he had decided to extend the proverbial olive branch to her?

Toni tensed when the elevator door opened. Expelling a nervous breath, she steadied herself and stepped out onto the knee-deep, royal blue plush carpet. As she walked down the hall, the blue silk wallpaper, overlaid with an opulent cream and gold-braided design, made her feel every bit as uneasy as Mr. John Victor Townsend Sr. intended her to feel. As one of a small, elite group of successful black businessmen to head up a brokerage firm of this magnitude in California, he wanted all who worked for him to be respectful of his power.

When Toni arrived at the executive office suite, Mildred Frances, Mr. Townsend's personal secretary, greeted her with a smile that was professional, yet at the same time coolly mocking.

"Go right in, Ms. Carlton."

As Toni walked over to the door, she looked back at the woman, wondering if that smile meant she was in for a hard time. Squaring her shoulders, she turned the knob. When she stepped inside, she found Mr. Townsend standing before a floor-to-ceiling window with his back to her. Toni cleared her throat and waited for him to acknowledge her presence. After a few long moments, he finally turned around. Her eyes widened in shock and concern at the distressed, sickly pallor of his face. He took several unsteady steps toward her.

"Are you all right, Mr. Townsend?" Toni asked.

He opened his mouth to speak, but no sound came out. The cup he was holding slipped from his hand and fell to the floor. When his eyelids started to flutter, and he began to sag, Toni rushed toward him, intending to catch him in her arms, but his weight drove them both to the floor. Coming onto her knees, Toni quickly loosened his tie and unbuttoned his shirt collar.

"Mr. Townsend, can you hear me? Is there some medication I can get for you?"

"I—was—wrong—about—" He gasped. "Tell—tell…"

"What, sir?"

A gurgling noise resounded deep in his throat, and then spittle dribbled from his mouth and down his chin.

"Miss Frances, call 911," Toni yelled. "Mr. Townsend—"

Before she could finish her sentence, his eyes closed and he was still. Toni screamed.

The secretary came rushing into the room. "I called 911." She gasped when she saw Mr. Townsend's head cradled in Toni's lap. "What happened?"

Toni gazed up at her. "I'm not sure. He just collapsed. I—I think he's dead."

CHAPTER ONE

Three Months Later

Mackinsey Jessup eyed John Victor Townsend Jr., the newly made president of Townsend Stock Brokerage and Investments with curious dislike. One thing for sure, he was a sorry imitation of his father. Mack had worked for the company five years ago under the senior Townsend, but sensed that working for the son would be a different proposition entirely.

Townsend cleared his throat. "As I mentioned when I contacted you, Mr. Jessup, I have found discrepancies in several of our premier accounts. I suspect an embezzlement scam is going on within the company. Will you take the case?"

"I'm considering it."

"Look, Jessup, if you—"

Mack watched as Townsend nervously moved his fingers through his thin salt and pepper hair.

"If I take the case," Mack cut him off, "the investigation will be handled my way, with no interference from you. Got it?" He smiled at the look of affronted dignity and controlled anger on the other man's face. He could tell that Townsend was aching to rescind the request for his services. But Mack was sure he wouldn't do that because he knew that Jessup Financial Investigations—specializing in corporate theft—happened to be the best in Los Angeles, in the state, Mack would go so far as to say. It was no brag, just fact.

"All right, Jessup," Townsend conceded through stiff lips. "Handle this your way."

"Good. Now the first thing I need you to do is get me a copy of all the portfolios that have been tampered with, or that you suspect have been tampered with. Oh, and I'll need to check out your account books, personnel files, computer disks, printouts; in essence, everything."

Townsend's exasperated brown eyes suddenly brightened. "Don't you want to know who I suspect is the thief?"

Mack arched his brows speculatively. "You have proof to support your allegations?"

"No, but—"

A sardonic smile curved Mack's mouth. "As I said before, Mr. Townsend, leave the investigating to me."

"How soon do you want the information?" Townsend gritted out.

"Now would be a good time since all of the employees have left for the day."

"But that means that I'll have to personally—"

"Retrieve the information? Exactly."

As she sat eyeing the stack of reports and sales figures yet to analyze, Toni sighed and brushed back stray wisps of wavy black hair that had escaped from her upswept hairstyle. The thought of working overtime this evening didn't appeal to her at all. She enjoyed her job as personal assistant to the CEO, but sometimes…

Pat Davis, the department's executive secretary, glanced at the clock on the wall. "It's almost quitting time, Toni. You're not working late again tonight, are you?"

Before Toni could answer, Hank Warren, the other personal assistant to the CEO, walked over to them and answered.

"Of course she is. Have to rack up those brownie points. Right, sweetheart? Lucky for you old Townsend conveniently up and died." He smirked. "Damn lucky, I'd say. It was like you arranged it. Sure you didn't knock the old guy off?" He laughed, then cleared his throat and said, "You think you've got it made now, don't you, Miss Efficiency? Save your energy, Toni. That directorship is as good as mine."

"You mean because you're male? That's not a prerequisite to success anymore, Hanky Panky," Toni said in a sugary-sweet voice. She watched his eyes flash and his jaw clench with barely suppressed temper, knowing good and well how much he hated being called that. Toni shifted her attention back to Pat, completely ignoring him, and smiled. "In answer to your question, Pat, not tonight."

Toni's phone buzzed. She picked up the receiver. "Yes, Mr. Clifford. If you need them for tomorrow's conference meeting, then of course I can stay. No problem."

"You'll be here alone with the boss," Hank said thoughtfully. "Could it be those brownie points will be racked up in, shall we say, more personal ways?" The look he gave Toni before arrogantly striding from the office was riddled with amused malice.

"Whew! If looks could kill," Pat quipped.

Toni shrugged. "Do I look like I'm scared?"

"You really shouldn't call him Hanky Panky to his face, even if most of the girls in the company do it behind his back."

"Maybe not, but the man is so full of himself I couldn't resist."

Pat shook her head, then turned off her computer. "I'd better get moving. Joe's waiting for me downstairs, and tonight I don't dare be late. It's Monday. You know what that means."

"Monday night football!" they chorused.

"What it really means is that I'll be relegated to playing waitress and serving my armchair quarterback popcorn and beer while he watches the game. I'm an executive secretary, for crying out loud." A comic pout shaped her lips and mock resentment tinged her voice. "You'd think I'd risen above that. But not as far as Joe is concerned." She glanced at Toni. "So it looks like you're going to be working over-time after all."

"Mr. Clifford needs my help."

Pat plowed on. "For the last six months, no, make it the last year and a half, you've worked late three or four days out of every week. You bucking for sainthood by way of an early grave?"

"Neither. I don't mind the extra work, so give it a rest, Pat."

"Is the possibility of getting the promotion what's driving you so hard?"

"It's not the only reason."

"You're out to prove something, then."

"No woman starts at the bottom of the success ladder and reaches the position I have in so short a time without drive and ambition."

"And don't forget hard work, above and beyond the call of duty. I hope Mr. Clifford appreciates the sacrifices you're making, like putting your love life on the back burner."

"Joe is waiting for you, Pat," Toni reminded her.

She sighed. "You're right, and he is." Pat grabbed her purse and sweater, then sliced her friend a curious look. "You do have a love life, don't you, Toni? You do go out?"

"On occasion." Toni averted her gaze.

"When was the last time?" Pat asked in a coaxing voice intended to draw out confidences.

"Pat!"

"Oh, all right," she said, slipping her purse strap over her shoulder. "I'm outta here."

As Toni watched her friend leave, a feeling of relief washed over her. She liked Pat, but sometimes…Toni glanced at the clock. If she hurried and finished the requested stock analysis, she could be ready to leave in an hour. Admittedly, she was beginning to feel more stressed lately. Maybe the long work weeks were getting to her, but it would all be worth it once she got the promotion.

Toni had worked for TSBI three and a half, going on four, years. She'd started out as a stock and investment consultant trainee, and in the short span of three years she'd taken classes and had worked her way up to assistant to the CEO, Frank Clifford. He had promised her a bright future if she could prove she was up to the challenge. Despite Hank's asinine insinuation that she was sleeping her way to the top, they both knew she was doing a damn good job. And that was what really rankled people.

It was Toni's dream to carve a permanent niche for herself at Townsend's. Most of the people—the majority of them in the top positions at Townsend's—stayed on until they retired. More than anything, she wanted job security, a feeling of belonging, permanence, something she'd rarely experienced in her twenty-six years.

Toni got up from her seat and walked over to the coffee machine to pour herself a cup. She drank her coffee black, allowing no additives to dull her senses. It was all-important that she be sharp, alert and ready for any challenge. She carried her coffee to her desk, sat back in the chair, and after a few swallows of the strong, steamy stimulant set the cup down and swiveled her chair around to face the computer screen. Then she accessed the accounts portfolio menu, then went right into the Harper Bond Exchange file.

She was ready to begin the sales comparison and stock analysis, but what she saw a minute later made her eyes widen in confusion. The sales figure for the common bonds this month and the previous two should have been recorded on the fifteenth. She checked the codes against the names on the bonds. They matched, but when she punched in confirmation, it showed they had been confirmed on the sixteenth in the two previous months. She would have to ask Pat about these entries. Evidently the dates or the codes or something had been wrongly entered.

How odd.

Pat was too good at what she did to overlook a mistake like this. Toni frowned. There had been similar instances in other accounts, but every time she'd gone in to investigate and shown it to the CEO, he had logically explained them away. So maybe she was going looney tunes.

All right, girl, get back to work so you can go home, fix yourself a quick dinner and relax in a hot tub.

Toni moved on to the next report. But the Harper account continued to prey on her mind. She stopped, cleared the screen and brought up the account again to check the percentage figures. According to what she was seeing the bonds had sold at 60% of their market value. But no details of the transaction had been recorded. She shook her head, wondering why they hadn't been.

"I'm ready to leave now, Toni," Mr. Clifford announced. "Have you finished the report?"

At the sound of her boss's voice, she shifted her gaze away from her computer screen and glanced up at him. "I have a few more things to check out before I'm done, sir. It won't be much longer."

He smiled, easing his hip onto her desk. "I've asked you to call me Frank." He cleared his throat as he continued to watch her. "You're certainly a conscientious young woman. It's a rare quality these days. I can tell you. I intend to see that you are amply rewarded."

She smiled. "Thank you, sir."

"Now, none of that sir business. Call me Frank."

Toni's smile faltered and she hurried to complete the report, waited for it to print, then handed it to him.

He took the report and checked through it.

Toni watched him. Something about the man disturbed her, even though she couldn't quite put a name to it. He seemed fair and supportive of his employees, her anyway. And he was an attractive older man, but there were times when she felt weird vibes coming from him.

He smiled, nodding his head. "As usual, you've done an excellent job. Come on, let me walk you out." He waved his hand for her to precede him.

Toni ached to examine the Harper account in more depth, but it would have to wait.

Several days after the monthly board meeting, Toni was in the hall outside the boardroom when she noticed the rigidity in Mr. Townsend's steps as he walked over to the elevator. She felt sorry for the man. His latest proposal had been shot down. It had to be a humiliating experience for a company president. He was certainly not the force to be reckoned with that his father had been. For one thing, he lacked the man's innate ruthlessness. Even though the senior Townsend was dead and his son was now president and chairman of the board, it was as though he were pulling strings from the grave.

"Maybe I was wrong about you playing hot and heavy with old Frank to get the promotion, Toni," Hank said, walking up behind her. "The way you were eyeing his son just now leads me to believe that you're setting your goals higher these days. Maybe it's Nina Townsend who should be worried."

"Has that thing you call a brain taken up permanent residence in the sewer, Hanky Panky? To you nothing is sacred, is it? You must want that promotion awfully bad."

"And I'm going to get it, too, never fear. No one, especially a woman, has ever beat me out of anything. And I don't intend to let a new trend get started."

"There's always a first time for everything. And you won't always be able to stop the wave of the future, Hanky."

"Don't call me that, damn it!"

The look in his cold, black eyes and harshly handsome African-American features chilled her to the bone. The menacing look on his face was so frightening, she jumped when he shifted the subject to the death of the elder Townsend.

"I wonder if a stroke was what really killed the old man. Maybe he was having an affair with you and it proved to be more than his body could handle." A nasty grin distorted his face. "You were alone with him when he died. I wonder, sweetheart, are you pretty poison or what?"

With that he walked away, leaving Toni seething.

"I'm glad you suggested we eat Italian today, Toni," Pat commented.

"Me too." Toni grinned. "Even if I don't know what I want to order."

"Just the thought of Mr. Angeletti's lasagna makes my mouth water," Pat confided as they followed the hostess.

The Italian Kitchen was Toni's favorite restaurant. And not because she happened to be part Italian. The prices were reasonable, the pasta was the best in town. The hostess showed them to a table near the garden, just off the outside terrace.

Minutes later a waiter arrived with the menus. Pat ordered lasagna; Toni decided on the pasta salad. The waiter had taken their orders and left when Toni saw Mr. Townsend, his wife Nina, and Frank Clifford being shown to a table in the restaurant's VIP section.

Toni's eyes narrowed in barely contained dislike as she studied Nina Townsend's long, brassy-blond, thickly weaved hairstyle, heavy makeup, and the way she dressed, as though she were a twenty-year-old hoochie mama instead of a forty-something wife of a wealthy black businessman. The overly long fire-engine red nails reminded Toni of dragon claws. And the way the woman flirted shamelessly with Mr. Clifford, with her husband sitting right there, turned Toni's stomach.

"It's enough to make you lose your appetite, isn't it?" Pat wrinkled her nose.

"Poor Mr. Townsend. I wonder how he could have ever married a woman like that."

"Isn't that the way it usually happens? There's just no accounting for taste."

After finishing their lunch, Toni and Pat returned to the office. Toni picked up the report she'd started working on before lunch and was deep into studying it when Hank Warren came storming out of the CEO's office and stalked past her. In his hurry to leave, he just missed colliding with Pat Davis. Toni wondered what had happened between him and the boss.

"What did you say to piss him off this time?" Pat asked.

"Not a thing, I swear," Toni answered. "Forget about Hank. Listen, Pat, I need to talk to you about the Harper account."

"The Harper account?" She frowned.

Toni swivelled her chair around to face the computer screen and accessed the Harper account, but when she did, she noticed that some of the facts and figures had been altered. What had happened to the mistakes? Who had changed them?

Could it have been Hank? And Mr. Clifford had found out and that was reason he'd stormed out?

"I found some mistakes the other day, but now they seemed to have vanished."

"Mistakes? What kind of mistakes?" Pat glanced over Toni's shoulder at the computer screen, then gave her a confused sidelong look.

"They were there, Pat. I swear to you they were."

"Well, they're gone now." Pat gave her a sympathetic smile. "I think you've been working too hard, girl. Look, I've got a lot to do before I go home. Joe is liable to go postal if I have to work overtime the way I used to. He was really bent out of shape about that."

Toni noticed that a distressed look came into her friend's eyes. Pat let out a definitely strained sigh and added, "I wasn't too crazy about that either." A bitter edge tinged her voice. "Anyway, it only added to our shared opinion that Mr. Clifford is a Simon Legree or worse. And of course everybody knows he works you like a slave."

"But he doesn't, actually."

"Try convincing Joe of that. Ever since I got promoted to executive secretary, he's been impossible to live with."

"That's because Mr. Clifford passed him over for mail room manager when he had assumed that it was in the bag. I'm sure Joe still resents it."

"But why should I have to suffer? My promotion has nothing to do with him not getting his."

"Evidently to Joe's way of thinking it does. I also think he's jealous."

"Joe? Jealous!" Pat made a derisive choking sound. "Of Mr. Clifford? Yeah, right."

"It's possible, you know. You're a pretty girl, Pat," Toni observed, looking her friend over. Pat had huge hazel eyes and wore her short, brown hair in a cute pixie cut. Although petite, she had a curvy figure and looked a lot like the actress Jada Pinkett-Smith.

Pat grinned. "You do wonders for a girl's vanity."

After Pat had gone back to her desk, Toni thought about her friend's reaction to what she'd said about Joe being jealous of their boss, and before that the crack about overtime. At other times there was something in the tone of her voice when her name and Mr. Clifford's were linked in any conversation. Toni wondered what her attitude about that was all about. She shook her head and recalled the look of pure unadulterated murder on Hank Warren's face when he came tearing out of the CEO's office.

Toni was asked to work overtime on Thursday; Mr. Clifford had a meeting in Chicago and was scheduled to catch the red-eye flight, and needed a last-minute analysis done to take with him.

Hank hadn't been back to work since the day he stormed out, which left all the urgent work on her shoulders. Toni had found out at lunch the day before, from Mazie in personnel, that the CEO had "urged" Hank to take a few days off. Anxious curiosity worked through Toni's system. She wondered what was going on and what effect it might have on her getting the promotion.

She finished her work and headed for the elevators. As she got out on the parking lot level and started toward her car, she saw Bill Watkins, head of parking security.

"Been working late again, I see."

"It's becoming an occupational hazard, I'm afraid." Toni laughed, continuing to her car.

"Good night, now," Bill called after her.

Toni stopped in front of her car, setting her purse on the hood, to rummage inside for her keys. She sighed in frustration when she couldn't find them. They had to be there somewhere. After making a more thorough search and still no keys, Toni concluded that they had fallen out of her purse into her bottom desk drawer. Damn it, she would have to go back upstairs to get them.

She saw the knowing smile on Bill Watkins' face when she headed back to the elevator.

"Left your keys upstairs, huh?"

"You guessed it. I should have checked to make sure I had them before leaving the office. Oh well."

The thought of going back upstairs was not in the least appealing to Toni, considering how dead tired she felt. During the ride to the seventh floor, she grumbled, scolding herself for her stupidity. According to the self-defense course she had recently enrolled in, every time a woman left home or work, she should have her keys in her hand with the two longest ones protruding between her fingers to use as a weapon against a possible attacker. Ms. Kymoto, her instructress, would be far from pleased by her carelessness.

Toni stepped off the elevator and strode into the office. Once inside, she made a beeline for her desk. Slipping her purse off her shoulder, she tossed it onto the desk, then pushing her chair back, opened the bottom drawer. She didn't have to search for the keys. They were in plain sight, gleaming up at her like the mocking grin of a lighted jack-o-lantern.

Toni's shoulders slumped and she groaned tiredly. She grabbed her keys and was ready to leave when her boss's voice snagged her attention.

Maybe the business trip wasn't that urgent after all and he would be catching an early morning flight. She wondered who was with him. When she didn't hear any answering replies, she assumed he must be on the phone. His next words not only confirmed the fact, but stopped her cold.

"She's finally left for the day. Our Miss Carlton is thorough, I'll give her that. Yes, we have almost everything we need. It's a good thing, too, because I think she's getting suspicious." A short pause. "No, not if we're careful. When the time comes everyone will believe our hard-working Miss Carlton is a clever, over-confident thief. The trail of evidence I've set up will lead right to the ambitious little lady's desk. The net will drop on her, completely entangling her." He laughed. "It's the perfect frame, don't you agree?"

He laughed again. "I am becoming eloquent in my prime, aren't I? You know, the gullible little bitch hasn't a clue why she's been singled out to work overtime all these months. She thinks it's because of the wholehearted confidence I have in her abilities. Isn't that a hoot?"

Toni swallowed around the lump in her throat and blinked several times. Mired in shock, she lost the rest of the conversation. This just couldn't be happening to her. All this time her boss had been using her to steal from the company. And was setting her up royally to take the blame! A hot anger came to life inside her and began to build in her blood. As she started shaking with the intensity of it, the keys slipped from her fingers and hit the floor with a loud clink, alerting her boss that he was not alone.

Toni heard the phone receiver crash down on its cradle and seconds later her boss came rushing into the outer office. He stalked over to her desk and stood glaring at her.

"Little girls who have big ears hear things they really shouldn't."

Toni's anger dissolved into stomach-knotting fear and her heart started pounding furiously in her chest. Every self-protective instinct she possessed screamed at her to take to her heels and run, but the numbing effect of shock slowed down her reaction time.

"What are you doing back here?" he demanded. "Were you by any chance spying on me?"

When she could answer, her voice came out sounding like a rusty hinge "No, I came back because I left my keys."

He shook his head. "That's unfortunate. Too much is involved to let you mess things up at this late date. If you happen to have an accident…"

Fear for her safety propelled Toni into action. She pushed her chair into Clifford and made a mad dash for the door.

"Why you—" He growled, then angrily thrust the chair aside and started after her. Moments before she could make it to the door, he grabbed her arms.

Toni tried to twist out of his grasp, but he was too strong for her. Then her self-defense training kicked in. Glad she had mastered at least a few basic moves, she ground the heel of her pump into his instep, then jabbed her elbow into his ribs with all her strength. When his grip loosened and she heard him groan in pain, it was all the opportunity she needed, and she wasted no time in fleeing from the office.

Toni ran to the elevator and pounded frantically, desperately, on the down button.

"Come on," she cried in mounting agitation and fear.

As luck would have it, all four elevators were downstairs in the lobby. She didn't have time to wait for them to come back up. Frank Clifford had recovered and was coming after her. Toni darted toward the stair exit.

He was hot on her heels!

"You might as well stop this, Toni. You can't hope to get away from me. It's going to be my word against yours. Can you guess who'll be believed?" he taunted.

Chest heaving and her breaths coming in hard jerky gasps, Toni ignored his words and sped down one flight of stairs, then the next. Clifford's long, menacing strides cut in half the distance her shorter, frightened ones made.

Toni stepped up the pace, but by the time she reached the third floor she could barely catch her breath. She could hear Clifford's labored breathing, but it seemed far away. Maybe he was tiring. She could only hope. He was, after all, a middle-aged man. She wrenched open the door leading to the floor of offices. If she could only find a place to hide. The hall lights had been dimmed, which meant that all the offices were probably closed. The dismal thought doused her hope of escaping Clifford. Could the cleaning people have left a door open?

"Oh, God, please, let them have forgotten to lock one. Please," she prayed.

Toni raced down the hall, trying one door after another, finding each one locked. When she'd given up hope of finding an unlocked door, the last one at the end of the hall opened and she rushed inside.

Toni turned the lock and leaned back against the door, allowing her breathing time to slow down to normal. She was safe for the moment.

The door to Toni's left eased open and the shadowed silhouette of a man filled the space.

"Oh, God, no!" she cried and slid to the floor as everything went black.

CHAPTER TWO

As Toni regained consciousness, she felt something cold and damp resting on her forehead. When she opened her eyes, it was to find a pair of concerned brown eyes intently watching her. When the rest of the man's face came into clear focus, she studied it.

His eyes were a shade of brown she'd never seen before, honey on brown velvet. He had an average-sized nose with a slight bump that made it fall short of perfection. His mouth had a firm, yet sensual, fullness. Add to that a head of short-cropped, curly black hair and a five-o'clock shadow and you had a ruggedly handsome man. Judging from the caramel color of his skin, she'd say he was a mixture of Spanish and black. A very handsome mixture, she might add.

The moment her mind jolted back to reality, she remembered how she happened to be there and why. Where was Mr. Clifford? She tried to get up from the couch.

"Hey, take it easy. You'd better lie back for a few minutes until you get your bearings."

The man eased off the couch, grabbed a chair, pulled it over to her and sat down.

"What's your name?" he asked. "Mine is Mackinsey Jessup, but you can call me Mack."

Should she tell him her name? For all she knew, he could be one of Frank Clifford's cohorts.

"Antonia Carlton," she reluctantly answered.

Mack noted her warm, golden-brown coloring and near-black eyes. Other then in skin tone, this woman reminded him of the actress Catherine Zeta-Jones. Her perfectly arched, midnight-black brows gave her face an exotic look. He'd say she was part Indian, or maybe Italian, and the rest black. The name she gave was familiar to him, but he didn't let on. He was curious to know why she'd run into his office, and what had frightened her to the point of passing out when she'd seen him.

"You work in the building?" he asked.

"Yes."

"Would you like a glass of water?"

"Yes, please," Toni answered, licking her dry lips.

Mack walked over to the water dispenser, pulled down a paper cup, filled it and handed it to his unexpected visitor. She was certainly no fountain spilling over with information. He wondered what she was trying so hard to keep from revealing.

"Were you—" he began.

The sound of voices intruded. Toni's eyes widened in fear and when she made to scramble to her feet, she swayed. Mack caught her."What's wrong?"

"Please, let me go. I…" As her voice faded, the others grew louder.

He could see she was frightened out of her mind. "You want to step into my private office and wait while I see who it is?"

She nodded.

Mack helped her into a chair in his office, then left, closing the door behind him. He moved the chair he'd occupied moments earlier back where it belonged. Just as he threw the paper towel and cup into the trash, he heard a knock at the door.

"Yes?"

"It's Jeff Andrews, head of security."

Mack opened the door.

"Sorry to bother you, Mr. Jessup, but I'm looking for Miss Antonia Carlton. I have her boss, Mr. Clifford, with me." He indicated the man standing next to him. "He's worried that something may have happened to her." The head of security held up a small, black purse and a ring of keys with a brass sunflower ornament dangling from it.

"Mr. Clifford found these on the floor by her desk and, recognizing that they belonged to Ms. Carlton, he called down to the parking lot. Bill Watkins, parking security, said she'd gone upstairs half an hour ago to get her keys, but hadn't come back down. No one has seen her since. Have you?"

"What does she look like?" Mack directed his question to Clifford.

He cleared his throat. "She's average height, slender, with wavy-black hair, golden-brown skin and dark brown eyes, very attractive."

Mack shook his head. "If I'd seen anyone who looked like that, I definitely wouldn't forget her." Glancing at his watch, he said, "I thought I was the only one burning the midnight oil this evening."

Frank Clifford glanced past Mack to the closed inner office door, then gave Mack a look. "Miss Carlton often works late. You see, she's a very conscientious employee. I wouldn't want anything to happen to her. Good workers are hard to find."

"Have you checked the ladies' room? She may have taken ill and gone in there," Mack suggested.

"Didn't think of that," Jeff Andrews answered, embarrassed at not having thought of it himself. "Sorry to have disturbed you, Mr. Jessup. Good night, sir."

Frank Clifford took the keys and the purse from Andrews.

"I'll wait in the office for her to return. Surely she'll come back for these."

Mack walked the two men out. As soon as he heard the elevator, he opened the door to his private office and walked in, sat on the edge of his desk and looked at Toni."Want to tell me what's going on?"

She rose from her chair. "Thanks for all your help, Mr. Jessup. I'd better be going."

"Without your keys and your purse?"

A panicked look flashed across her face.

"Is there something you should tell me, Miss Carlton? Maybe I could be of more help to you." When her silence continued, he studied her for a moment. "You're afraid of someone or something, aren't you?"

Toni's heart lurched and she lowered her gaze to her hands, clenched tightly in her lap. Could she trust this man? Other than his name, she knew next to nothing about Mackinsey Jessup. As she looked around the room, searching for something reassuring, her attention snagged on the plaques of credentials on the wall. She also recalled seeing the name Jessup on the lobby directory and returned her gaze to the man sitting on the edge of the huge mahogany desk in front of her.

"I work for Townsend's Stock Brokerage and Investments and Frank Clifford is my boss."

"Was he trying to be more than friendly? Did his actions send you running?"

Mackinsey Jessup had given her the excuse she needed to keep Mr. Clifford at bay, at least temporarily, and she relaxed.

"He threatened to make things impossible for me if I didn't—you know."

"I take it this isn't the first time he's tried to come on to you. You should have reported him to your personnel department and had him charged with sexual harassment."

"I could have done that, but I thought I could handle him myself."

"Famous last words. Look, if you want your things, you're going to have to go to him and get them."

Toni chewed her bottom lip, not eager to face her boss at all, let alone by herself.

Noticing that the fear was back in her eyes, Mack stood up.

"If you want me to, I'll go upstairs with you."

Even if she got her belongings from Clifford and he didn't try anything, there was no guarantee she'd be safe from him once she got home. Toni shivered at the thought of what he might do.

She gazed at the tall, ruggedly handsome man standing before her. He looked completely professional in his perfect-fitting dark blue suit. Again she wondered if she could trust him. He had an aura of danger about him that she couldn't put her finger on, but knew it existed.

"Or you could come home with me."

Toni balked at that suggestion.

"Mr. Jessup, I—"

He grinned. "Please, call me Mack."

"Mack, I don't really know you."

"We can easily remedy that. I'm Mackinsey Jessup," he introduced himself, "and I run Jessup Financial Investigations." He added to get a reaction, "We specialize in corporate theft."

He noted how her dark eyes momentarily widened before returning to normal. He wondered what the look meant. In their last meeting John Townsend Jr. had said he strongly believed that she was their thief. Mack wasn't convinced, though. Too many things just didn't add up. He'd have to get Ms. Toni Carlton to open up to him. When he took her hand in his, the contact was electric.

Toni's lips parted in shock and her body instantly came alive with sensual awareness.

Mack felt her reaction to his touch. It was similar to his own for her. This wasn't at all what he'd expected, and he didn't like how she made him feel. Admittedly, an aura of innocent vulnerability surrounded this woman, drawing his protective instincts to the fore.

Her eyes were like pools of black gold. And her lips reminded him of dark cherries swollen tight with juice. Her hair, black as his own, had felt like silk when he brushed it back from her forehead after she'd fainted. He shook his head to clear it. Why was he waxing poetic all of a sudden?

Mack mentally strove to free himself from his arousing thoughts to concentrate on the present situation. He knew he would have to be careful around this sexy lady. Mack had an idea that it wouldn't take much for her to turn a man's mind to mush. Although he could believe that Clifford had tried to get her into his bed, Mack had a gut feeling that it wasn't the reason for her fear of the man.

Mack smiled. "Antonia sounds so formal. Do you mind if I call you Toni?"

"No, that's what people at the office call me."

"Isn't that what your folks call you?"

She laughed. "No, to them I'll always be their little Antonia."

"You must be an only child."

"Yes, I am. How did you know?"

Mack shrugged. "Just a lucky guess." He could feel the tension in her ease. "Well, Toni, what do you want to do?"

Something about this man encouraged Toni to confide in him. He had an underlying honesty and a unique brand of charm. She was sure it helped him in his line of work as well as his personal life.

"Don't you have an extra set of keys?"

"Yes, but they're at home."

"Not much use to you right now, are they?"

"No."

"It looks like we'll have to get your things from your boss tonight."

Toni moved uneasily in her chair.

"Don't sweat it." Mack held out his hand. "Come on, let's go."

Toni rose reluctantly to her feet and squared her shoulders. Pretending a composure she was far from feeling, she took Mack's hand and they left the office and headed for the elevators.

"How long have you worked for Townsend's?" Mack asked conversationally, as they waited for the elevator.

"A few months short of four years."

"All of them working for Frank Clifford?"

"No, only the last two."

"Listen, Toni, I'm asking these questions to draw you out of your shell. Clifford has obviously frightened you into clamming up. Won't you tell me what's really wrong?"

The elevator came and they stepped inside. Toni pressed the number seven up button, then moved back against the wall. She stood, nerves taut, eyes aimed at the doors. "I don't know quite how to begin."

"Or whether you even want to. Am I right? I can understand that. You don't know me from Adam. I could be worse than the person you're afraid of."

"I never said that I was afraid of anybody."

The elevator bell dinged, the car came to a stop and the doors slid open. Toni swallowed the rest of her reply and looked up at Mack. He cupped her elbow, and smiling at her, gently guided her in the direction of the Townsend offices. Mack tried the door and, finding it locked, knocked. They heard no answering reply.

Toni realized that her boss had purposely left with her keys and purse. What was she going to do now? Suddenly this latest complication proved too much and her knees buckled. Mack offered support.

"You're coming home with me."

It wasn't a request; it was more like an order. She was too shaken to call him on it. Toni wasn't sure how she knew it, but she felt she could trust him not to take advantage of her, given the circumstances. Without a word she let him lead her back to the elevators.

When they reached the parking level, Bill Watkins walked up to them.

"I'm glad to see you're all right, Miss Carlton. Mr. Clifford left a little while ago."

Toni cleared her throat and smiled. "Mr. Jessup has kindly offered to take me home. I'm not feeling well enough to drive so…" She let her voice fade, purposely encouraging him to draw his own conclusions.

Bill smiled at Toni. "You couldn't be in better hands. You do look a little peaked. Better take it easy when you get home. Good night now."

Mack escorted Toni over to his silver-blue Jag parked a few feet away. She looked back longingly at her car for a moment, then let Mack help her into his car.

"Better fasten your seat belt."

Toni sighed as the warm concern she heard in his deep rich voice poured over her senses like heated syrup.

Mack glanced at Toni. "I'm sure Clifford guessed you were in my private office. I wonder why he didn't leave your things with security?"

Toni hunched her shoulders. "I don't know." But that wasn't true. She had an idea why. It was Frank Clifford's way of letting her know he held her future in his hands. Although they were at a stalemate of sorts, he was no doubt reveling in her helplessness.

Mack could tell by her expression that Toni knew exactly why, but she wasn't going to tell him, and it irritated the hell out of him. He had to find out all he could about her.

For business reasons, or for more personal ones, Jessup? an inner voice taunted.

As he drove Mack noticed how Toni quietly gazed out the side window. He remembered how appealing her expressive eyes had been when her attention was focused on him. And the graceful way she swept the errant strands of hair back from her face made him wonder how long her hair was when it was down. He mentally shook himself. He had to stop doing this and keep an objective mind.

When they came to a traffic light, Mack glanced at Toni's profile. His gaze slid down her face and throat to her chest. Her breasts were voluptuous, considering her slender build. He remembered how her hour-glass figure molded into slim thighs, tapering into a pair of long lovely legs that ended at her delicate ankles had aroused him. Yes, she was definitely dynamite to a man's senses.

He was attracted to this woman and definitely didn't want to be. He had a job to do and he felt sure she was somehow involved in the Townsend problem. Until he knew her role, he would proceed with caution, stay alert and not allow her beautiful face and luscious body to distract him from his purpose.

Toni sneaked sidelong looks at Mack. She guessed his age to be somewhere around thirty-four or five. He had impossibly long lashes that were at variance with his ruggedly handsome features.

"Why are you inviting me to your place? I could be Jill-the-Ripper for all you know."

"Yeah, right. I bet you can't step on a bug without feeling guilty."

She laughed. "You're right, but I still want an answer to my question."

"Contrary to popular belief there are modern-day knights who rescue damsels in distress."

"Oh, really?" She pretended to consider what he'd said. "Are you saying you're one of the scarce few who do?"

He grinned. "I am, my lady."

"You haven't answered my question."

"Oh, didn't I?"

Toni shook her head. She had a feeling she wasn't going to get an answer that would completely satisfy her. Mackinsey Jessup was a mystery man. She would have to play it by ear and see what happened.

Mack parked his car beneath a stucco-arched carport beside a beautiful Spanish-style house. Toni was amazed. She had expected him to live in a suave bachelor apartment or condo. "You look surprised." After switching off the ignition, he turned toward her. "I'll bet you expected me to live in a different kind of place, didn't you?"

"I confess, I did."

"When I was a little boy, I promised myself that one day I would buy myself a house. You see, my two brothers, my sister and I grew up in the East L.A. projects. To live in a house holds a special appeal for me. I don't know if you can understand that."

"Oh, I can and I do. To me a house represents stability, security, whatever you choose to call it. It's something I've always wanted," Toni confided. "You see, I'm a navy brat. My father met my mother when he was on shore leave in Italy. They were married and she followed him around the world. I was born in Australia and grew up moving from one country to another. I can't even count the number or remember all the names of the schools I've attended."

"I see you understand what living in a house means," Mack said, unlocking his front door.

He turned on the lights and waved for her to precede him. Toni took in the decor of the room as she entered. She didn't know what she expected but it wasn't what she saw. The room, though tastefully done, had a lived in look and feel about it.

The walls were a warm beige. On one, a collection of African landscape paintings and Spanish hangings woven in oranges, browns and reds dominated the room. A hearth-style fireplace was beneath one of the hangings. A chocolate-brown carpet with a deep rich pile that she knew would surely sink two inches if put to the test covered the floor.

Large louvered windows took up the entire front wall. The mahogany furniture was modern, with a Spanish flare.

Mack flashed her a pearl white smile. "Are you impressed with my house?"

"Yes, very." Toni returned the smile with an approving nod.

"Look, are you hungry?"

"I'm starved. Don't tell me you're a gourmet chef, too?"

"No, I won't tell you that, but I do know my way around a kitchen. Are you willing to take a chance on my culinary skills, Toni?"

She knew he was asking more than that of her; he was asking her to trust him.

"You need any help?" she volunteered.

Mack saw the fatigue shadowing her eyes. "No. Sit down and let me take care of you."

At his words a feeling of warmth and security covered her like a blanket. The idea of someone taking care of her was nice. but she'd better not get used to it; after all, it was only a temporary situation.

"Okay. I'm too tired to argue." She yawned and dropped down on a beige and brown earth-toned, nubby-textured couch. Toni eased her head back and laid her cheek against the nubby surface, enjoying its softness.

"You rest while I fix our dinner."

Toni let out a tired sigh and closed her eyes. Mack moved his lips into a wry, knowing smile. Miss Antonia Carlton would probably fall asleep before he finished making dinner. Striding to the kitchen, he headed straight for the fridge, took out the makings for a salad, and a plate of sliced turkey for the sandwiches. He decided to open a bottle of sparkling apple cider instead of making hot coffee. The last thing his houseguest needed was something that would keep her awake.

All at once a scream rent the air and Mack ran out of the kitchen.

CHAPTER THREE

When Mack reached Toni's side, tears were streaming down her face and she was shaking.

"What's wrong? Why…" his voice faded when he saw the stark terror in her eyes. She must have dozed off and had a bad dream. He sat down next to her and drew her into his arms and held her close, stroking her back until she calmed down. "It's all right, I'm here for you, Toni. You had a bad dream, but it's over."

She sniffed. He felt one last renegade shudder quiver through her body before she regained control.

"Want to talk about it?"

"I can't. I don't remember what it was about."

Another evasion, he thought. "Maybe you should come out to the kitchen with me while I prepare our dinner."

"I'd like that."

He looked right at home in his comfortable kitchen. It was painted a bright lemon yellow. An island cooking range with a butcher-block preparation surface occupied the center of the room. Copper-bottom pots hung suspended from a rack on the ceiling.

As she looked around she couldn't help admiring the clean, shiny red brick tiles on the floor and the wood cabinets of varnished oak. She appreciated that he had a latest state-of-the-art dishwasher and other labor saving devices.

"Come sit down on this stool." He indicated one near the butcher-block counter and pulled it closer to him. "I'll do all the work while you do all the relaxing. All right?"

"All right." She flashed him an agreeable smile. A girl could get used to a handsome attentive man and a wonderful place like this and become as spoiled as a pampered cat. Toni shook her head to clear it.

She'd been in Mack Jessup's house all of twenty minutes and here she was fantasizing.

Mack watched the play of emotions on Toni's face and made a guess as to what was going through her mind. He felt as though she belonged here. But how could that be? They'd only just met a matter of hours ago. In the past he'd made the mistake of caring too much too soon about a woman, and lived to regret it. He wasn't about to repeat that mistake.

Toni observed Mack as he rinsed fresh vegetables, chopped them up and put them in the juicer for the soup. Then he opened a can of broth and poured it into a saucepan, added thickener and seasoning, then waited as it simmered on the range. While it was cooking, he fixed sliced turkey sandwiches. The way he deftly moved about in his kitchen fascinated her.

"Don't look so shocked. My mother made sure all us little Jessups knew our way around a kitchen. She's Spanish, and very practical. She used to tell me and my brothers that we had better learn to cook because in this day and age no woman would allow herself to be chained to the stove."

He shot her a solemn glance. "Don't laugh, I'm serious." Then he laughed, spoiling the effect. "Now, what would you like? A soda or sparkling apple cider to go with dinner?"

"Cider."

"I thought that would be your choice."

Humor sparkled in her eyes. "Think you're coming to know me, do you?"

"The way to a woman's heart is through her stomach."

"Haven't you got that turned around? I thought it was the way to a man's heart."

"You could be right." He gave her a crooked smile.

They ate their meal in silence, both attempting to analyze the other.

Toni wanted to tell Mack everything, but she hesitated.

"Now that I've fed you, I think it's time we organized the sleeping arrangements." He watched her reaction. "Don't look at me like that, Red Riding Hood. I only eat little girls every Tuesday and third Thursday of the month." He glanced at the calendar on the wall and gave it an exaggerated look of realization. "So it's the third Thursday. What can I say?" He grinned wolfishly.

She laughed, shaking her head. "You're crazy, Mackinsey Jessup."

They pushed away from the table and Toni followed Mack into the living room, then down a hall to the bedrooms. When they came to a very masculine bedroom, she slowed her steps, taking in at a glance the king-size bed with its unusual Hollywood style headboard of padded forest green leather inset with slivers of mirrors. A comforter, the same forest green, was folded back, revealing striped forest green and cream satin sheets which seemed to conjure up some particularly tempting sensual images. She cleared her throat and quickly hurried after Mack.

They moved on down the hall to a room Toni assumed was a guest room. The flowered drapes, comforter and sheets matched the blue, cream and mauve color scheme of the room. The final distinctively feminine touch to the room was the creamy white wall-to-wall carpet.

"So, what do you think? Does it pass inspection?"

"It more than passes. I like it. Do you do your own decorating?"

"Mostly. My sister and mother helped. Actually, this room is their creation." He noticed the tired slump of Toni's shoulders. "Hey, you must be dead on your feet. To your right you'll find an en suite bathroom. I'll get you some towels and something to sleep in." He turned and quickly left the room.

As she waited for Mack to return, Toni took a deep, rejuvenating breath, walked over to the bed and wearily sank down on it. Easing her shoes off, she wiggled her toes. She gazed at her reflection in the mirror on the dresser. Her face showed signs of strain and her eyes had a haunted look. Her mouth trembled. She saw that her hair had partially come undone.

Her navy blue linen jacket was rumpled. And the collar of her white blouse lay limp and blotched with makeup stains. Toni glanced down at her skirt, equally unappealing in its wrinkled state. What was she going to do for a change of clothes? She didn't much care at the moment; she was just too wiped out.

"Here you go," Mack said, walking into the room and handing her towels and a T-shirt she assumed belonged to him. "Sorry, I couldn't find any of my sister's nightshirts. I think when she was here last she must have taken them with her."

"It's all right. I'll manage." She took the proffered items.

"If you need anything, I'll be down the hall."

After Mack left, Toni ran water for a bath, sprinkling in some of the bath beads she'd found on a rack. She removed her clothes and underwear, rinsed out her bra and panties, then towel-dried and draped them over the top of the sliding glass door enclosing the tub.

Minutes later Toni eased her exhausted body into the water and soaked until the water cooled. By the time she put on the makeshift nightshirt and slipped into bed, she was so relaxed she drifted right off to sleep.

"You thought you could escape me, didn't you, Toni? No, don't get up. From where I stand, I can see you just fine." Frank Clifford came away from the window swinging her purse tauntingly on his fingers. "Did you think anyone could keep me from getting to you?"

He came closer. Toni gulped in fear and terror and pulled the comforter closer while at the same time inching away from him until she felt the headboard against her back.

"You aren't a bad looking woman. If I didn't need you for cover I might cut you in for a share. But as it is I have to—"

She swallowed hard. "I'll go away and no one will know."

"I'm afraid not."

He came closer still. Every nerve in her body seemed to riot and her muscles screamed with tension, urging her to run, to escape.

"Please, I—"

Smiling, he said, "You plead so prettily, Toni."

The next second he pounced on her. She screamed and screamed, struggling wildly with all her strength to get away.

She had to get away!

Mack lay in his bed, hands locked behind his head as thoughts of his houseguest filled his mind. He could imagine how she looked in his T-shirt. Considering the difference in their sizes, he knew it would be way too big on her.

He could visualize the way her wavy black hair looked spread loosely around her shoulders like a silk veil, the way her voluptuous breasts with aroused nipples pushed against the soft clingy material of his T-shirt, the way the T-shirt exposed her firm, shapely thighs and long, slender legs. The thought of it all made the lower part of his anatomy harden uncomfortably.

Mack closed his eyes, mentally tamping down the desire building inside him. He had to stop this! Raising himself onto his elbow, he thumped his pillow, then lay back down. He glanced at the clock on his nightstand. It was almost two a.m. He had to get some sleep. Just as he finally fell asleep, a now familiar scream rent the air. He jumped out of bed and ran from the room.

Mack wrenched Toni's bedroom door open and turned on the light. "Toni, are you all right? I heard you scream."

Toni sprang upright and gazed wildly around her.

"Oh, Mack. He was here!" she cried, struggling to escape the tangle of bed covers. "Frank Clifford was here! He came in through the window and…" Her voice faded into a shudder.

Mack strode over to the bed and sank down beside her, taking her in his arms. "Shh, Toni. Calm down." When she did, he went to the window and checked it out, only to find it securely locked with no sign of tampering.

He returned to the bed and pulled her trembling body into his arms. This was getting to be a habit. And since it brought her soft body into such intimate contact with his, he was finding it increasingly difficult to resist her. All his male instincts to offer protection and comfort threatened to give way to another feeling entirely.

Toni raised her tear-wet face and looked into Mack's eyes.

He smiled reassuringly and kissed her forehead. "I'm afraid you had another nightmare. Now, do you want to tell me the real reason you were running from your boss?"

"You didn't believe the answer I gave you!" she accused.

"No. I just gave you the out you needed because I could see you didn't trust me with the truth."

"You were right about my being afraid of him. I am, and with good reason. I heard him admit to framing me."

Mack frowned. "Framing you? Framing you for what?"

"Considering my job, I'm sure it's embezzlement. I happened to overhear him discussing his plans with someone on the phone. He said he was ready to implement his plans, but I got the feeling he hadn't yet."

"That's a serious accusation. Are you sure you—"

She pushed out of his arms. "You don't believe me?"

"It's not important what I believe."

Toni was disappointed and more than a little hurt by his lack of faith in her because what he thought was important to her, although she knew it shouldn't be.

"Why did you help me?"

Mack ran his fingers through his hair. "Damned if I know. Something about you…"

Toni suddenly realized he only had on pajama bottoms which were riding dangerously low on his hips. Heat seemed to emanate from his hard-muscled chest. She was captivated by the V of dark body hair arrowing down, disappearing inside the waistband of his pajamas. She didn't remember ever being as drawn to any other man as she was to this one.

Mack moved to leave the bed.

Toni looked at the window, remembering her nightmare in vivid detail. "Don't leave me, Mack," she pleaded, her eyes dark with fear.

She sounded and looked so forlorn, he thought.

"You afraid the dream will become a reality?"

Toni nodded.

Mack went to turn off the light. When he returned to the bed, he eased Toni between the covers, then went around to the other side of the bed and got in next to her, being careful to leave a layer of top sheet separating them. He drew her into his arms, then pulled the comforter over them.

A sigh of relief eased from her like the purr of a contented cat when the warmth of Mack's arms and upper body wrapped around her.

After a few minutes the hypnotic thudding of his heartbeat beneath her ear lulled Toni to sleep. When Mack moved to make himself more comfortable, she stayed the motion by tightening her arm around his waist. Mack groaned inwardly at his predicament, knowing the thin layer of sheet, his T-shirt and his pajama bottoms were the only barriers keeping her naked body from making skin-to-skin contact with his. God, he was glad she had fallen asleep. The obvious hardening of his manhood would be impossible to hide and quite embarrassing.

As he thought about what Toni had revealed, sleep eluded him. Could he believe her? He had to admit that he did, just a tiny bit, or else he wouldn't have insisted that she come home with him. Would he?

Mack felt dangerously close to compromising his position where Townsend's was concerned, not to mention his own sense of professional and personal pride. Once before he'd laid both on the line for a woman and paid a high price, a price he refused to pay again.

He ran his fingers through Toni's hair, sweeping the silky, errant strands away from her face, reveling in the feel of her soft skin. If what she said about Frank Clifford was true, he could make her life at work hell. More importantly, she was in real danger.

On the other hand, if Toni was lying and in partnership with the man, threatening to betray him would be reason enough for him to come after her. Self-preservation always won out in the end. He knew this firsthand from his past experiences working as a detective in the L.A. Police Department.

What was he going to do about Toni Carlton? When he could not come up with one single satisfactory answer, he finally closed his tired eyes and slept.

The smell of coffee woke Toni the next morning. As she stretched and yawned, she realized she was definitely not at her place. There there would be no one to make coffee but herself. Then everything came back to her. Glancing at the closet, she wondered if Mack's sister had left something behind she could wear.

Toni swept the covers back and climbed out of bed and padded across the room to investigate. She found a pair of gray slacks and a white blouse hanging in the closet. Luckily, they were close to her size. She hoped Mack's sister wouldn't mind her borrowing them. Toni showered quickly and dressed. Before leaving the bedroom, she looked in the mirror. She could stand a dash of makeup, but that couldn't be helped; Frank Clifford had her purse and keys, damn him. She headed for the kitchen.

"That coffee sure smells good."

Mack looked up, instantly recognizing the familiar gray slacks. They'd never fit his sister Mariah the way they hugged Toni's curvy figure. "Sit down and pour yourself a cup. The cream and sugar are on the counter."

"No thanks, I take it black. If your sister gets this kind of star treatment I'm surprised she hasn't taken up permanent residence."

"I don't spoil her. When she's here we take turns being domestic drudges."

"You don't have a trace of male chauvinism in your body, do you?"

"Don't fool yourself. The right circumstance hasn't presented itself."

"Yeah, right."

"Don't you believe that?"

"I have my doubts." Toni's expression turned serious. "What should I do, Mack? Should I go to the office and act like nothing has happened?"

"You should definitely go in. If you don't, it'll look suspicious. You don't want to give him any more ammunition to use against you."

Toni thought it over and decided that Mack was right. She would have to go to work, if for no other reason than to throw the CEO off balance. Besides, she had to get her keys and purse from him. But she wasn't looking forward to the prospect.

Mack watched Toni as she ate breakfast. For a slender girl she certainly had a healthy appetite. He could only imagine what was going through her mind. His gaze narrowed. Either she was an Oscar-winning actress or she had been telling him the truth.

"I'll return your sister's clothes as soon as I can."

"Hey, don't worry about it. Ready to leave for work?"

"Not really, but I know I have to go." Toni excused herself to go to the bathroom. When she came out, she made up the bed and neatly folded her clothes, then laid them across the arm of a chair. She'd come back for them later and return his sister's clothes at the same time.

During the ride to the office, Toni tried to keep her mind occupied, but it didn't work; instead it raced ahead to the coming encounter with her boss.

Mack occasionally glanced at Toni. She was very quiet, contemplative, he would have to say. "I'll go up with you if you want me to."

"It's kind of you to offer, Mack, but this is something I have to do. He can't do anything to me with witnesses around. I don't think he will anyway, once he realizes we're at a stalemate, although a somewhat tenuous one."

The brave, yet frightened, sound in her voice made Mack feel an urgent need to ease her distress. Minutes later he parked the car and they took the elevator up. When it stopped on his floor, Mack was reluctant to get out.

Toni looked at him. "I'll be all right. I can do this."

"If you need any help—"

She gave him a bright smile. "I know who to come to for it."

He stepped out of the elevator and as he turned the doors closed.Toni looked at her watch, then took several deep, calming breaths. It was only 8:45. She suddenly remembered that her boss wouldn't be in until late in the afternoon since he had to attend a meeting this morning in San Diego. That should give her plenty of time to search his office for something to help prove her innocence.

When the elevator stopped on her floor and the doors opened, Toni mentally pumped herself up to go into the office. When she walked in, Pat Davis was about to turn on her computer.

"How are you feeling? Bill told me what happened last night. You look a little ragged. Maybe you shouldn't have come in to work today."

She shrugged. "I'm fine, Pat. I've got a lot to do and I need to get cracking so I don't fall behind."

"You work too hard, Toni. What you need is a man in your life, girlfriend."

"How do you know I don't already have one?"

Pat lifted curious brows. "Do you have one? Is he anyone I know?"

"You're priceless."

"Does that mean you're not going to tell me who this mystery man is?"

"I've got work to do and so do you. Talk to you later," she answered and walked away.

Once inside her office cubicle, Toni let out an anxious breath. This cloak and dagger stuff just wasn't conducive to calm nerves. She needed to get into Frank Clifford's office, but she would have to be careful not to let Pat, or anyone else, see her go in.

Toni checked her in-basket and smiled. She'd found several things she could have Pat do that would require her to leave the office.

After Pat had left, Toni checked the office. Hank's cubicle was empty. She smiled, remembering that he was still off on his "vacation." Toni tried the door and, finding it locked, swore under her breath. Usually the boss's office door was left unlocked. Toni, Pat and Hank had keys to the outer door, but only the CEO had a key to his private office.

Her body tensed. It meant that whatever he was up to was reason enough for him to lock his personal office. She had to think. How was she going to get in there?

Toni walked back to her desk. Her eyes lit on a box of mini paper clips and the light of an idea turned on in her head. Taking one out, she unbent it and stepped over to his door, then inserted it in the lock, turning and twisting. When the clip wouldn't unlock the door, she chewed her bottom lip in frustration.

"Damn," she swore. She let out a defeated groan and went back to her desk, sat down and rifled though the drawer, trying to find something else she could use. Then she remembered there was an emergency key in case the CEO misplaced his. Now the question was, where did Mr. Clifford keep it? She glanced around the room, first at the coffee machine cart, then the wall clock. Her gaze locked on the supply cabinet. Could the key possibly be stashed in there?

Toni walked over to the cabinet and checked every shelf. Then ran her hand underneath the last shelf. Bingo! She'd found it! Her lips quirked into a triumphant smile.

She unlocked the CEO's office door, slipped inside and went straight to the desk. She searched it thoroughly, but didn't find anything. Just as Toni started to open one of the drawers in the file cabinet, she heard the doorknob turn. Her heartbeat quickened. Surely her boss hadn't cancelled his meeting!

Her mouth went dry.

The door opened.

CHAPTER FOUR

After the elevator doors closed, Mack hesitated for a moment, tamping down the overpowering urge to get right back on and ride up to Townsend's to be by Toni's side when she faced Frank Clifford. Finally, with a resigned sigh, he strode down the hall to his office.

"Good morning, boss." Daphne Frazier, Mack's secretary, cheerfully greeted him.

Mack's reply consisted of an absent-minded grunt. He didn't look up, just headed for his private office.

"Who had the nerve to mess with your head so early in the morning?" Daphne asked.

Mack stopped and glanced back at his secretary. "What did you say, Daffy?"

Daphne frowned, her expression curious, her huge brown eyes sparkling with interest. "All right, who is she?"

"She?"

"The woman you can't keep your mind off of."

Mack quirked an eyebrow, ignoring her words. "Has my brother come in yet?

"Ah ha! Changing the subject. She must really be something."

"Daffy!"

"All right, boss. No, he hasn't. He has an early appointment with Phelps Electronics and won't be in until ten o'clock. Don't you remember?"

"Oh, yes." He cleared his throat. "If a Toni Carlton calls, I don't care what I'm doing, put her call through."

"What if you're—"

"Daffy, just do as I said. Okay?" he snapped.

"All right. But you don't have to bite my head off."

Mack blew out a weary breath. Hunching his shoulders, he muttered, "Sorry." Then he went into his office and closed the door. Taking off his jacket, he glanced at his desk. He had a thick stack of papers awaiting his attention. Ignoring them for the moment, he sat down and checked his desk calendar. He had several afternoon appointments scheduled.

After a few minutes of trying to concentrate on his work, he stopped and loosened his tie. Fifteen more minutes passed before he gave up the fight, rose from his chair, walked over to the window and looked out.

How had Toni's confrontation with Clifford gone? He wondered, raking his fingers through his hair. Had he simply handed her her things? Or had he tried to...

Mack strode over to his investigations file cabinet, retrieved the Townsend personnel file, and then pulled out Toni's information. He wondered how she'd feel when she found out he would in all likelihood be investigating her? Would she still want his help?

The more he thought about Toni and what could be happening with Clifford, the more anxious he became. Finally unable to stand it anymore, Mack decided to go up to the seventh floor.

"Daffy, if Marcus gets back before I do, tell him I've gone up to Townsend's." Mack didn't wait for an answer, just left the office and sprinted to the elevator.

Anxious impatience clawed at Mack's nerves as he waited for a car to come. He imagined how Toni must have felt when she ran for the elevator to escape Frank Clifford and it didn't come. Because he understood this didn't mean he believed her story, however.

"Oh, come on," he cursed, furiously stabbing the up button. It was taking the damned elevator forever to get to his floor. Maybe he should have taken the stairs. At last the elevator came. As soon as the doors opened, he rushed inside and punched the seventh floor button.

Finding the office empty threw him into a panic. His heartbeat quickened. Where was Toni? He eyed the door to the CEO's office.

He could only imagine what could be happening if she was in there with him.

Should he knock or just go in?

Not hearing any sound emanating from within, he turned the knob. What he saw when he opened the door was Toni standing in front of the file cabinet with her hand in a drawer.

"Oh, Mack!" She pulled her hand out, then fell back against the file cabinet. "You almost scared me to death."

"Where's Clifford?"

"He had an early morning conference. When you turned that knob, I thought he had cancelled the meeting and decided to come into the office."

"You never mentioned anything about a conference."

"It slipped my mind with everything that happened. I only remembered when I came in and found he wasn't here."

Mack folded his arms. "And decided to do what?"

"See if I could find something to figure out what he's planning for me."

"If he's as clever as you say, he wouldn't be stupid enough to leave anything like that lying around."

She sighed, her face crumpling in defeat. "I thought because the door was locked...You're right, he wouldn't."

"If it was locked, how did you—never mind. Come on and go across the street and have a cup of coffee with me."

"I sure need one." She smiled. "All right."

Toni and Mack left the office and headed for the elevator. When the doors opened, Pat Davis stood inside. She looked from Toni to Mack, then back at Toni with a questioning smile on her face.

"I'm going across the street to the Coffee House," Toni said, hoping to get away without revealing her companion's name, but knowing Pat, she shouldn't have wasted the energy. The woman didn't move.

"Pat, this is Mackinsey Jessup. Mack, Pat Davis, Townsend's best executive secretary, and my friend."

"Pat," he said, beaming a charming grin on her.

THE PERFECT FRAME

Shifting the papers to her left hand, Pat extended her right hand. "Mack."

Toni looked up at Mack. "We'd better be going. I have a lot of work to do before Mr. Clifford gets back from San Diego."

Pat gave Toni a you-have-some-explaining-to-do-later smile before heading for the office.

During the ride down to the lobby Toni and Mack were silent, each deep into their own private thoughts.

Toni shot a quick look at Mack's profile, wondering what he was thinking. Had he really believed her reasons for searching the CEO's office? For a moment she could have sworn that a tinge of doubt had seeped into his face and voice.

Although Mack continued to face the elevator doors, he managed to observe, out of the corner of his eye, Toni's expression as she tried to guess his frame of mind. He wished he could completely discount her as a suspect, but he couldn't.

The Coffee House was crowded when Toni and Mack walked in. It took a few minutes before the hostess came and showed them to a small corner table. After the waitress had taken their order and left, Toni focused her attention on Mack.

"What should I do?"

"I don't know. You'll have to wait until he gets back and see what happens."

"But how can I possibly work with him, knowing what I know? And especially after he intimated that I might have an accident."

"He can't follow through on any of his threats now. He neutralized the situation when he involved me and the security people. What you have to worry about is how he set things up to frame you, and then try to counter his next move. Basically the ball is in his court."

Toni definitely didn't like the idea of that man being in control of any aspect of her life or her career. She had believed him when he'd said that honest work had its own reward and he intended to see that she received hers. She'd been foolish to trust him.

The waitress returned with their coffee.

"To be on the safe side, I think you should have your locks changed once you get your keys back."

"I think you're right."

Mack covered her small cold hand with his large warm one, caressing the soft back with his thumb as he gazed into her dark, anxious eyes.

"It's going to be all right. You can trust me, sweet Toni."

She wanted to, but she'd trusted Clifford and look where that had gotten her.

Mack saw the wary glimmer in her expressive eyes and he let her hand go, picked up his coffee and sipped it.

Toni followed suit, quietly studying him as she did so. She was suddenly concerned with the way Mack's lips lingered on the rim of his cup and her urgent desire to feel the warmth of his lips moving sensuously over hers.

Mack felt her eyes on him and sensed the shift in her thoughts. He didn't look up, just continued to drink his coffee as though he were savoring it instead of thinking about how much he wanted to taste the sweetness of her mouth. For a moment he was lost in his own vivid imaginings. Then reality reasserted itself. He was a professional and right now he wasn't acting anything like one.

"If Clifford is setting you up, how close do you think he is to achieving his goal?"

If? Toni frowned. Did Mack doubt her? "According to the person he was talking to on the phone, he's almost there." She thought for a moment. It had to be the Harper account he intended using to close the frame tightly around her. "I don't know," she answered.

Mack could tell by the look on Toni's face that she was holding out on him. What could he say to get her to open up to him? And how was he going to handle things with her once she knew his position regarding the case?

Mack glanced at his watch. "I think we'd better be getting back. I have some calls to make and a desk piled high with work."

Toni stiffened at his sudden change of mood, wondering what had brought it on. "I have work to do, too," she muttered.

As they rose, Mack realized what he had done and wanted to say something to make up for it, but what could he say? They stopped at the cashier counter and Mack paid for the coffees. Before heading across the street, he took her arm. With his next words, he tried to get back to their earlier closeness.

"My brother should be back at the office by now."

"Your business is a family business, then?"

"Marcus is the only member of the family who works with me. My brother Matthew is a lawyer and has his own practice. Mariah is still in college, although she has threatened to join me at the office when she graduates."

Toni laughed. "I've noticed that all of your names begin with the letter M. Not a coincidence, I take it?"

"No. It's my mother's romantic obsession, I'm afraid. Her name is Marianna and my father's was Mali. She felt his branch of the family should start their own tradition. I remember hearing them laugh about it when we were kids." Mack's voice changed from one of sharing confidences to one of remembered pain.

"My father died when I was ten. He was born and raised in Liberia, and was a chemist by profession. Several months after arriving in the States, he met my mother and six months later they were married. During the seven years he waited for his citizenship to become permanent, he took any job he could find close to the line of work he was qualified in."

"And did he finally get a chemist position once he became a citizen?" Toni asked.

"Yes, at a metal and graphics plant in Vernon, California." Mack's jaws clenched and he paused a moment before continuing. "He was killed a year and a half later. He was the victim of a drive-by shooting while on his way home from work. My mother was expecting Mariah at the time."

"Oh, Mack, I'm so sorry."

"It happened a long time ago." His jaw flexed and he gave her a small smile. "I don't know how I got off on this subject. Whenever I'm with you..."

"What?"

He shrugged. "I can't explain it."

"Jessup doesn't sound African to me."

"My father changed it. In its original form you would have difficulty pronouncing it."

They walked into the lobby of the Townsend Building. An elevator stood waiting. When they reached Mack's floor, he held the door open.

"What time are you going to lunch?"

"At one."

"I'll come for you then. Be ready."

"Yes, sir." She saluted.

He grinned, then let the doors close. Toni smiled, allowing the warm feeling of connecting with Mack flow through her. When the elevator stopped on the seventh floor, she stepped out, then headed down the hall to the office. Her smile disappeared when she saw Frank Clifford standing beside Pat's desk talking to her. Toni noticed the strained, pinched expression on her friend's face. She wondered what they could possibly be talking about to put that look there. When Mr. Clifford saw Toni, he straightened to his full height and beamed a charming, guileless smile on her.

"Toni, I'm glad you're back. I need to talk to you. Come into my office." Then he strode into it.

"Listen, when you get time, I want to hear all about Mack Jessup," Pat commented. "I know he has offices in the building, but until today I'd never seen him. I was off on maternity leave when he did some work for Townsend's five years ago." She smiled. "I'd have to say he's a real hunk. Evidently you've been holding out on me, girl. How long have you been seeing each other? Is he your mystery man?"

"Pat!"

"Oh, all right, I'll wait until later, but not much later."

"Thank you," she said. The time to confront her boss had arrived. She smoothed her hands down the sides of her slacks and walked over to his door. Taking breath to gather her composure, she turned the knob and entered.

Frank Clifford was sitting behind his desk thumbing through some papers when she walked in. He looked up. "I have some things that belong to you, I believe."

He put the papers down on the desk and delved inside his bottom desk drawer and extracted her purse.

"The keys are inside. I was worried about you, Toni. I waited for you to miss them and come back. But when you didn't, I went home." He cleared his throat. "As you'll remember, I had intended to catch a late night flight to San Diego. But before I could leave for the airport, John Riley's secretary called to say the meeting would have to be rescheduled for next Wednesday because her boss had suddenly taken ill." He sent her a contrite smile. "I feel bad about having asked you to stay last night to do that report. As always, you did an excellent job."

"Thank you." That was all she could manage as she reached for her purse, bewildered. Was she losing it? Had she just imagined the previous night? He was acting as though nothing out of the ordinary had happened! As if he hadn't told someone the trap he'd set for her was almost ready to be sprung! As if he hadn't threatened to end her life!

"You look tired, Toni. Why don't you go home early today? Whatever you have to do can wait until Monday."

"But—"

He gave her a fatherly smile. "No buts. That's an order." He picked up the papers he'd laid down minutes before and started studying them.

Toni stood fingering the strap on her purse for a few seconds before turning to leave his office. She went back to her desk, stowed her purse in a bottom drawer and dropped into her chair. What kind of mind game was he playing with her? She turned on her computer and reviewed the Harper account, as well as several others, and found absolutely nothing out of the ordinary.

By lunch time, Toni was more then ready to get away from the office. She evaded Pat's determination to question her about Mack and hurried to the elevator. When the doors opened, she saw Mack standing inside.

"Are you all right?" he asked, studying her intently.

"I don't know."

"You look poleaxed."

"That's exactly how I feel," she said, stepping into the elevator beside him and pushing the close button.

"What happened? He didn't try anything with you, did he?"

"No, quite the opposite. Mack, he's acting as if nothing happened." How could she explain this without sounding like a raving lunatic?

"He did give you back your keys and purse, though, didn't he?"

"Yes. But, Mack, I want you to know I wasn't lying about what he said. Everything I told you really happened. You do believe me, don't you?"

"I believe he frightened you," Mack said carefully.

"But you don't believe me about his scheme to frame me?"

"I didn't say that, I—"

The elevator stopped on the third floor and the doors opened.

"Mack!"

"Marcus."

"I would ask where you rushed off to," Marcus gazed appreciatively at Toni, "but I can see the answer to my question is standing before me." He grinned. "Well, Mack, aren't you going to introduce us?"

"Toni Carlton, my brother, Marcus."

She extended her hand. There was more than a passing resemblance between the brothers. They were both tall and had that same sexy, magnetic mixture of Latin and African charisma.

"Pleased to meet you, Marcus."

"Call me Marc. And believe me, the pleasure is all mine."

"I think we should be going," Mack said to Toni.

"I think that maybe you should go alone," she answered coolly.

"Toni."

"I'm really not hungry now, Mack. We can have lunch another day."

"But we need to talk."

"I don't think we have anything more to say to each other," she said, but her look told a different story.

Mack knew he'd blown it. He stepped off the elevator. For a moment Toni stood glaring holes through him before pushing the close button.

"Toni, wait we—"

The doors slid closed.

"Damn it," he growled, banging his fists on them.

"It can't be you, the original silver-tongued devil, who usually talks his way out of any unpleasant situation with a woman."

Mack glared at his brother. "You're asking for a world of hurt, my brother."

"Why? Because I dare to criticize the great Mackinsey Jessup?"

"All right, all right, you've made your point," he gritted out, stalking past his brother, back to his office.

Toni got off on the seventh floor and marched down the hall to Townsend's. Pat started to grill her on the subject of Mack the moment she walked through the office doors, but stopped short when she saw the warning sign to back off flashing in Toni's eyes.

After clearing her desk, Toni stopped by Pat's on her way out. "I'm leaving early."

"Why?"

"Mr. Clifford insisted."

She frowned. "Weren't you supposed to go to lunch with Mack?"

"I changed my mind and decided to go home instead."

"Are you sure you're feeling all right?"

"Just because I chose not to go out to lunch with Mack doesn't mean I need my head examined."

Seeing the hurt look on her friend's face, Toni relented.

"I'm fine, Pat, really. See you on Monday." And she headed for the door. As she waited for the elevator, Toni glanced back at Pat and thought about her friend's attitude toward their boss and concluded that whatever her reason for it, she was no doubt justified, as Toni herself felt justified considering what he was doing to her.

On the way down to the parking lot, Toni's feelings about her own situation were intensifying. Frank Clifford was evidently playing a game of cat and mouse with her, keeping her wondering how, when and where he was going to make his next move. And make no mistake about it, she was sure he would do that in his own good time. What could she do in the meantime to save herself? Knowing he was planning to destroy her, but not when, would surely shred the threads of her composure.

If she tried going to the president with this without any proof, he not only wouldn't believe her, but he'd think she was crazy.

Toni got off the elevator and, flashing her keys in front of her, smiled at Bill as she moved on to her car. She fastened her safety belt and glanced down at her clothes. She would have to return Mack's sister's clothes and get her own things from his house. The thought of facing Mack again made the nerves in her stomach jerk. She had been willing to trust him, but that was before he'd showed her his true colors.

Thirty minutes later, Toni eased her car into her assigned parking space beneath her apartment building. A wave of loneliness washed over her. After spending one night with Mack, she now dreaded going up to her empty apartment. How could she be missing him this much when they'd only just met?

Once inside her apartment, Toni showered, then wrapped herself in a mint-colored terrycloth robe. Realizing how hungry she was, she went to the fridge and took out the makings for a salad and a sandwich. It wouldn't be anything like the meal Mack had prepared for her.

Oh, Mack.

When the door buzzer sounded, her heart started racing.

CHAPTER FIVE

Toni pushed the com button. "Yes."

"It's Mack, Toni."

She let out a relieved breath at the sound of his voice and held the button down to unlock the outside door.

An eternity passed until she heard his knock. Toni rubbed her hands down the sides of her robe. Then, pulling the tie tighter around her waist, she opened the door.

"I know it's late, but I had to see you. I couldn't let an entire weekend go by without letting you know how sorry I am." He grinned crookedly. "I think I'd better come inside and offer a proper apology."

"All right." Toni signaled him inside, closed the door, then led him into her living room.

Mack took in the ambiance of the room at a glance. It was totally feminine, but with none of the frilly touches some women added that could make a man feel as out of place as an elephant in a flower garden.

Toni's furnishings were comfortable, yet had a subtle elegance about them. The recliner couch set was made of a tweedy material done in mint green, peach and cream. A brass and glass tree branch lamp extended across the back of the couch. The pictures on the walls were of homey scenes with houses surrounded by trees and shrubs. Thomas Kincade, if he wasn't mistaken.

Mack smiled warmly at Toni. "You'll have that house with the picket fence one day."

"And the husband and children to go with it, I hope."

"Listen, I didn't want you to think that I didn't believe you. It's just that you took me by surprise when you said what you did about Clifford."

Now is the time to tell her about your part in the investigation. Yet if she knew, what would she think of him?

"I know I probably overreacted," Toni began, "but it seemed to me that you—oh never mind." Sensing that she needed to put some distance between them, she walked over to the windows.

Mack, picking up on her reaction to him, quickly came up behind her and pulled her back against his body, then nuzzled the space behind her ear. The rose-scented fragrance of her skin thoroughly intoxicated his senses. He felt desire for her rising inside him. All he had to do was be anywhere near her and his self-control threatened to desert him.

Toni's damp black hair glistened and her skin had a flushed attractive rosiness about it from her shower. When he turned her to face him, he became aware of how little there was between her naked body and himself. And the fact that the lapels on her robe had gaped open, revealing the enticing swell of her breasts, hadn't escaped him.

"Mack?"

"Yes," he groaned.

She eased away from him and turned to look into his eyes.

"Should we be doing this?"

He kissed her deeply. "I want you, sweet Toni."

She wanted him too, but they hardly knew each other. Things were moving way too fast.

When he kissed her throat and behind her ear again, the sensation nearly drove her out of her mind.

"Mack, I think—"

"Baby, don't think, just feel," he said, continuing his onslaught of desire-spiking kisses over her throat and next to her collarbone. When Mack felt Toni shudder and heard her moan, what little control he still possessed vanished completely and he pulled the belt to her robe loose, exposing her naked body.

A shower of cold reality splashed Toni and she sought to maneuver her body out of his embrace, but Mack's mouth found an aroused nipple and he sucked strongly, draining the last of her resistance. Her fingers took on a will of their own and rushed to unbutton his shirt, seeking the warmth of his bare skin.

Mack groaned and started helping her undress him. In a matter of seconds his lean athletic body stood magnificently naked before Toni's devouring gaze. She'd seen his bare chest at his house the night before, but seeing all of him this way made her insides dissolve like sugar dropped into a cup of hot coffee.

"Oh, Mack, I want you so much."

"Don't worry, baby, I intend to see that you get me." He lowered her slender frame to the carpet and followed her down, kissing her again and again, urging his fingers to explore every curve, every hollow of her body. When he felt her quiver with need, he reached for his pants to get their protection. Seconds later, he moved between her thighs and thrust deeply into her femininity, glorying in the feel of her hot damp sheath clenching tightly around him. Desire took over and everything else melted away under the heat of his throbbing passion.

Toni gasped, rocking the cradle of her hips against him again and again and yet again. Any reservation she had left about what she was doing vanished under the enveloping tide of ecstasy.

Toni reached for her robe. "I think we'd better get dressed."

Mack's hand encircled her wrist, staying her movements. "I have a better idea. Why don't we adjourn to your bedroom?"

"Maybe later. Right now, I'm starved."

Mack flashed her a wicked smile.

"I meant for food. I've made a salad and was about to fix myself a sandwich when you came. If you're hungry, I'm sure there's enough for two."

Conceding defeat, Mack shrugged his shoulders and reached for his pants. "Whatever you say, my little chickadee. I'll make us some coffee."

"W. C. Fields." She laughed.

"I must have sounded like him if you recognized who I was imitating."

"I wouldn't say that, exactly."

"What would you say exactly?"

"Oh, Mack, you're priceless."

"You really think so?"

"Yes." She gave him a sexy smile. "And I loved your imitation."

"You're just saying that. My brothers claim the imitations I do don't even come close to being good; in fact they say they suck." His expression turned serious. "We need to talk about Frank Clifford, Toni."

Her smile faded and she let out a sharp breath. "I told you how he was acting."

Mack arched a dark brow. "And you have no clue what he could be up to?"

"Not a one." When she saw the skeptical twist to his mouth, she added, "I thought at first that he would use certain accounts that I've worked on, but when I checked the files I saw nothing to indicate that he had. I found no mistakes or inconsistencies."

Mack thought about what he had already managed to uncover when he examined the company files. Whoever was doing the tampering hadn't done as good a job of covering their tracks as they had assumed. Or maybe it could be deliberate. And judging from what he'd seen, he was beginning to believe Toni might be innocent. God only knew how much he wanted to believe that. Especially now that they had been intimate.

Mack swept Toni up in his arms with the intention of taking up where they had left off. Then the phone rang.

She reached down and picked up the receiver and said hello.

"You think you've got it all figured out, don't you, sweetheart?"

"Who is this? Hank?" She signaled for Mack to put her down.

"Yeah, it's me, baby. You and Clifford think you're going to edge me out of that promotion. But I've got a news flash for you. It ain't gonna happen."

"Hank, I—" Toni heard the sharp click, followed by the hum of the dial tone, and pulled the phone away from her ear as though it were a snake shaking its rattle. She stood wondering what the call was all about. What could Frank Clifford have possibly said to Hank?

"What is it, Toni?" Mack asked, carefully monitoring her reaction.

"Oh, it's nothing important, just somebody from work."

His doubts began to resurface. Hank Warren was as much a suspect as anyone else. Could they be in on the embezzlement scam together? Mack's insides churned at the thought of Toni's possible involvement with the man. He didn't know if it was because of the theft or Hank Warren. What did he mean to Toni?

Mack felt damned confused right now. He realized only too well that he'd done what he'd promised himself he would never do again— get emotionally involved with a suspect. And to make matters worse, he had complicated things by taking her to bed. He quickly finished dressing, his ardor having completely disappeared.

Toni and Mack ate their dinner in silence. Then, afterward, he helped with the cleanup.

He bent his head to kiss her lips when they were done. "I'd better go. I'll call you. Oh, and don't forget to get your locks changed," he reminded her.

"I won't." Disappointment filled her at his sudden eagerness to leave. The effect he had on her was mind-altering and she couldn't understand it. She had been unable to control her reaction to him. And that realization had scared the hell out of her. How could she feel so connected to this man so fast? And you've allowed him to make love to you, her conscience nagged.

Mack kissed her good night and then left. None of the passion they'd shared earlier was evident in that kiss. He had wanted to stay at first. She had certainly wanted him to. What had made him change his mind?

Had Hank's call cooled Mack's desire? Maybe he thought that something was going on between her and Hank. He had no idea how much she despised the man.

That night, as Toni sat in bed reading, it dawned on her that Mack knew where she lived. She hadn't told him, so how had he found out? She thought about it for a moment. He could have gotten the address, along with her phone number, from Pat, the eternal matchmaker, she supposed.

And another thing: Hank Warren, of all people, had called her. She'd never in a million years give him her phone number, yet he had it. But if he'd really wanted it, all he had to do was hack into the personnel files. Although those files were presumably confidential, for someone as well versed in computers and determined to find out certain information as he was, it wouldn't be a problem.

She was more puzzled than ever since that phone call. Why had he called her and said what he did? A few minutes later she put her book down, turned off the light and closed her eyes, but sleep didn't come right away. When it did, she was still no nearer to finding the answers she sought.

On Saturday Toni had a locksmith come out and change her locks. For the rest of the day as she did her laundry and housecleaning, her thoughts swung from Mack to Frank Clifford and back again. Each posed a threat in his own way. Clifford was a danger to her professional life, and Mack her personal one.

Toni knew by Sunday afternoon Mack wasn't going to call. She couldn't help wondering what was in his mind. All of the passion he'd displayed couldn't have just evaporated overnight, could it? Why hadn't he called? Surely he wasn't a love-'em-and-leave-'em kind of man. He owed her an explanation, and she intended to get one.

One of the few times since she'd started working at Townsend's, Toni was late getting to work. She'd stayed up most of the night thinking about her situation, worrying, wondering if she would be able to extricate herself from it without suffering too much. In addition, her relationship with Mack was bothering her. Where was it headed? Although she knew a little about his family life, she knew next to nothing about his personal side. He was a very enigmatic man where his private life was concerned.

The moment Toni stepped off the elevator, a strange tension enveloped her. She felt much like an animal sensing danger, alert and ready for the predator's attack. The first indication that her instincts were on target came when she saw Pat Davis. Her friend spoke to Toni in an oddly strained voice when she said good morning.

"Is anything wrong, Pat?"

"No." She cleared her voice. "Mr. Townsend has called a staff meeting for ten o'clock."

"Do you know why?"

"No, I don't," she said, looking away evasively, pretending an interest in the papers on her desk.

Something was going on, but what?

Hank came from behind his office cubicle with an evil gleam dancing in his eyes and said, "So you finally decided to grace us with your presence. Did your sugar daddy, our esteemed boss, say it was all right for you to be late?" he asked nastily.

"You're rude, crude and disgusting, Hanky Panky," Toni answered. Without uttering another word she disappeared behind her own office cubicle.

The hands on the clock seemed to take forever to reach ten. When meeting time finally arrived, Toni eyed each employee speculatively as they filed into the conference room. After everyone was seated, Mr. Townsend called the meeting to order.

"I've called you all here to discuss discrepancies in a number of our premier bond exchange accounts and the disappearance of negotiable securities this company is responsible for."

Murmurs of disbelief filled the room. Townsend cleared his throat and continued speaking.

"We've hired an expert to help sort out the situation."

The murmuring stopped when he said those words. Toni read the look of satisfaction on the president's face, sensing that it was some kind of major coup for him. She felt a sudden rush of pity for the man. His father was a hard act to follow. He had demanded respect, whereas his son had to practically beg for it.

For a moment Toni had let her thoughts wander, and just as she returned her full attention to the proceedings, Mr. Townsend signaled for the side door to be opened.

Mildred Frances, Townsend's secretary, opened it and Mack Jessup strode into the room.

Toni's eyes widened and her mouth fell open in shock.

Mack! What was he doing here?

Townsend introduced Mack when he reached the podium. "This is financial investigator Mackinsey Jessup. His company specializes in theft and other corporate irregularities. Many of you may remember that he helped us with another problem five years ago. You also may have seen him in the elevator or the lobby. He has an office suite on the third floor of this building."

Mack searched the room until he found the face he sought. When he saw the stunned hurt and disbelief freeze-framed on Toni's face, it felt like a barrage of hailstones pelting his conscience. Damn it, he should have told her the truth, but how could he have known that Townsend would call an emergency meeting to introduce him?

Mack spoke in a firm, professional voice. "I'll be talking to each and every one of you over the next few days. I'll try not to disrupt your routine. If you think of anything that might be helpful to the investigation, I want you to feel free to discuss it with me."

Amidst the buzz of employee reaction, Toni blinked in confusion at the words 'helpful to the investigation.' What she'd told Mack could be used against her. That feeling of danger she'd felt when she first met Mack came back to haunt her.

One burning question begged for an answer. How did he really feel about her?

Why hadn't he been honest with her from the beginning?

It had to mean she was just a part of the job.

She closed her eyes after that distressing thought. When she opened them again, eyes were riveted on her. Frank Clifford was studying her as if she were a butterfly staked to canvas. A sly look of triumph glittered in his eyes. Toni glanced at Mack, who was conversing with Mr. Townsend. Surely he wasn't reporting what she had told him!

She noticed that her boss wasn't the only person watching her. Toni caught Pat Davis and Hank Warren eyeing her strangely, too. She could only guess what was on their minds.

Minutes later, Mr. Townsend adjourned the meeting and everyone moved to leave the conference room and return to their respective jobs. At the door Joe Davis stopped and gave Toni a hard, sidelong glance before walking out.

What was going on? Why had Pat's husband looked at her like that? Was everyone suspicious of her?

The room was soon empty of people, except for Mack. Toni had hoped to avoid a confrontation with him by lagging behind. Resigned to the fact that he wasn't going to leave, she rose and headed for the door. Mack stepped in front of her, blocking her only avenue of escape.

"We need to talk, Toni."

"I think we've 'talked' enough, thank you very much."

"Damn it, would you listen to me, please. It's not what you think."

"Oh, isn't it?"

"No, it isn't, and you damn well know it." Suddenly he was all business. "I'll be in your office in an hour."

She glared at him. "Why? So you can officially grill me?"

His facade faltered and his jaw tensed. "Don't be like this, Toni."

"What other way do you expect me to be, Mack? I confided in you, trusted you and gave you a special part of myself."

"I know that. You can still trust me, baby. Believe me, I would never do anything to hurt you."

"You already have."

"If I did, I'm sorry." He sighed deeply. "I didn't know how to tell you who I was at first without—"

"Without revealing your part in the investigation? Are you sure you aren't in league with my esteemed boss?"

"A question like that doesn't deserve an answer."

She shifted her gaze uncomfortably. "I'm sorry."

A sharp jab of pain seared through his gut when he saw the unhappy, disillusioned look on her face. It was his fault for not being straight with her from the jump. He hadn't wanted to reveal himself until he was sure…Sure of what? Right now he wasn't sure of anything.

"I was hired to find a very clever thief. If you're not that thief you have nothing to worry about."

"If?" She laughed humorlessly. "That's the million dollar question, isn't it?"

"Don't say that. Give me a chance, will you?

"A chance? A chance to do what? Lie to me again? Use me again?"

"I never lied to you. And I certainly didn't use you. What happened between us was mutual."

"Maybe you didn't mean to lie, at least not outright. But there is such a thing as a lie by omission, you know. And about what we did on Friday—"

"It had nothing to do with this, no matter what you think of me right now. I have a job to do and I'm going to do it."

"Like the Northwest Mounties who always get their man, in this case, woman." She shot him a hard, contemptuous look. "And some people say I'm obsessed with my job."

Seeing the obstinate expression on her face, Mack moved out of Toni's way and watched her leave the room.

Every time she heard her office door open, Toni tensed, expecting it to be Mack. She might as well prepare herself for his visit, because he would be there just as he said. The thought of him questioning her in his official capacity shook her. What did he know that she didn't? The object of her thoughts suddenly appeared.

"I have to talk to the CEO first, Toni. Be here when I come out," Mack said, his tone determined, threatening retribution if his wishes were ignored.

Before she could answer, he was knocking on Frank Clifford's door. After he'd gone in, Hank Warren appeared.

"No man is safe around you, is he, sweetheart?"

"You certainly have nothing to worry about, Hanky."

His grin faded. "Why you—One day you're going to pay for talking to me like that." That said, he stalked away.

The evil intent in his eyes chilled her to the bone. Was he the one her boss had been talking to that night? Toni let out a weary breath, shifting her thoughts back to Mack. She dreaded talking to him. She could leave, but if she did, it would only be putting off the inevitable, and besides, not only was she not a coward, but she had nothing to hide.

Fifteen minutes later Mack came out of the CEO's office, and then the man himself followed.

"You can use my office if you need to speak individually with my staff, Jessup," he offered. "I have a lunch appointment with a prospective client." He pushed up the sleeve of his suit coat and glanced at his watch. "If you will all excuse me…" With that he hurried out of the office.

Toni waited expectantly, her nerves taunt, stretched to the breaking point. What would Mack ask Pat? And more to the point what would he ask Hank Warren? And what would that lying snake say against her?

CHAPTER SIX

Toni gazed at the computer screen, trying her best to get involved in her work, but it was no use. Her concentration was shot to hell because of Mack's presence in the office, and the subject he was discussing and the people with whom he was discussing it.

She glanced at the clock. Mack had been talking to Pat a long time. Why? When Toni had talked with her a few days ago, Pat had denied knowing anything about any discrepancies.

At the sound of the door opening, Toni looked up. She read Pat's expression as one of unease when she came out of the office. Her gaze avoided Toni's. And her manner was evasive, guilty even. And that was definitely not like her friend. Why should Pat look guilty? What had Mack asked her?

"Warren, you can come in now," Mack instructed.

The calculating smile on Hank's face when he looked at Toni set her teeth on edge. Anything bad he could think of to say about her she was sure he would relate to Mack with relish. How she despised the man.

"Sit down, Warren," Mack said, striving to keep his tone neutral.

"If you want to know what I think, our Ms. Carlton is as guilty as sin."

Mack's eyes narrowed. "What makes you think so?"

"It's obvious. She had access to the accounts and the authority to act on them. Stands to reason she's the one responsible for the irregularities."

The man's arrogance irritated Mack to no end. What bothered him even more was the venom in his voice when he bashed Toni. Was he a jealous ex-lover seeking revenge because she had dumped him? Just what was the relationship between him and Toni?

"You have proof to substantiate your allegations? And I don't mean an opinion; I'm talking about hard evidence."

"Well no, but—"

"All I want from you are the facts as you know them, not your suspicions, not your opinions. You got that?" Mack relished the look of angry hostility his words brought to Warren's face. He couldn't help wondering if he was the one Clifford had been talking to on the phone the night Toni ran into his office. What also interested Mack was finding out why he had called Toni Friday night.

"I got it, all right. You'd like to get your hands on Toni's luscious little body. Or maybe you've already sampled the merchandise and you're eager to post a no-trespassing sign."

Mack gritted his teeth, calling on every ounce of control he could summon to keep from smashing his fist into Warren's face. But in the end he found the temptation to do something too great and grabbed the man by his jacket lapels, jerking him up from the chair.

Hank laughed. "I see you're going to get primitive."

Mack let him go.

"Don't back down now, Jessup. Things were just beginning to get interesting. I can understand how you feel, man. I've seen the effect she has on men often enough. Maybe she and Clifford are getting it on."

Mack felt a jerking in his stomach at those words. "As I said before, if you don't have proof to back up what you say…"

"Old Frank and our little Toni work late together almost every night, and have done so for the last year and a half. I'd say they have the perfect setup, not to mention the perfect opportunity to steal. Wouldn't you say?"

"That'll be all," Mack ground out. "You can go back to your work."

"But don't you want to know—"

"I said you can go."

With a smirk on his face that made Mack feel like punching his lights out, Hank Warren left the office. Mack slammed his fist down on the desk, wishing it was the jerk's gut. What he wasn't looking forward to was questioning Toni. But it wasn't as though he had a choice. He straightened his shoulders and headed for the door.

When Toni thought she couldn't stand the suspense any longer, the door to the CEO's office opened and Hank walked out. After flashing her a smug smile, he stepped behind his office cubicle.

Mack observed the byplay, wondering again if anything was going on between them. "You can come in, Toni—Ms. Carlton," Mack corrected himself, striving to ease back into a professional persona.

Toni rose and smoothing down her skirt, coolly started toward the office door. Inside, her nerves were rioting, but on the outside she projected a cool, calm front.

Mack moved back, allowing her passing room. Once she stepped inside, he closed the door.

Toni felt a moment of trepidation at the ominous click.

For a brief few seconds all Mack did was stare before asking Toni to sit down. He perched a lean hip on the corner of the desk, then crossed his arms over his chest.

"I get the impression from your boss that you're quite an ambitious lady."

She lifted her chin proudly. "Anything wrong with that?"

"On the surface, no."

Toni frowned. What did he mean 'on the surface'? What was he implying?

"He said you've been more than helpful, volunteering above and beyond the call of duty."

"What are you trying to say, that you believe I'm a thief?"

"Don't put words in my mouth. According to your personnel record you—"

"My personnel record!" She felt so exposed. Those records were supposed to be confidential. "When did you see them, before or after you took me to bed?"

Mack moved off the desk and walked over to the window and thrust his hands into his pockets. Then he turned to look at Toni and answered, "Before."

"Then you knew about the discrepancies the night we met."

"Yes, I did." He cleared his throat. "I knew that your name appeared on the authorizations to buy and sell on several of the company's major accounts."

"Of course they would. It isn't unusual since I was put in charge of them by the CEO. I am his PA."

"Don't get defensive with me." Mack felt the easy rapport they'd shared from the start slipping away, and he didn't like it. "I'm just stating a fact. Where is the paperwork that goes with those accounts, explaining the action you took?"

"The originals go to the client and the copies are kept on file."

Mack shook his head. "They're missing from the files and several clients didn't receive them."

"Well, I can't explain it. I didn't deliberately misplace or destroy them."

"I think we need to start from when Mr. Townsend first suspected there were, as he put it, irregularities with the sale of certain stocks and securities. According to him, they began to show up five months ago, when his father was still president."

"Five months ago?" Toni thought back to that time. It was when Mr. Townsend Sr. began to scrutinize her work and everything having to do with her. Had he been suspicious of her? Was that the reason he'd called her into his office?

"From what I could gather it was when the elder Townsend, who was a naturally suspicious man, began to notice the shifts and discrepancies in the accounts. He hadn't gone so far as to accuse anyone, but if he hadn't died I'm sure he would have done so."

Toni watched the blank expression on Mack's face. Was he trying to say that Townsend's death went beyond coincidence? And because she had been with him when he died she was suspect? That was ridiculous. No one could possibly blame her for his death, could they? He'd died from a stroke, hadn't he?

Mack studied Toni for a few seconds. "You can go, but don't leave the office. I have something else I need to discuss with you."

Toni sat worrying her bottom lip with her teeth, wondering why Mack had changed the subject so abruptly. The look in his eyes told her the other subject he wanted to discuss was one he considered of equal importance. After all that had happened today, she wasn't sure she wanted to talk to him about anything else, personal or otherwise.

This was Mack, the man who had made such tender love to her, the man she had trusted with not only her life and her body, but her vulnerable emotions.

"You're telling me you need to talk to me about something else, yet giving me my walking papers? Can't you simply tell me what you think?"

"It's not that simple."

"Why isn't it? Either you believe what I've told you or you don't."

Mack ran his fingers through his hair. "Damn it, Toni, right now I'm not sure of anything, okay?" He inhaled a deep breath. "I need to check out a few things before I can begin to form an opinion."

"And you're not going to tell me what those things are, right?"

"I can't. Don't you see—"

"Oh, I see all right." She got up and started for the door.

Mack reached it first and clamped a hand around her wrist, swinging her around to face him. He gazed into her eyes for a moment before lowering his mouth to hers.

The doorknob rattled and they broke apart.

Frank Clifford strode inside. He glanced at Toni's flushed face and Mack's discomfited look and smiled knowingly.

"I assume you're done 'questioning' my staff—to, ah, your satisfaction?"

Mack cleared his throat. "For now I am, yes, although I'll probably be questioning all of you again as the investigation progresses."

"We'll make ourselves available."

Toni put her hand on the doorknob.

"Won't we, Toni? Don't leave, I need to discuss a few things with you," Clifford said to her, giving Mack a dismissive look.

The intimacy his words suggested angered Mack. Had Clifford intended to give the impression that something was going on between him and Toni? Mack glanced at Toni, and then Clifford, before exiting the office.

CHAPTER SEVEN

"Now, Ms. Carlton," Clifford said from his perch on the edge of his desk, "come over here and sit down." He indicated the chair in front of his desk.

Toni didn't want to be alone with this man, let alone that close to him, but decided that if she wanted to find out what he had to say she would have to do as he suggested. She sank down on the chair.

"I know you're probably wondering why I haven't come after you since the other night. Well, I've had time to rethink the situation. I was a bit premature in resorting to threats of violence.

"The net is very close to hopelessly entangling you." He laughed. "I don't know what you hope to accomplish by cultivating a relationship with Mackinsey Jessup. It won't do you any good, you know. He can't save you. My plan has already been set into motion, and there is nothing you can do to stop or alter its progression."

"What do you mean?"

He smiled. "You'll find out soon enough. It was unfortunate that you found out about things when you did. Soon your Mr. Jessup will discover more evidence against you. And believe me, despite whatever is going on between you two, he will begin to doubt your claim of innocence. When that happens, I won't have to do anything. He'll do it for me.

"Until then, you can do one of two things: You can continue to work the same as usual and try to vindicate yourself, or you can cut and run. It's that simple. You may go now, Toni. I have a lot of work to do. Oh, and be sure to close the door on your way out."

Toni sat staring at him for a moment, too stunned to say anything, much less move to leave. "You can't—"

"I already have." He grinned triumphantly. "You are dismissed."

When Toni rose from her chair, her legs felt weak and she stumbled slightly. He reached out to steady her, but she jerked away.

"I'm going to stop you."

"You'll try, but you won't succeed."

Toni left his office with a renewed determination to save herself and thwart his plans. Somehow she'd find a way. There had to be something he'd overlooked or neglected to do, she told herself, but fear that he might not have made her shiver despite her new found confidence.

Mack was right; they did need to talk. Toni returned to her desk and looked up the number for Jessup Investigations.

"Jessup Investigations. Daphne speaking."

"Is Mack Jessup in?"

"He's in a meeting at the moment. Would you like to leave a message?"

"No, I'll call back."

"If you'll leave your name and number, I—"

"That won't be necessary."

"Are you Toni Carlton?"

"Yes, but how did you know?"

"Hold on and I'll let him know you're on the line."

Had Mack left word to put her calls through no matter what? He had to believe in her a little to do that, didn't he?

"Toni, what is it? Did Clifford try to hurt or threaten you?"

"Yes. I need to see you right away, Mack."

"Come down now. I'll be waiting."

Toni gazed at Pat. She had some questions she wanted to ask but she decided to wait until a better time.

"Pat, I'm leaving the office for a few minutes."

"Toni."

"Yes?"

"I didn't want to say anything to hurt your relationship with Mack."

"What does my relationship with Mack have to do with the investigation?"

"I can tell that he's crazy about you, and I didn't want to mess things up."

"Don't worry about Mack and me. What did he ask you?"

"What I knew about the irregularities in the accounts, and I had to tell him the truth."

"What truth?"

"Toni, I had to tell him that you said some sales confirmations were wrong, but that when I went into the files, I didn't find the kind of errors you mentioned."

"It probably looks like a cover-up to Mack. The errors were there, Pat. I'm being set up."

"Set up! Oh, my God! I thought you were just tired from overwork when you mentioned them. I never dreamed that anything could be really wrong. I'm sorry if I made you look bad."

"It's not your fault," Toni said, staring at the CEO's closed office door. "I've got to leave now."

"Are you coming back to work later?"

"I don't know."

"What do you want me to tell Mr. Clifford?"

"Don't worry about it, Pat, I'll do the honors." Toni noted the relief on her friend's face and shook her head and walked back to her desk and picked up the phone and punched the com button to her boss's office.

"Yes, Toni."

"I'll be out of the office for a few minutes."

"Going down to Jessup to plot and plan your strategy? Like I said, it won't do you any good. No one can save you. But knowing you and that clever capable mind of yours, you'll try."

He laughed, then severed the connection.

"The arrogance of the man."

"Have a fight with your sugar daddy?" Hank inquired, leaning against the compartment separation wall. "Did he not do as you wanted?"

"Why don't you slither back into your hole and pull the ground over you."

"Now if I did that, I wouldn't get that promotion when you're exposed as the thief."

"It's unwise to count your chickens, Hanky." She rose in one fluid motion and, grabbing up her purse, walked around him and out of the office.

On the way down in the elevator Toni wondered what she could say to Mack. Would he believe her if she told him everything Clifford had said? When the elevator door opened, she stepped out and headed for Mack's office.

"You must be Toni Carlton. I'm Daphne, Mack's secretary and girl Friday." She smiled. "Go right in, he's waiting for you."

Mack opened the door to his private office. "Come in, Toni." He closed the door on Daphne's curious gaze.

Mack took Toni in his arms and kissed her. Her response was immediate and hot as she returned it with ardor.

"Wow, you are one dangerous woman. Now what prompted this visit? I sensed by your voice that something must have happened." His eyes darkened. "He didn't touch you, did he?"

"No, not literally."

"What did he say? Did he threaten you?"

"Not precisely. It was more a prediction of my doom. Oh, Mack, I'm scared."

"If you're innocent—"

She pulled away. "If?"

"Sorry, bad choice of words. I believe what you've told me."

"Believe, or want to believe?"

"You're not a thief. The thing is how to prove it."

"But what if we can't?"

He pulled her back into his arms and eased her head onto his shoulder and stroked her hair. "Together we can do anything, sweet Toni." Toni rubbed her cheek against his chest and tightened her hold around his waist. How she wanted to believe that. Mack was saying all the right words, but she got the feeling he wasn't as confident as he would have her believe.

After Toni had gone Mack called Marcus into his office.

"Yeah, what's up?"

"Did you track down the cancelled checks for the accounts I gave you?"

"Sure did."

"And?"

"All of them were dated on the fifteenth."

"What dates were they cashed?"

"Harper, 20th; A. C. Holdings, 23rd; Modern Day Investments, 30th; Barnes Group, 31st, Profit-tech, 31st."

"All on or after the 20th of each month."

"Your point is?"

"Were confirmations of sales attached?"

"No, but there are probably reasons for that. They aren't always immediately available. It's not unusual for them to be sent at a later date."

"No, but it's our job to find out why they weren't in this instance. Something tells me we'll need to with all the rest too. Did you talk to the mail room manager?"

"He said he'd just taken over the job and I would have to talk to the assistant, Joe Davis."

"And did you?"

"He'd gone home sick."

"Damn."

"Mack?"

"I'll talk to him when he gets back. You find out anything unusual?"

"There are at least five days between the dates the checks were issued and when they were received."

"Townsend's delivers the checks to the companies by same day messenger, don't they?" Marc asked.

Marc's eyes narrowed as he glanced at his brother. "All right, Mack, what are you thinking?"

"I'm not ready to say."

"When will you be?"

"Possibly after I've talked with Joe Davis."

CHAPTER EIGHT

Mack prowled the confines of his office, imagining that a caged animal must feel as frustrated and angry as he did. In his case it was frustration and anger born of his own actions. Would another beautiful woman be his downfall?

He stopped pacing and brushed his fingers through his hair. The memory of silky jet-black hair and warm caramel skin had invaded his thoughts, keeping him awake all night. God, he had to stop thinking about what it felt like to make love to Toni and concentrate on solving this case.

And proving her innocence.

Was he so certain that she was innocent?

Mack stalked over to his desk and punched the com button. "Daffy, did you find out if Joe Davis has reported for work yet?"

"If I had, you would be the first to know, boss."

"I'm sorry. I know I would."

Damn it, he had to get control of himself.

The door to his office opened and Daffy walked in with a cup of coffee.

"You sounded like you need this."

"Thanks. You're a real lifesaver. I don't know what I'd do without you."

"Luckily for you I have no intention of letting you find out. You'd have an easier time stripping Crazy Glue off your desk than getting rid of me," she said on her way out the door.

Mack had just finished his coffee when Daffy returned.

"According to Bill Watkins down in parking security, Joe Davis has arrived."

"I'll be in the Townsend mail room if you need to get in touch with me." With that he hurried out of the office.

Mack watched the workings of the vast mail room through the window in the door. At least forty busy people were milling around in a huge room that had evidently been created by removing walls between several smaller rooms to accommodate the company's ever-growing mailing needs.

He spotted Joe Davis giving orders to several messengers. Mack recognized him from his personnel picture. Joe Davis was a huge, rough-hewn man. More brawn than brains one would assume by looking at him, if you didn't know that Joe was a college graduate with a degree in management.

Mack shifted his attention to the manager. The man looked the part of manager, but from talking to him, Mack thought he was definitely not the aggressive type needed to run this fast-paced department. Mack frowned, wondering why Clifford hadn't given the position to Joe Davis. Office politics, no doubt.

The more he found out about Frank Clifford, the less he liked the man. Not that he'd liked him from the jump. He was a master manipulator and had likely manipulated Toni. Unless there was a conspiracy going on between—No, he couldn't, he wouldn't believe that, though so many questions remained unanswered.

Mack activated the door buzzer. A security guard came to the glass and slid it aside.

"Yes."

"I'm Mackinsey Jessup." He produced the access pass Townsend had issued him.

"Looks to be in order," the guard confirmed.

As Mack strode inside, a sea of expectant, curious eyes focused on him, and the room quieted almost immediately. He glanced at Joe Davis and gestured for him to come over. The man was reluctant, if not down-right wary, instantly putting Mack on alert.

"Yes, Mr. Jessup?" Joe answered.

"Davis, I need confirmation from you about certain records."

"What records?"

Mack handed him the list he'd compiled and studied his reaction as he examined them.

"I don't understand."

"Don't you? You have set standards of running this mail room, right?"

"Well, yes, but—"

"After examining the list, wouldn't you agree that standard procedures must not have been adhered to?"

A guilty look suffused the man's face.

"Now, would you like to explain why they weren't?"

Joe cleared his throat. "When the outgoing mail came in on those occasions, I was told to delay it."

"By whom?"

"The CEO's office."

"Be specific, Davis." Mack was becoming impatient with his reluctance to answer. "Out with it, man. Was it your wife? Is she the reason for your unwillingness to tell me the truth? Are you trying to protect her?"

"No! My wife doesn't need protection; she's not at fault."

"Then who is?"

"I don't know."

"Come off it, Davis."

Joe looked around at the people pretending to work; in fact, they were listening intently to their conversation.

"Your wife has already said that she didn't find any irregularities. Did she lie to me?"

Joe's Adam's apple bobbed up and down. He sighed. "Pat said to okay the deliveries using whatever date was on the envelopes."

"Did you personally seal them?"

"Yes, I did."

"And were the dates on the papers inside the same?"

"No, sir. They were dated two days earlier."

"Approved by?"

"Toni Carlton."

Not only did Toni have the authority to approve and change the confirmation of sale dates, but also the dates when they left the company, regardless of the date on the contents of the package. This bit of information seemed to imply one thing: That Toni could be guilty of manipulation, if not outright theft.

He was sure now that Pat Davis knew more than she had revealed to him. Did the woman know for a certainty that Toni had 'cooked the books,' so to speak? Or was Pat herself involved with Clifford?

He had to talk to Pat Davis and Toni again, ASAP.

Toni had told him about mistakes in the dates but said she hadn't been the one to make them. He didn't know what to believe now. He took the elevator up to the seventh floor.

"Mrs. Davis, I need to have a word with you."

Pat's head jerked up. "Mack, I mean Mr. Jessup. I didn't hear you come in."

Mack thought she looked a little unsure. He asked, "Is Frank Clifford in?"

"No, he's away for the day on business."

"Then we can go into his office and talk."

Mack followed Pat. Once inside, he asked her to sit down. When she'd done as he'd suggested, he began. "I've been in the mail room talking to your husband. And I uncovered certain facts. I'm sure you know what I'm referring to."

"Mr. Jessup, Mack. I can explain."

"I'm all ears."

"When Mr. Clifford promoted me to executive secretary, I was given specific duties, one of which was to help the PAs. You know, to make the job easier for the whole department."

"Are you now, or have you ever been, intimately involved with him?"

"No! I swear it." she said quickly.

Much too quickly, Mack observed. He sensed that she was holding something back, what exactly, he wasn't sure. "What is the status of the relationship between you two?"

"One of employer and employee."

He shot her a skeptical look. "He never tried to come on to you?"

She lowered her head. "One time when…"

"When what?"

"When Joe was up for mail room manager."

"Come on, Pat. I want to know the truth."

"I refused to cooperate and—"

"He made sure your husband didn't get the promotion, right?" Mack now began to understand her reluctance. That bastard Clifford, he swore under his breath. "Then what?"

"Nothing. He acted as if the incident had never happened."

"Did he want you to do anything else, like help him frame Toni Carlton?"

Her eyes sparked. "I resent that remark. Toni and I are friends. I'd never agree to do anything like that," she said in an affronted voice.

"What did you do?"

"Continued to assist Toni in doing her job, the same as always."

"Not quite."

A puzzled look came into her eyes. "What do you mean?"

"You knew it wasn't policy to delay outgoing documents, including the confirmation of sale documents, yet you did it anyway."

"Toni was very busy during that time, and I figured she had forgotten, that's all. I'm sure of one thing: She's not a thief!"

"All right, Mrs. Davis. You can go back to your work."

As Mack followed her out, Hank Warren appeared in the outer doorway. A sarcastic grin spread across his face.

"If it isn't the enterprising Mr. Jessup."

"Warren," Mack gritted out.

"Our lovely Ms. Carlton isn't here, as you no doubt already know."

"Look, Warren—"

"Come to give us all the second degree? Or is it the third or fourth? I've lost count."

"Step into Clifford's office," Mack urged.

Hank glanced at Pat before preceding Mack inside.

Once they were inside Mack indicated the chair he wanted Hank to take. "All right, Warren, on the list of accounts Toni Carlton is responsible for, I found that several were originally assigned to you. Why were you taken off those accounts, and why were they given to Ms. Carlton?"

Hank worked his mouth into a smirk. "You'll have to ask the great man himself."

"He didn't give you a reason for his decision?"

"He's the boss, Jessup, he doesn't have to." Hank cleared his throat and smiled, refusing to say any more.

Mack was getting a little bit tired of the evasions he'd come up against in this company. "You may as well tell me, Warren."

"And if I don't, will you break my arm?"

Mack noticed the way the man's eyes narrowed when he looked at him. Mack smiled knowingly. Warren must have realized that he was pushing his luck.

"If you must know, he said those particular clients preferred to deal with a woman. But it was a lie. He was just trying to keep his affair with Toni intact."

Mack laughed. "You sound like a jealous colleague or a jilted lover. Which is it?"

Hank quirked his mouth. "Now, you don't really expect me to answer that, do you?"

Toni hurried into the outer office. "Any calls or messages for me, Pat?"

"Ah, no, but—"

Hank and Mack walked out of the CEO's office.

"Mack!"

"You're just in time to be, ah, interrogated. Right, Jessup?" Hank drawled, flashing Mack a vicious sneer.

"I have questions that need answers," Mack said to Toni.

"I'm sure she'll be more than glad to give them to you. And anything else you might want." With that parting shot Hank disappeared into his cubicle.

"What's with that guy?" Mack asked once they were inside the office. "Have a seat."

Toni sat down in the chair he indicated. "To say he dislikes me would be a gross understatement."

"He's obviously a jerk. Forget about Warren. He's not the reason I want to talk to you." Mack walked behind the desk and sat in his chair, then slid some papers across the desk.

"What are these?" Toni glanced at them. "Why they're copies of confirmation documents on several of my accounts." She lowered her gaze to the dates. "This can't be right."

"According to the mail room it is."

"But that would mean—"

"They're either not copies of the originals or—"

"I lied to you about the mistakes I'd found." Toni gritted her teeth. The initials looked like hers, but she hadn't put them there. Her boss must have. Damn him!

"I didn't sign these, Mack."

He got up from his chair and walked over to the file cabinet and leaned his back against it. This could all be a part of Clifford's scheme to frame Toni or...

"Well, do you believe me?"

"Toni, I..."

She left her chair and started for the door.

"Toni, wait."

"For what? To hear you condemn me as a liar or worse, a thief?"

"I wasn't going to do that."

"What were you going to say?"

Mack was at a temporary loss for words. Toni stormed out of the office.

He wanted to go after her and explain.

And then what? Tell her things looked bad for her, that in fact they couldn't get much worse?

Why wouldn't they if, as he suspected, Clifford was behind it? Toni had already told him what the man planned to do. But was it an attempt at cover up? It wouldn't be the first time he'd been the victim of silken lies from a woman he cared about. But Toni was different.

Can you be sure of that, Jessup?

Toni sat at her desk wondering what Mack really thought after seeing those papers. She was pretending an interest in her work when she heard the door to the CEO's office open. Mack looked as if he wanted to say something more when he glanced her way. Instead, he left the office without a word.

Frank Clifford's prediction of doom was becoming more of a reality with each passing day. Toni was scared. Was she completely trapped? Would Mack be the one to send her to jail? Those papers were forgeries, but the copies of the originals were supposed to be in the company vault. She looked at her watch. The automatic timer was set to open the vault at two o'clock. It was almost that time now.

With briefcase in hand, Toni left the office in a rush and rode the elevator to the floor where the Townsend vault was located. Milton Jameson, the security officer, smiled at her, checked the dates on her access card, and waved her through to the inner door.

Toni shoved her plastic key in the slot. Once inside, she walked over to the accounts section and took out the ones she remembered seeing in the files Mack had shown her.

Her legs nearly buckled. The stocks had all sold at different percentages than what was quoted on the papers Mack had shown her. Toni felt chilled to the bone.

"May I see those?"

Toni jumped at the sound of that all-too-familiar voice. She handed Mack the documents and waited for him to say something.

He frowned. He was beginning to have his own suspicions about who was framing who and why. And that didn't necessarily mean Frank Clifford was the one doing the framing. "I'll have to show these to Townsend."

"I know." Toni lowered her gaze to the floor.

"But not right away."

She lifted her face, her eyes narrowing in confusion. "Why not?"

"These don't really prove anything. It's nothing more than circumstantial evidence. You're not the only one who has access to these documents."

Toni blinked back tears of relief. Mack wasn't convinced of her guilt.

"Hank Warren could very well have produced the forgeries and not Clifford."

Toni recalled the day Hank had stalked out of the office on his forced vacation. Maybe he wasn't in on this with their boss. He could have done it for his own reasons. From the way he looked at her sometimes, he certainly seemed to hate her enough to pull something like this, or something even worse.

Mack saw the fear in Toni's eyes and his insides tightened. How dangerous a threat was Hank Warren to Toni? "You're coming to live at my house for a while."

"But, Mack—"

"I don't like the way things are shaping up. It's the only way I can protect you. Since the vault will be closing soon, we'd better take these and get out of here."

Toni wondered as they rode down in the elevator if Mack was really trying to protect her by insisting that she come to his house. Or was it his way of keeping a closer eye on a suspected thief? If that was the case, it was an extreme measure to take. She shook her head. She had to stop thinking like that. If Mack was anything, he was honest and caring.

As Mack watched Toni get off on her floor, he wondered if he was doing the right thing. He had to ask himself why he wanted her with him. Did he really fear for her safety or was it an excuse to keep her with him?

His feelings for Toni were putting him in danger of completely losing his objectivity, not to mention risking his and his company's professional reputation. But what could he do? He was falling in love with the chief suspect.

CHAPTER NINE

While Mack waited, Toni packed enough clothes for a one-week stay. She didn't think she'd be at Mack's any longer than that. She wasn't sure she agreed with the reason he gave for the move. True, Hank was despicable, but was he a physical threat? Somehow she didn't think resorting to violence was his style. His mouth was his weapon. But Frank Clifford was another matter entirely. She knew from personal experience that he could be violent. He'd said that he wouldn't have to physically harm her now, but should she believe him?

"You may have to come back for more later," Mack remarked.

She looked questioningly at him. "You really think I'll be staying that long?"

"I don't know, but I'm not willing to take any more chances. I don't like the way or the speed with which things are closing in around you. It's all so perfectly planned, and is being executed like clockwork."*According to Frank Clifford's time clock*, Toni reasoned bitterly.Mack pushed her suitcase off the bed and pulled her down onto it. "I've grown fond of you, Ms. Carlton," he said huskily.

She smiled. "Have you really?"

"Absolutely. I think I'm more than fond actually." His mouth covered hers hungrily. "That should give you some idea."

"Only a drop in the bucket."

He arched his brows in mock surprise. "You want more?"

"Maybe later. Let me go so I can finish packing."

"You're a cruel-hearted woman, Antonia Carlton."

"No, I'm practical."

"Practical?"

"If we continue along these lines, I'll never get moved."

"You won't have an excuse once I get you home."

"Home. I like the sound of that when you say it."

"I'm glad."

Later, after settling Toni into her room, Toni and Mack went into the living room. He put on soft music as they relaxed on the couch.

"I've been wondering about Frank Clifford's personal life," Mack muttered. "You know anything about that?"

Toni shrugged her shoulders. "No, nothing. He keeps his personal life private." A memory of seeing him in the restaurant flirting with Nina Townsend flashed through her mind.

From her expression Mack knew she wasn't telling him everything she knew. He hated it when she did that.

"What about Hank Warren?"

"I can't stand the man." Toni glowered. "And could care less about his personal life."

Was her dislike as impersonal as she made it sound? Mack wondered. Had something gone on between her and Warren at one time which had led to her hostility? Could she possibly be a woman scorned? He wouldn't like to think so, but anything was possible.

"Are you only interested in his professional life, then?"

She tilted her head, a questioning look in her eyes. "What do you mean by that?"

"You're both vying for the same promotion, aren't you?"

"And?" She inched away from him.

He placed a restraining hand on her shoulder. "And you both want to appear at your best."

She made to pull away. "If you've got something to say, say it, Mack."

"I'm not ready to do that. I need to check out a few things first."

"When will you know whatever it is you need to know to solve this case?" Mack shrugged.

Toni knew he was keeping what he thought and knew close to his chest, and it irritated her that she couldn't get him to reveal any of it. "Is that all you're going to tell me?"

"Prickly, aren't we?" He kissed the tip of her nose. "But, yes, it is."

The next morning at his office while Mack was checking through the papers he'd gotten from the Townsend vault, Daffy buzzed him. He punched the com button, then picked up the receiver. "Jessup."

"This is John Townsend. It has come to my attention that certain papers are missing from the vault. Would you happen to know where they are?"

"Why would you assume that I would know anything about them?"

"I got a call from Frank Clifford this morning. He's concerned about the investigation. He's been doing some checking on his own and discovered that certain documents are missing. You and your associate were allowed access to the vault as a part of the investigation."

"That's true. But believe me, I'm on top of this investigation."

"I know you said you would handle it your way, but your way doesn't seem to be producing any significant results."

"Oh, it is. I'm just not ready to reveal my findings yet."

"When will you be ready?"

"Soon."

"All right, I'll give you time, but you had better show me something concrete. I'm answerable to the board on this matter."

Mack frowned as he hung up the phone. Clifford hadn't wasted any time. Mack had a gut feeling the man was close to completely ensnaring Toni in his trap. What could he do to save her? Mack punched the com button.

"Daffy, get Frank Clifford on the phone."

Seconds later Daffy buzzed. "He's not in his office, Mack. His secretary said he was in a meeting."

"Is Marc back in the office?"

"Not yet. You want me to have him come see you when he does?"

"Yes, please."

Hank's attitude toward her when she went into the office puzzled Toni. Usually he didn't pass up an opportunity to run her down, but for the last few days he'd done his work and kept to himself. Frank Clifford had eyed her with the-cat-that-swiped-the-goldfish-from-the-bowl look a few minutes ago when he left the office.

How she hated this game he was playing with her. When would the final blow come? The suspense as well as the dread was killing her an inch at a time, and he knew it. She didn't know how much longer she could stand the pressure without cracking up.

Her phone rang. "Toni Carlton speaking."

"Ms. Carlton, this is J. V. Townsend. I'd like to see you in my office right away."

"But—" She heard the sharp click of the receiver. What now? She stood up and walked over to Pat's desk.

"I'll be in Mr. Townsend's office, Pat."

A feeling of déjà vu washed over Toni as she rode the elevator to the tower suite. The last time she'd been in the president's office Mr. Townsend Sr. had summoned her. And that interview had ended on a tragic note. This one had the feel of—she didn't know what. What could Mr. Townsend want with her? Nothing good, she would venture to guess.

Mildred Frances shot Toni a curious, probing look when she instructed her to go into the president's office.

Toni knocked on the door.

"Come in, Ms. Carlton," she heard Mr. Townsend say.

She walked in.

"Have a seat, please."

As she moved to do as he asked, she noticed Frank Clifford standing by the coffee maker.

He smiled. "Would you like a cup, Toni?"

She cleared her throat. "No, thank you."

"Ms. Carlton, Frank has brought certain information to my attention. Is it true you're staying at Mackinsey Jessup's house?"

Toni glanced at her boss. He had a smug, self-satisfied smirk on his face.

"For my protection, yes."

"Your protection? Is someone stalking or threatening you?"

"Yes, in a manner of speaking."

"Then why haven't you contacted the police? It seems to me they could offer you more help and better protection."

"Mack—Mr. Jessup is an ex-policeman."

"I was given to understand—" Townsend glanced at Frank Clifford, then back at Toni, "that you and he were personally involved. What I want to know is, is it true?"

"We're close friends, yes."

"From what I've observed, I'd say it is more than that, Toni," Frank Clifford interjected into the conversation.

Townsend cleared his throat. "You may return to your work, Ms. Carlton."

Toni wanted to say something to dispel the impression Frank Clifford had given Mr. Townsend, but she had been dismissed. She rose to her feet and headed for the door. When she looked back, she sensed an almost sinister plot hatching between the two men. How could they be on such friendly terms when Townsend's wife and Frank Clifford were obviously involved? Toni recalled how the woman had blatantly flirted with him in front of her husband the day she and Pat had seen them at the Italian Kitchen. As she walked out of the office, Toni glared at her boss, hating him with a passion.

Toni sensed that the tense atmosphere in the office was fast approaching the breaking point when Pat Davis, usually cheerful and friendly, turned uncharacteristically quiet and withdrawn. Hank was actually civil to Toni. Joe Davis, on the other hand, avoided Toni like the plague. Several other employees shot sly, knowing looks her way. Still others acted wary of her. The fact that she was staying at Mack's house had gotten around the office with the speed of wildfire, thanks to her boss. It had been a week since Mr. Townsend had called her into his office. Mack was as close-mouthed as ever about the investigation. In the evenings at his house Toni had caught him staring at her with a grim expression on his face.

While they sat embracing and listening to music in the living room after dinner one evening, Toni broached the subject they had avoided discussing since her summons to the president's office.

She eased out of Mack's embrace and gazed into his face. "Mack, what's going on? I have to know. A leper couldn't receive any more negative attention than I have at the office. And here with you the atmosphere is almost as bad."

"I'm sorry if I've been neglecting you lately," he said, drawing her back into the curve of his arm. "Things don't look good for you. I don't know what else to tell you right now. Every scrap of evidence so far points to you as the guilty party, with or without the help of an accomplice."

"But I'm innocent. There has to be a way to prove it."

"If there is I haven't found it—yet." He wanted so badly to reassure her that everything would turn out all right, but he couldn't and it frustrated the hell out of him. That scared, lost, betrayed look in her eyes ripped his guts apart. Damn it, he had to find a way to expose Clifford, and quick.

"What are we going to do, Mack?"

"I don't know, but we'll come up with something." He hoped they did before it was too late.

Was that an edge Toni detected in his voice? Was it one of determination to help or acknowledgment that he didn't really believe he could save her after all?

CHAPTER TEN

Two days later Toni stepped off the elevator on the seventh floor and glanced down the hall. She dreaded going into the office. The feeling of impending doom was bearing down on her like a runaway freight train.

Toni squared her shoulders and marched into Townsend's like a proud queen.

"Here's a message for you to call Mazie in personnel," Pat informed her in her most professional executive secretary voice.

Toni took the message from her. "What is it, Pat? And don't tell me it's nothing, because I won't buy it. Have I done something to offend you?"

"No," she said, but looked decidedly uncomfortable.

Toni moved away from Pat's desk and headed for her cubicle. After lowering her purse onto the desk, Toni sat down, picked up the phone and punched in Mazie's extension.

"I need you to come down here right away."

"Why? What's up?"

"It would be better if you just came down. Okay? I'll explain everything when you get here."

Toni picked up on the strained cadence in Mazie's voice. The same bad vibes she'd felt earlier came back to haunt her.

"All right, I'll be right down."

Fifteen minutes later Toni returned from personnel in a state of shock. Clinched in her hand was a blue slip of paper. Mr. Townsend had suspended her until further notice, pending the outcome of the investigation. She couldn't believe it! But then, why shouldn't she? It was all Frank Clifford's doing. If she had learned anything at all, it was how devious and ruthless he could be. What was going to happen now? What would the man do next?

"Are you all right, Toni?" Pat asked.

"No, and I won't be until the truth comes out. No matter what anyone thinks, I'm not a thief, Pat."

For a moment the other woman looked as if she wanted to say something, but refrained from commenting, cleared her throat and returned to her work. Pat had been her closest friend before this thing with Clifford.

"How I hate that man," Toni said in a low, angry voice as she glanced at the CEO's office door. Pat heard her and let out a shocked little gasp. Toni headed for her ex-office space. Once within the cubicle she plopped down in her chair. After a few moments she started methodically clearing her desk. Then she heard Frank Clifford's voice. Her nerves tensed and a knot of bitter frustration tightened in the pit of her stomach.

"I'd like to see you in my office before you, ah, leave, Toni," he called to her.

She could hear the smug triumph in his voice and see it in his mocking eyes as he waited for her to precede him into his office. She hated him enough to kill him for all he'd done to ruin her career. Taking a cleansing, strengthening breath she entered.

"Have a seat, " he said, stepping behind his desk. The smile on his face reminded her of a crocodile licking his chops.

"I'd rather stand, thank you."

"Have it your way—at least for the moment."

Toni gritted her teeth. "Just get on with it."

"You can be a vicious little spitting cat, can't you, Toni? Well, you can hiss and spit all you want, it won't do you any good."

"I have you to thank for the suspension, I suppose."

"I told you your downfall was assured," he said confidently. "I don't know why you refuse to accept that. My plan is flawless. I'd say it's the perfect frame. The next step is your arrest and trial, eventually leading to your imprisonment."

Why was he telling her these things? To gloat? How she would love to deliver a sharp karate chop to his arrogant neck. She'd had just enough self-defense training to try it if she dared. The thought left her mind as soon as it entered. As he had said, it wouldn't do any good. She would only succeed in making things worse.

"If looks could kill…I'd advise you to do whatever you like now, before your freedom to do so is permanently curtailed." Toni didn't bother responding, just turned and stalked out of the office, slamming the door behind her. She grabbed up her purse and other personal items from her desk and marched out of the office.

"You haven't handled this case to the board's satisfaction, Jessup, so we're dismissing you from the case," Townsend said to Mack from his chair behind the desk.

"Is it to the board's satisfaction or yours?" Mack pointedly asked.

"The board and I both feel that you aren't moving swiftly enough on this."

"Frank Clifford wouldn't have anything to do with this decision, would he?"

"He is the CEO of this company. Of course his opinion carries a certain amount of weight, especially in this matter since it concerns his personal assistant."

"I see. What's your reasoning for doing this, may I ask?"

"Since you're no longer officially associated with the case, I'm under no obligation to share that information with you. Send us a bill for whatever expenses you've incurred up to this point."

"Like that, I'm off the case?" Mack snapped his fingers. "What about Toni—Ms. Carlton?"

"She's been suspended with just cause. In my opinion we have our thief. I know you don't agree, but then you and Ms. Carlton are—shall we say—close. Believe me, I know how a woman can color a man's judgement," he uttered bitterly under his breath, his mind having wandered off the subject of Toni Carlton on to something, or someone, else.

His wife? Mack wondered.

"So do I. But I think you're making a mistake in this instance. By taking me off the case and assuming that Toni Carlton is the guilty party, you're in essence allowing the real culprit to get away with the crime."

"I don't believe I'm mistaken about who the thief is. She may have you fooled, but that's because you've let yourself become personally involved."

"I wouldn't say any more if I were you. I may be off the case, but I still intend to help Toni Carlton prove her innocence."

"You're going to have a problem there, Jessup, because she's guilty."

"I don't happen to believe that. And I don't think I'll have a problem," Mack said, and confidently strode from the office.

A worried frown beetled Mack's brows moments later when he stepped into the elevator. The screws were tightening on the trap set to ensnare the woman he had fallen in love with. He got off on the seventh floor, hoping to catch Toni before she left.

"Sorry, Mack, she's already gone," Pat informed him when he stopped by her desk. "It doesn't look good for her, does it?"

"I'm afraid not," he said in a strained voice.

Clifford opened his office door and, seeing Mack, strode over to Pat's desk.

"Jessup, I'm sorry about your lover—I mean Ms. Carlton. She's on indefinite suspension, pending the outcome of the investigation."

Anger darkened Mack's eyes to the deep gold of a dangerous cat's. "Just what did you tell Townsend?"

He answered, oblivious to the danger. "I didn't have to tell him very much. You really should have shown him the documents immediately instead of waiting. Was it Toni's idea?"

Mack gritted his teeth. This man was cocksure about being in complete control of everything. His sights were beaded on Toni. But Mack would be damned if he'd stand by and let him destroy her.

"No, she didn't have to convince me to do anything. Since I wasn't even close to completing my investigation, I saw no pressing reason why I should give them to him. You made a very basic mistake framing Toni, Clifford, and believe me, you're going to pay for it."

"Threats, Jessup?"

"No, a solemn promise."

Mack had to take care of several important appointments he couldn't get out of before he was finally able to leave the office. By the time he'd finally managed to do so it was almost five o'clock. He parked the Jag in the drive next to Toni's car and crossed the lawn to the front porch and unlocked the door. He heard music when he entered the living room and saw Toni on the couch with a half-filled glass in her hand.

"Is this a private party? Or can anyone join?"

"By all means join me," Toni answered, her voice sounding not quite steady.

"We're going to prove that you're not the thief, baby."

"I don't see your magic bag, Mr. Felix. You're going to need it if you're going to thwart Dr. Destructo."

He took the drink from her hand. "I think you've had more than enough."

"I don't agree. I haven't had nearly enough."

"Look, Toni, I know things don't—"

"Oh, don't feel so bad, Mack. I was the stupid one for believing Frank Clifford's lies. He knew how eager I was for that promotion and he took advantage of it. I thought I'd be one of the lucky ones. Did you know there have only been two women directors ever at Townsend's? I was determined to be the third."

"Nothing is wrong with aspiring to success, Toni."

"You're so sweet, Mack."

"I'll make us some coffee; then we can talk."

"Are you suggesting that I'm less than sober?"

"No, I'm hinting that you're more than a little bit drunk. After the blow you received today I can hardly blame you for wanting to dull the pain."

A while later Mack smiled at Toni. "You want some more coffee?"

"I've had enough already, thank you. I'll be sloshing in it if I drink another cup."

"What set you off? Did Clifford say anything?"

"Before I left, he called me into his office to inform me that I'd be arrested soon and that I'd end up in prison."

Mack's eyes slitted with rage. "The bastard, I'd like to—"

"You'd have to get in line, maybe even take a number. I've learned that no one at work really likes the man. How could I have been so blind, Mack?"

He pulled her into his arms. "When we want something so badly that we can almost taste it, we tend to ignore anything that will divert us from our goal."

"All those evenings I worked overtime and weekends—for what?"

"It isn't over until the fat lady sings. You've heard that expression, haven't you?"

"Don't misunderstand me. I'm not giving up. I've only been temporarily shut down."

"That's my girl."

"Am I really your girl, Mack?"

His mouth devoured hers, drawing a mind-boggling response from her. "Does that answer your question?"

"It looks like you were right."

"Right about what?"

"About me needing to go back to my apartment for more clothes. It looks like I'll be staying indefinitely."

You'll never leave if I have my way, Toni my love.

The smell of bacon cooking woke Toni the next morning. Mack was up working his magic in the kitchen, she thought with a smile. A girl could get used to this. She took a quick shower and padded into the kitchen in her robe and bare feet.

"Did I say the best route to a woman's heart is her stomach?" Mack quipped.

"You know you did," she said, easing onto a kitchen stool, lifting the coffee pot and pouring herself a cup of the wonderful smelling brew.

"French toast or waffles?" he offered, producing a plate of each.

"I'll let you chose."

"Such an accommodating woman all of a sudden. I must be dreaming." He placed the waffles in front of her and poured on her favorite strawberry syrup. Then taking a bite, he kissed her.

The taste of his lips was delicious. "Umm, so sweet. Is this a part of my breakfast?"

"But of course, compliments of the house, mademoiselle," he said in an awful French accent.

Toni frowned.

"Bad, huh."

"It's not that. What do we do next, Mack?"

"I want to make—"

The doorbell interrupted.

"I'll get it, Toni. Drink your coffee and enjoy my out-of-this-world bacon waffles."

"Such modesty in a man. I love it," she said, reaching for more syrup.

As she took a bite of her waffle, Mack appeared in the doorway flanked by a tall man with a short-to-the-scalp haircut and the most piercingly dark eyes she'd ever seen.

"Antonia Carlton?"

"Yes."

He whipped out his badge. "I'm Lieutenant Robert Barnes, L.A.P.D. You're under arrest. You have the right to remain silent. Anything you say may be used against you in a court of law. You have the right to have an attorney, and to have him present during questioning. If you can't afford one, one will be appointed at no charge."

Toni swallowed the bite of waffle and rose to her feet after her rights had been read to her.

"What's the charge, Bob?" Mack demanded.

"You know him?" Toni's brows arched in surprise.

"We were partners when I was a cop with the L.A.P.D. And we're still good friends."

The man looked uncomfortable but answered. "The charge is embezzlement. I'll have to take her down to the station and book her, Mack."

"I'm coming with you. Don't even think about giving me a hard time."

"I wouldn't dream of it." The man smiled. His expression turned serious when he looked at Toni. "You'd better get dressed, Ms. Carlton."

"Yes," she said numbly, and all but stumbled out of the kitchen.

"What have you got?" Mack asked as soon as Toni had gone.

"Number one, we have the president of the company pressing charges against her. Two, we have evidence provided by her immediate supervisor, Frank Clifford."

"It's all circumstantial, Bob."

"That may very well be the case, Mack, but I have to do my job."

"I know you do."

Lieutenant Barnes smiled. "If you're going down to the station you'll need to get dressed yourself," he said, eyeing his friend's low-riding pajama bottoms.

Toni had never felt so humiliated as when they took her fingerprints and mug shots, but the ultimate humiliation was being intimately searched as if she were some dangerous, despicable criminal. She felt completely dispirited by the time she went before the judge the next morning. She was relieved when Mack arranged bail so fast that she got out of jail that evening.

"Clifford is going to pay for this, baby," Mack vowed as they walked to his car.

"I intend to personally see that he does," Toni said with conviction.

Mack frowned at the coldness in her voice. "Now don't do anything you'll be sorry for."

"Anything I do to that—that man, I won't ever feel sorry for."

"Don't let anyone else hear you say those words," he teased.

"What next, Mack? Everything that rotten man has predicted has come to pass."

"We'll have to snap his winning streak then, won't we?"

"I'm scared, Mack."

"Don't be, sweet Toni. I'll take care of you."

Toni hoped he would be able to keep that promise. The only thing Frank Clifford had predicted that hadn't happened was that Mack hadn't been the one to send her to jail.

"What's going through that fertile brain of yours?" Mack asked as he drove them to his house.

"I wondered if I should call my parents. I don't want to worry them. My mother is a typically emotional Italian and tends to get upset easily and since I'm her only child…I hesitate to call. For the first time in their entire marriage my parents are free to do what they want to do. My father retired from the navy a few months ago, and they're all set to take a long-awaited vacation. I hate to lay this on them."

"Wait up on calling them. Maybe you won't have to."

"Only if I'm able to clear myself."

"We'll do it, baby."

Toni hoped it wouldn't prove to be only wishful thinking on his part. Frank Clifford was a frighteningly clever man. The question was whether he was clever enough to pull this off. He had to have made a mistake somewhere along the line. There was no such thing as a perfect crime.

"It's a good thing I made copies of everything," Mack told Toni as he pulled his car into the drive next to hers. He turned to Toni and took her hand. "I hate seeing you so upset. We'll go over every shred of evidence with a fine-toothed comb. We're bound to find something we can use to clear you."

"I hope you're right."

Mack took his briefcase out of the trunk of his car and he and Toni went into the house. Together they carefully checked through the disks.

Hours later Mack yawned. "Let's call it a day. You look all done in, Toni."

"You look like you could use some rest yourself."

"Let's go to bed."

The next morning was Saturday and they didn't move to leave Mack's bedroom until noon.

"I should go to my apartment and get some more clothes and clean up the place."

"And you'll be needing a work detail, right?"

She shot him an encouraging smile. "Well, I was kind of hoping."

"I don't have a problem with that. Let's get moving."

Toni shook her head. "You never fail to amaze me, Mackinsey Jessup. You're not like any other man I've ever known."

"Are you telling me I'm an original, that my parents broke the mold when they created me?"

"Your modesty overwhelms me."

He pulled her on top of him. "I want other things about me to overwhelm you."

She felt the evidence of his desire pulsing against her femininity.

"Now none of that or we'll never get out of this bed."

"Killjoy."

"Is this it, Toni?" Mack asked over the computer equipment he was helping her put in the back seat of his car.

"All I'll need for now. I know we were supposed to be just getting some of my clothes, but I feel lost without my own computer."

"Don't you have a laptop?"

"I do, but it's being repaired. Are you trying to get out of helping me, Mr. Jessup?"

"Not me."

She laughed. "Surely my desktop isn't that heavy?"

"It isn't. Are you questioning my manhood, by any chance?"

"Would I do that to you?"

"I don't know. Maybe."

She kissed him deeply. "Not a chance after last night and this morning. No more stalling. I have on this computer several of the programs we used during inventory. There might be something in them that could help clear me."

Mack didn't want Toni to pin too much hope on that possibility, but what could he say to make her feel better?

Toni took her keys out to lock her door and noticed an extra one. She didn't have a clue what it went to. Maybe it was an extra luggage key. But it didn't look like that kind of key. How and when had it gotten there?

Frank Clifford. He had to have put it there when he had her key chain. Wouldn't she have noticed it when she had her locks changed? Not necessarily. She'd only been interested in getting the old apartment key off.

"What's keeping you?" Mack grumbled.

"Nothing, I just kind of hate to close up the place is all. It's like trading in an old friend for a newer one."

"Sentimental females."

"That's what I am, all right." She wouldn't tell Mack about the key just yet. She wanted to find out about it on her own. The more she thought about it, the more the possibility that it went to a safety deposit box grew. What would be in such a box? Or was the key another one of Frank Clifford's meticulously constructed traps designed to ensnare her? The question was, should she risk finding out?

Mack knew something was bothering Toni. He hated it when she kept things from him. Would she ever come to completely trust him?

When will you come to trust her the same way, Jessup?

Remnants of the past edged their way into his present. He'd trusted a woman without hesitation once and she had nearly destroyed him. Her betrayal was hard to forget when it had been the cause of so much pain. He no longer had feelings for Linda Hutton, but what she had done to him occasionally bobbed to the surface to taunt him. She was a part of his past, and it was exactly where he wanted her to stay. Toni was nothing like her.

You're beginning to sound like you're falling—Oh, hell, you're already in love with Toni.

He knew it was wise to proceed with caution when his heart was so deeply involved. But how was he going to do it? He couldn't turn his feelings off and on to suit the circumstance.

"You're kind of quiet. Is anything wrong?"

Mack smiled. "No."

Toni wasn't sure she believed him. Something had taken him away from her for a few moments. She wondered what it could have been.

CHAPTER ELEVEN

Mack got a call from his mother. While he was on the phone, Toni went to her room, booted up her computer and accessed BankScape, sure the extra key on her key chain went to a safety deposit box. She surfed through the listings of banks, and using the serial number on the key, found out which bank the key was registered with.

To her shock, her name came up as the user of the safety deposit box. Too bad the computer couldn't tell her what was in it.

As she exited BankScape, Mack knocked on her door and walked in.

"What are you up to, Miss Marple?"

Toni smiled. "I was surfing the 'Net, that's all."

Mack wasn't sure he believed that was all she was doing. He'd get her to tell him later.

"Are you going to spend all night in here?"

"You wouldn't be trying to seduce me into joining you in your room, would you?"

"Maybe. You considering letting me?"

"Maybe."

"You think I could change that maybe to a yes?"

"It's a distinct possibility."

Toni let out a sigh of relief when Mack left to go to his office the next morning. They'd gone over the information again and again and had still turned up nothing. She ached to find out what was in the safety deposit box. The bank opened in thirty minutes, and she intended to be their first customer.

Toni showered and dressed in record time, gulped down another cup of coffee and got out her street guide. She didn't know exactly where Farrell Street was, but after a few minutes she located the street and was ready to go.

Mack returned to the house to collect an important file he'd left on his desk. When he didn't see Toni's car in the drive, he wondered where she could have gone so early, and so fast. Then he saw the street guide lying open on the coffee table. He glanced at the place she'd circled. There was something familiar about the street number, but he couldn't recall...Then it came to him. Surety Bank was in the center of the circle. He'd done investigations for them two years ago.

Why would Toni go there? He knew it wasn't her personal bank. He'd seen the name of her bank in her personnel file and then again when she wrote out her rent check.

Toni parked her car and headed across the street. The bank had just opened its doors when she reached it. With a smile she entered and walked past the security guard. She observed the safety deposit service area and realized that she would have to show some form of identification to get into the box.

Toni stepped over to the customer service area. A tall, slender gray-haired woman approached her.

"May I help you? I'm the Service Rep."

"I seem to have misplaced my card pass to get into my safety deposit box."

She smiled. "We can fix that. Have a seat. If you'll show me your identification we can issue you another pass."

Toni couldn't believe it would be this easy. When had Frank Clifford set this up? She wondered. In all likelihood what she'd find in the box would just be another macho attack meant to frustrate her. Even so, she still wanted to know what was in there. What was that old saying? Curiosity killed the cat, but satisfaction brought him back.

Toni took out her wallet and showed the service representative her driver's license and credit cards. Minutes later the woman returned with a duplicate pass card. She walked with Toni to the safety deposit service desk.

The deposit officer greeted them with a smile. The representative explained the situation. After she walked away the officer asked Toni to follow him.

The officer retrieved the bank key and together they unlocked the door to the box, and he lifted it out for her and guided her to a small enclosure so she could view the contents in private.

As soon as he had closed the door behind him, Toni opened the box.

"Where did you rush off to this morning?" Mack asked Toni that afternoon when he walked into the house and found her in the living room sitting on the couch, completely oblivious to her surroundings.

Toni was pondering what she had discovered in the safety deposit box and how she could use it to clear herself.

"What do you mean?"

"Don't tell me you've been in all day. I had to come back this morning to get a file I'd left on my desk. You weren't here. So where did you go?"

"Mack, is this some kind of interrogation?"

He frowned. Why was she getting defensive with him? "No, I'm just curious to know where you went, that's all."

Toni made a decision and, with a resigned sigh, said, "The other day when you went with me to my apartment, I noticed there was a strange key on my ring. It looked like a safety deposit key so I went to the BankScape Website and discovered I was right."

"So you went to the bank where the key was registered."

"Yes."

"Okay, what did you find?"

"Let me show you."

Mack followed her into the guest room and then watched her as she stepped over to her computer.

Toni picked up the collection of disks. "These contain dated transaction documents made out to the heads of several of the companies Mr. Clifford assigned to me. You know what this could look like to the police?"

"I have a pretty good idea. I want to see these documents."

After reviewing all the information, they returned to the living room. Mack signaled her to join him on the couch.

"We're going to have to show these to the police."

"Why? Mr. Clifford is sure to tell them about it. What I want to know is why he did this. He's already gotten Mr. Townsend to suspend me."

"I don't know, but if the police find out you have these and didn't show them to them, it'll look like you were trying to hide something."

"It's going to look like that regardless. According to what is on the disks, I bribed the heads of those companies. Damn Frank Clifford to hell. How I hate that man."

"You're not the only one. From what I've managed to find out, half the employees at Townsend's feel the way you do. The man is one first-class rat."

"I second that emotion."

As Mack pulled her into his arms and bent to kiss her, the doorbell rang. He reluctantly moved away from her and went to answer the door.

"Bob! What's wrong?"

"I need to talk with Ms. Carlton." He looked past Mack and when he saw Toni sitting on the couch, he advanced toward her.

"I received a call from Frank Clifford. He saw you go into the safety deposit area of Surety Bank and come out carrying a computer disk carrier. May I ask where these disks are and what's on them?"

"If I choose not to tell you?"

"I'd have to get a court order and insist that you accompany me to the station."

"You'd better show them to him," Mack suggested.

Without another word she went to get the disk carrier.

"Bob, can't you see what Clifford is doing?"

"Mack, I don't like the man any better than you do, but there's nothing I can do. We'll have to review the disks down at the station."

Toni returned, taking in the looks that passed between Mack and his friend. She handed the carrier to the lieutenant.

"You'll have to come down to the station with me."

"I figured as much. I'll get my purse."

Mack moved to put his jacket on.

"You wouldn't consider—"

"Save it, Bob. I'm coming in with you."

Toni and Mack followed Bob into the police computer lab. They waited while a technician brought up the information on all six disks.

The names, places and dates suggested unusual activity taking place in several accounts over a period of a year and a half. After an hour of reviewing the information, the lieutenant reached a conclusion.

"What now, Bob?" Mack asked.

"The information will be cataloged, tagged and put with the other evidence we have in this case. Then a judge will decide whether he'll revoke bail and have Ms. Carlton taken into custody."

Mack's stomach dropped to his feet. From what he could deduce, things couldn't look any worse for Toni.

Toni didn't say anything. What could she say? Frank Clifford had driven another nail in her coffin. And dummy that she was, she'd fallen into yet another one of his intricately set booby traps. When would she learn not to underestimate the man? It was impossible to predict what he would do next and how he would carry it out. But one thing she knew for sure was that his plan would roll on to its eventual conclusion, whatever that was.

"Are you going to detain me?" Toni asked Lieutenant Barnes.

"No, but I'd advise you not to leave the city."

"I'm taking her home with me. The evidence you have is only circumstantial, Bob."

"That may be true, but convictions have been won on less."

Mack wanted to say more. He wanted to say that Frank Clifford was succeeding so far with his plan: framing the woman he loved. And that he wanted to kill the bastard with his bare hands. But he didn't say anything. He just placed his hand under Toni's elbow and escorted her out of the station.

That night, after Mack had fallen asleep, Toni got out of bed and padded into the bathroom to get something for her headache. She returned to the bedroom, but not to the bed. She stood gazing into the face of the man she loved. She didn't want to wake Mack with her restlessness. For Toni, sleep was an elusive goal right now. Damn Mr. Frank Clifford. She realized this was how he wanted her to feel; so on edge she couldn't function, let alone sleep, and it made her furious.

And every time she thought about how he was manipulating her like some master puppeteer, she wanted to—No, she wouldn't think like that. His expert ruthlessness was proving to be lethal not only to her career, but her very life. If only she could figure out a way to stop him, expose him for the lying, thieving monster he actually was.

He had to be watching her every move, or how else would he have known she'd gone to the bank? When he'd seen her go there he must have realized that she had found the key and taken the bait. He'd read her like a book.

Toni glanced at the clock on the nightstand. It was 11:15, too late to confront her boss. Or was it? Maybe if she caught him off guard she could find a chink in his armor and manage to save herself.

She left Mack's bedroom and went down the hall to her own and got out a pair of jeans, a shirt and a jacket, then quickly dressed. She couldn't let Frank Clifford continue to do this to her. She had to put a stop to it and she would, one way or another, whatever it took.

CHAPTER TWELVE

Mack groaned and turned over in the bed. When he reached for a warm curvy body and instead encountered a cold empty space, he woke up, blinking away the lingering effects of sleep. Where was Toni? He glanced at the clock on his nightstand. It was midnight. Maybe she was in the bathroom. After time passed and she didn't come out, he checked. When he didn't find her there, or anywhere else in the house, he cursed under his breath.

As he dressed, several possibilities streaked through his mind. What she'd said earlier came back to haunt him. He could almost touch the hatred she felt for Frank Clifford. Damn it, surely she hadn't gone to his place to confront the bastard!

He must have really been knocked out not to have heard her car drive away. How long ago had she left? He checked through the addresses of the employees at Townsend's and found the one he sought. If Toni had gone there, how much of a head start did she have on him? he wondered as he rushed out to his car.

God, please don't let her have done something stupid, he chanted over and over as he drove.

Mack's heart began to pound when he heard the sirens and saw the flashing red and blue lights on the tops of several police cars as he turned onto Frank Clifford's street. He realized when he saw Toni's car he had been hoping that she hadn't come here.

Where was she now?

He knew something terrible had happened, but to whom?

After parking his car, he hurried down the block to the Park Condos. Yellow caution tapes were stretched across the front entrance gate to Clifford's condo.

A uniformed policeman put out his arm to stop Mack when he moved to get past him.

"Can't let you—"

"It's all right, Dave," came the voice of Lieutenant Barnes.

Mack's jaw tensed. "Has something happened to Clifford?" He gulped. "Or Toni?"

"It's Clifford, and he's dead."

Relief that it wasn't Toni washed over Mack. "Where is Toni?" he asked anxiously. "I saw her car."

"She's over there." Bob pointed to a nearby squad car. "She's in a dazed condition."

"I don't understand. How? Why—"

"Someone, probably a neighbor, reported hearing gunshots. When we arrived on the scene, the door was open and Ms. Carlton was kneeling beside the body. There was a gun lying a few feet away."

"What did she say?"

"Not much of anything. Said she couldn't remember." His look was skeptical.

"Well, isn't that possible?"

"Anything is possible, Mack. A Mr. Morris who lives across the street saw her enter the building at around eleven thirty. He's a night watchman, and had left to go to work. He'd forgotten his glasses and came back to get them. When he climbed into his car to leave again, he heard something that sounded like gunshots or a car backfiring. He couldn't distinguish which it was or exactly where it came from, but it seemed to originate from the vicinity of Clifford's condo."

"Is that all you have?"

"The time element is enough for me to take her in."

"I want to see her."

"Mack—All right, but only for a few minutes. She appears to be in some kind of shock. We need to get her to a hospital to be examined."

Mack walked over to the police car and opened the back passenger door and climbed in beside Toni. He noted the ashen cast to her skin.

"Toni, are you all right?"

"Mack?" Her head lifted. "How did you—"

"Your side of the bed was cold and empty. I had to find out why my best girl had left me."

"He's dead."

"I know. Can you tell me what happened?"

"The blood. There was so much blood all over him. Some of it got on me," she said, rubbing the front of her shirt. "I don't remember how it got there, but I can't get it off," she said, rubbing frantically at the stains.

He grasped her hands, stopping her agitated movements, then gently cupped her face in his hands. "It's all right, baby. It'll all come back to you. Why did you go to see Clifford? I thought we agreed that you wouldn't do anything stupid?"

"I was so angry, Mack. I was tired of that man controlling my life."

"You were tired and angry, but not angry enough to kill him?"

"No."

"Where did the gun come from? You don't own one, do you?"

"No. It was already there, I guess—I remember seeing it on the floor moments before the police arrived."

"Do you remember anything prior to that?"

Lieutenant Barnes opened the door and said to Mack, "We'll be taking her to Westwood Hospital. You can follow us in your car."

All kinds of things went through Toni's mind as the doctor examined her. She hadn't killed Frank Clifford. Who did? She tried desperately to remember exactly what happened, but every time she did her head throbbed unmercifully. The doctor found a lump the size of a bird egg on the side of her head above her left ear. How had she gotten it? Had someone struck her, or had she fallen and hit her head?

"Why can't I remember?" she asked the doctor.

"You have a concussion," the doctor said. "We want to run some tests, so we'll be keeping you in the hospital for observation."

Toni looked to the policewoman standing by the door and said, "I want to see Mack."

"I'll get Lieutenant Barnes," the officer replied and stepped outside the examining room.

What now? Toni thought. Why hadn't she followed her best instincts, and Mack's advice, and stayed away from Frank Clifford? She was bound to look guilty in the eyes of the police.

While Lieutenant Barnes was talking to the doctor, Mack entered the room, taking in Toni's fragile and disheveled appearance. She was unusually quiet now and looked so vulnerable his heart turned over.

Toni saw Mack and held out her arms to him. He went to her and pulled her close to his body. She circled her arms around his waist and laid her head against his chest.

"Oh, Mack."

"How are you feeling, baby?"

"I have a hurricane of a headache, but other than that I'm all right."

He wondered if she was because he could feel her body tremble. She appeared to be suffering from the delayed effects of shock.

"Mack, what's going to happen now?"

"Bob wants to take you in for questioning when you get out of here. Can you tell me anything?"

"I can't remember past the moment I walked into Frank Clifford's apartment."

"How did you get in?"

"I don't—I think the door was already open, but I'm not sure. I just can't remember. I've tried, but I keep drawing a blank," she said, frustrated and verging on tears.

"Don't get so upset. It'll all come back to you."

"Oh, Mack, I hope so or else—"

"You didn't kill him."

"No, but—"

"Then don't borrow trouble."

"You're right. Heaven knows I've got enough on my plate without doing that."

"You haven't been charged with anything."

"Not yet, but Mack, it's only a matter of time."

He silenced her with a quick kiss. An orderly came to help her onto a gurney, and the doctor stepped over to her. Lieutenant Barnes instructed the policewoman to follow Toni to the room.

Mack hugged her one last time before they wheeled her away.

When the door closed behind them, Mack approached his friend.

"All right, Bob, give it to me straight."

"It doesn't look good, Mack. She was found at the scene of the crime with a gun that appears to be the murder weapon. Considering the situation at Townsend's…"

"Are you going to arrest her?"

"Listen, man, I feel for you, I really do. If the woman I cared for was involved in something like this, I'd be a basket case."

"She didn't do it. She couldn't have. Anyone who can't even step on a bug sure as hell couldn't murder anyone."

"Even if that someone is responsible for her being arrested on embezzlement charges? Even if that same someone was a threat to the career she prizes?"

"Bob."

He held up his hand. "Believe it or not, I'm not the enemy, Mack."

"I never thought you were. It's just that—"

"You're personally involved and can't see the forest for the trees."

"Yes, I am, damn it."

The lieutenant squeezed his friend's shoulder. "I understand where you're coming from."

Mack wondered if Bob really did understand. He wasn't sure he did at the moment. He left the emergency room.

Mack opened the door to Toni's hospital room. "You should be asleep."

"Mack," she said, watching him enter. "A nurse keeps coming in every half hour or so to check on me, making it hard for me to sleep. It's so late. I'm surprised your friend let you in to see me."

"Bob isn't your enemy, Toni. He's only doing his job. It's nothing personal." Mack pulled a chair over to her bed. He didn't like the way she looked, as though she were going to pass out. "I won't stay long. You should be resting, not lying awake worrying."

"I can't help it. I want—I need—I have to remember." She started breathing fast and swallowing hard.

"You can't force it, Toni."

"I'm scared, Mack."

He took her hand in his. "I know you are, but I'm not going to let anything or anyone hurt you."

Toni let the conviction she saw in his face and the confidence she heard in his voice temporarily soothe away her fears and anxieties.

As Toni closed her eyes in sleep a few minutes later, Mack watched her lovely face for long moments before placing her hand across her waist. He realized that he had never cared for Linda Hutton, or any other woman, the way he cared for Toni.

When he moved to leave, Toni's eyes opened and he noticed that they had begun to dilate. Her breathing changed, coming in quick gasps and she swallowed repeatedly. She was going to be sick. He reached for the container by the bed and rushed to her side just in time, and she emptied the contents of her stomach.

When she was done, he pushed the nurse's call button. The nurse, realizing the situation, took over.

"It's not unusual with patients suffering from concussion," she explained to Mack.

Toni was sick several more times. It practically unnerved Mack. The doctor was called in and Mack was ushered out of the room by the policewoman.

After a while the doctor came out of Toni's room.

"She might be sick again during the next few hours due to the effects of the concussion. I'm going to have the nurse stay with her the rest of the night, or should I say morning now." He glanced at his watch.

"She is going to be all right?" Mack asked.

"The injury over the left ear is in a delicate area. We want to keep her for an additional twenty-four hours to be on the safe side."

"The safe side?" Mack frowned.

"It's rare, but she could go into a coma."

"A coma?" Mack felt stupid repeating everything the doctor said, but he couldn't help himself.

The doctor went on. "We don't anticipate that happening, but…"

Mack understood. He had to find the person who really killed Clifford and struck Toni so savagely.

Mack left the hospital a few minutes later, relieved but just barely.

He glanced at his watch. It was five o'clock in the morning. God, he was tired, yet he knew he wouldn't be able to sleep. Toni wasn't the only one who hated Frank Clifford. The man had had more than his share of enemies. Mack had to include himself on that list. The question was, who besides Toni hated him enough to kill him?

Mack went home and headed for the bathroom to shower and dress before going down to the police station. Bob should know something more about what happened by the time he got there.

"I knew you'd come. I've been expecting you," Bob said matter-of-factly to Mack as he walked into his office. "What I have to tell you won't brighten your day or your disposition."

"All right, spit it out."

"One, Toni Carlton's fingerprints are all over the gun. It looks like I'll have to take her in."

"She doesn't remember touching it. And she doesn't own a gun."

"That's the strange part. The gun is registered to Henry Warren. Can she explain what it was doing near the body?"

"Since it's Warren's gun, it stands to reason he's the one who put it there."

"Maybe, and then again, maybe not. In any case, I've already sent someone over to his place to bring him in for questioning."

Mack knew that although his friend recognized the determined look on his face indicating he would want to be present when he questioned the man, Bob wouldn't let him.

Mack sat cooling his heels in Bob's office, waiting for him to finish questioning Hank Warren. Needless to say, he was mad, even though he knew procedure wouldn't allow it unless he was Toni's lawyer or Warren's. Finally Bob returned to his office.

"Well? Did he explain how his gun happened to be at the scene of the crime?"

"Says he gave it to Ms. Carlton for protection months ago."

"Yeah, and I'm General Schwarzkopf. Toni hates the guy, and from what I've seen when the two of them are together, the feeling is mutual."

"I hate to be the one to tell you this, but it might not have always been that way between them."

Mack considered his friend's words, but he couldn't believe that there had ever been anything between Toni and Hank Warren. None of this was making any sense to him. It was as though he and Toni were in a maze and couldn't find the way out.

Clifford had hinted at something between him and Toni, but he hadn't believed anything the bastard had said about that.

Against his will, Mack started remembering another time when he hadn't believed something about another woman. And he'd been proven wrong. Suddenly it was shades of Linda Hutton all over again.

Mack had quit the force because of that woman and what she had driven him to do with her lies, evasions and deceptions.

Don't forget she almost made you abandon your honor.

Mack closed his eyes. As if he could.

One thing was sure: He had to come to grips with his feelings concerning Linda and the present situation, or he'd be no good to Toni or himself. He'd thought he was done with that part of his past, and faced everything he'd had to face, but he was evidently wrong. He owed it to Toni, and himself, to wash away the residue of the emotional garbage Linda Hutton had dumped on him.

CHAPTER THIRTEEN

As Toni slowly awakened and her eyes began to focus, it took a few moments for her to remember where she was and why. Then it all came back to her in a flash. Her first clear vision was of Mack slumped in a chair beside her bed, deeply asleep. Her lips molded into a smile. He looked so uncomfortable in the chair that she felt sorry for him.

She wondered what time it was and how long he had been in the hospital.

Mack groaned, moving his body this way and that, trying in vain to find a comfortable position in the hard chair. Unable to find one, he slowly began to awaken. Opening his eyes, he yawned, stretching out the kinks in his arms and legs. When his elbow connected painfully with the arm of the chair, his senses quickly cleared and he swore under his breath. This certainly wasn't his bed.

Toni laughed. "Such language."

"Toni! You're awake." Mack's brown eyes darkened in concern. "How do you feel?"

Toni moved to raise her head and a throbbing pain shot through her brain and she moaned, closing her eyes and gingerly resting her head against the pillow.

Worry brought a frown to his face. "You're obviously in pain. Do you want me to get the nurse?"

"No. I'll be all right in a minute."

Mack wasn't convinced of that. He straightened in his chair and reached for her hand. "You need to take it easy and not move around too much until the doctor says you can."

"Is that an order?"

"You'd better believe it." He grinned.

Her heart did a crazy flip-flop whenever he did that. Her smile faded when thoughts of her situation intruded.

"What is it, Toni?" Mack asked, watchful.

"Nothing, just reality setting in. Has Lieutenant Barnes said anything to you?"

Mack looked away evasively.

"I want the truth."

He wasn't eager to discuss this with her, but knew he wouldn't get any peace until he did.

"The gun beside Clifford's body is registered to Hank Warren."

"Hank!" Her faced brightened. "It must mean he's the one who killed Clifford."

"The way he tells it, he gave it to you months ago for protection."

"Say what?" Toni raised up on the bed. The dull throbbing in her head forced her to lie back. "Mack, he's lying through his teeth."

"According to Bob, he sounds pretty convincing."

Toni sensed that there was more behind Mack's words and her temper flared. "What do you believe?"

"You can't stand the guy; everyone knows that."

"But do you know it? And do you believe it? Is the reason you have a problem discussing it because he called me the night you and I first…"

"Made love?"

Seeing the question in his eyes, she glared at him. "I told you I didn't know why he called. I don't even know how he got my phone number, since it's unlisted. And for your information, I wouldn't give it to him if he were the last human on the planet."

The line, 'the lady doth protest too much,' flickered through Mack's mind, but only for a split second. He shook the doubt away.

Toni noticed the gesture and guessed what it meant. Her hot Italian and African American temper flared again, even hotter this time.

"You can choose not to believe me, I—ooh, my head." She stopped and carefully touched the area above her left ear before limply collapsing against the pillow.

"Toni!" Mack gently eased her into his arms. "For your information, you little wildcat, I believe you. I just couldn't stop my male jealousy from rearing its head." He lovingly stroked a stray lock of her hair away from her face. "Hey, I don't like the idea of you working anywhere near the guy, let alone him having anything personal to do with you. Okay?"

"But he hasn't. It baffles me why he would hint that he had. Even more than that, I want to know what prompted him to call me." Her brows arched in thoughtful contemplation. "I wonder if Clifford said something to him. In the past, Hank has insinuated I was having an affair with the boss and that I was attempting to use it to edge him out of the running for the director's chair."

"His lies could make it look like you had both a personal and a professional reason for killing Clifford."

"And if anyone believes I was involved with Hank, they might assume he and I were actually—"

"In on it together," they said in unison.

Toni was quiet for a few moments. The trap her dead boss had so cleverly set for her was clamping ever tighter, bearing down ever heavier as time went on. She closed her eyes on her agonizing thoughts.

"I think I'd better leave. You're looking peaked, and you're trembling."

Her eyes fluttered open and she protested. "I don't want you to go, Mack."

"And why not?" he inquired.

Toni's faced heated. "You know why."

He grinned. "I do? Maybe a little mutual reassurance is needed here. Do you think?"

"And just how can I give you that?" A teasing look lighted her face.

"Like this." Mack lowered his mouth to hers in a tender yet arousing kiss. "I want your head to ache for an entirely different reason.

Let's not forget how much I want to make love to that beautiful body of yours."

"Just my body? You're so cruel," she said, feigning hurt feelings and turning her head away.

"I want all of you, sweet Toni. Every lovely inch of you." His lips found hers.

"I want you, too, Mack, so bad." She moved her mouth over his, savoring every nuance of the contact. Then she slipped her arms around his neck. "But at the moment it's a little difficult." She glanced around her hospital room.

"You have a point," he said, unwilling to give up what they were sharing. "You're not in any shape to handle me right now anyway."

"I'm only temporarily out of commission," she answered wryly. "Temporarily being the operative word."

Reluctantly Mack moved away and headed for the door. Then, turning when he reached it, he gave her a smoldering look. "I'll be back later. I'm going home and get some sleep. Hang in there, kid," he said, the last in a passable Humphrey Bogart imitation.

Toni smiled to herself. Mack was everything a woman could ask for in a man and more. He was warm, loving and had a wacky sense of humor. And he was good at what he did. But would he think so if he couldn't keep her from going to prison? She didn't want to think what it would do to him, so she intended to save herself. But where should she start? For sure, she had to get out of this hospital.

Any time now Lieutenant Barnes would come in to question her. She could tell him the truth as she knew it, but would it be enough to satisfy him, the D.A. or a judge? She doubted it. Then what?

They'll arrest you.

She had to think of something before that happened. Half an hour later she heard a knock at the door. Toni tensed when it opened.

"Ms. Carlton?" Lieutenant Barnes stopped in the doorway. "How are you feeling?"

"Does it matter?" When she saw him grimace, she was instantly ashamed of her attitude. As Mack had said, the man was only doing his job. "If you want to talk to me, I'm ready."

He seemed relieved as he walked across the room and stood beside her bed.

Toni's lips quirked into a wry smile. "You may as well sit down."

"Such a gracious invitation." His lips did a similar quirk.

"I'm sorry. I know this can't be easy for you since you and Mack are such close friends."

"No, it isn't. Just know it's nothing personal." He took out a notepad and pen and started writing. "We discovered that the gun at the crime scene belongs to a colleague of yours. And according to Hank Warren, he gave it to you months ago for protection. Is that true?"

Her mouth thinned to an angry line. "No, it isn't. The gun may belong to Hank Warren, but he never gave it to me for protection, or any other reason. The man is a liar if he said otherwise."

Lieutenant Barnes glanced at her, appearing momentarily thrown by the vehemence in her answer. He wrote something down on his pad. Glancing up from it, he asked, "How did the gun come to be at the crime scene?"

"I have no idea." She gritted her teeth. "Hank must have put it there," she answered simply.

"And how do you explain that your fingerprints were on it?"

"My fingerprints? I—I don't remember picking up the gun, let alone handling it. Since the gun belongs to Hank, it stands to reason that he's the one who killed Mr. Clifford, hit me in the head, pressed my fingers onto the gun, then left it and fled."

"That would be a logical assumption, except that he claims to have an alibi for the time of the killing and adamantly insists that he gave you the gun months ago when the two of you were involved."

"We were never 'involved,' as he put it. I'd never sink that low."

Toni realized that she shouldn't be discussing this any further without a lawyer. She also realized it was her word against Hank Warren's until his alibi could be checked out. Snake that he was, and deserving of the name, he wasn't the one accused of embezzlement and now murder.

"If I allegedly killed my boss, can you explain how I came to have a concussion?"

"According to the doctor, you could have sustained the injury in a fall."

"Meaning?"

"You could have tripped. When we arrived on the scene, you were on your knees beside the body."

"So, I killed the man and then tripped over the body, giving myself a concussion?" she said, her voice incredulous. "Give me a break, Lieutenant."

He looked uncomfortable. "We're not getting anywhere with this. I can see you're not feeling well. I'll come back later. The doctor says he'll probably release you tomorrow morning. We'll have to take you down to the station for more in-depth questioning. I think you'd better have your lawyer present."

"Of course. We wouldn't want my rights violated, would we?"

"Look, Ms. Carlton...may I call you Toni?"

"Yes, if you want to."

"Toni, I have no personal axe to grind. I'm, as you said, only doing my job. Mack is a friend of mine and has been for years. We were once partners when he was on the police force. He believes you're innocent and will do all he can to help you." The lieutenant rose from his chair and shoved his notepad and pen into his jacket pocket. "I'll be back this evening after you've had some rest."

As Toni watched him leave, a feeling of impending doom closed in around her. Tomorrow they would be sending her to jail. They might call it protective custody, or just simple questioning, but she knew better. She thought about what Lieutenant Barnes had said about Mack. He was right. He would help her—if he could. The question was, could he? Could anybody?

Toni laid her head back against the pillow, feeling completely drained—both physically and mentally. When she thought about

Hank Warren and the lies he'd told, she wanted to scream and rant and rave and all around pitch a fit, but she was just too tired at the moment. What good would it do, anyway?

She'd never find out the truth sitting in jail. Although she wasn't officially under arrest, a policewoman was stationed outside her door. And she believed that once they got her down to the station, they'd arrest her for murder. She had to think of a way to distract the policewoman and escape this craziness.

Toni got out of bed and, on shaky legs, walked over to the closet and pulled her jeans out and struggled into them. It took her a few minutes to recover from her efforts. Then she made it back to the bed and collapsed on it, pulling up the covers. She had to rest and conserve her energy for later.

Toni closed her eyes and tried to concentrate. She still had one hell of a headache and her arms and legs felt so weak. How was she ever going to get away from here? And there was no mistaking that that was exactly what she had to do if she wanted to find the real murderer and clear herself.

She eyed the nurse's call box hanging on the side of the bed.

That was it!

Several hours later Toni initiated her escape plan. She knocked the pitcher of ice water on her food tray onto the floor. The policewoman peeked her head inside the room to investigate.

"I was thirsty and reached for the water pitcher." She shot the woman an embarrassed smile. "Needless to say, I felt weak and I'm afraid it slipped out of my hand. I tried the call button, but it doesn't seem to be working." She flicked the button and nothing happened.

"Do you want me to get you some more ice water?"

"If you wouldn't mind."

"No problem. And I'll get someone to mop up the mess." She picked up the pitcher and went into the bathroom to rinse it. As she left the room, she said, "Be right back."

Toni threw back the covers and eased herself out of the bed and grabbing her shirt and jacket from the closet, dashed into the bathroom to finish dressing. Seconds later she opened the door and stood behind it, flattening herself against the wall.

A few minutes later the policewoman returned with a fresh pitcher of ice water. Seeing that the door to the bathroom was open and Toni wasn't in there, she turned and rushed to the closet. Finding it empty, she ran out into the hall to search for Toni. Toni left the bathroom and hurried from the room. She breathed a sigh of relief when she spotted a nearby supply closet and swiftly darted inside.

Toni was crouched down behind a canvas-covered receptacle filled with dirty linen when she heard voices outside the room. Luckily she wasn't discovered when the door opened seconds later. Realizing that the policewoman wouldn't waste any time summoning help to search for her missing charge, Toni knew she had to get out of the hospital fast.

When Toni looked out into the hall, she found it empty and stepped out of the supply closet and headed for the stairs. The way she was feeling, she would have loved nothing better than to take the elevator, but that was definitely out. Even though her room was on the second floor and all she had to do was make it down to the ground floor, she put going down the stairs right up there with running the L.A. marathon.

Just as she opened the stairwell door, Toni saw a policeman hurrying to the elevators and quickly closed the door. She swallowed her fear and stayed still until he got on the elevator and the doors closed behind him. She casually walked over to the telephone alcove. It was then that she realized she didn't have her purse or any money in her jeans pocket. She would have to make the call collect.

"Hello," a sleep-husky male voice answered.

"Collect call from Toni. Will you accept the call?"

"Yes."

"Mack?"

"Toni?" He cleared his throat.

"Yes, it's me. I haven't got time to explain, but I'm leaving the hospital. Meet me at the corner of Wilshire and Westwood in fifteen minutes and please hurry." She hung up before he could answer.

Toni thanked God Mack didn't live that far from the hospital. Just then she saw an elderly lady shuffling out of the elevator and walked over and offered to help her. Keeping her face averted so that the security guard couldn't get a clear look at her, Toni and the lady walked past the security desk and out of the hospital. Moments later, Toni helped the woman into a waiting taxi, then made her way to the corner to wait for Mack.

Mack was wide awake now. Why was Toni leaving the hospital? What could have happened to panic her into running? He scrambled out of bed and stumbled into the bathroom.

A few minutes later, as he was leaving the house, his brother Matthew drove up in his mini van.

"Matt, you caught me on the way out." It occurred to Mack that the police would be, thanks to his friend Bob, on the lookout for his car and license plate number.

"Mama is worried about you, so she commandeered me to come check on my big brother since Marc is out of town for the weekend."

"Why should she be worried about me? I just talked to her a few days ago."

"Now, you know Mama. She says the last time she talked to you, you sounded strange."

"Strange how? Don't answer that. Tell her I'll come by later."

"I'll tell her, but you'd better show up."

"I will." An idea came to him. "Listen, Matt. How would you like to borrow my Jag for a few hours? I know you've been dying to try it out ever since I got it. Rachel told me you have no love for the mini van she insisted the family needed and coerced you into buying. I really need a favor, Matt. I'll explain everything later."

Matt's brows arched skeptically at his brother, the look saying he doubted he would get the whole story.

"Are the keys to the beach house on this ring?" Mack held it up for inspection.

"Sure, why?"

Mack could see the wheels turning in his brother's brilliant lawyer brain. "I'll return the van to your house this evening and pick up my car."

Matt frowned. "You aren't in any trouble, are you?"

"Matt, this is important, man."

Although his brother had gotten out of the van and tossed him the keys, Mack was sure he hadn't overlooked the fact that he had purposely evaded answering his question.

Matt glanced longingly at Mack's Jag. "The thought of driving this baby becomes more appealing by the moment. As for the beach house, you can use it for as long as you need to."

"Thanks, Matt, I won't forget this."

"Don't worry, I don't intend to let you. Take care, big brother."

Mack smiled. "I will. You make me feel so ancient. I'm only two years older than you." With that he slid behind the wheel and backed the mini van out of the driveway.

Ten minutes later Mack pulled up at the corner of Westwood and Wilshire. He spotted Toni standing beneath the palm frond canopies belonging to a stand of short palm trees.

"May I offer you a ride, my little chickadee?"

Toni hesitated for a moment before walking toward the van. She opened the door and climbed in back. "You nut. One day you're going to get enough of doing those imitations. Whose van is this, anyway?"

"My brother Matt's," he said, turning the vehicle around and heading for the beach.

"Where are we going?"

"That same brother has a beach house in Santa Monica. I'm taking you there. No one will think to look for you there."

"What about your good friend Lieutenant Barnes?"

"Bob doesn't even know about the place. By the way, what made you decide to leave the hospital so suddenly?"

"I couldn't stay there any longer, Mack. I think your friend is close to arresting me."

"I think he is, too," he answered grimly.

"He's going to be gunning for you, too."

"Yeah, I know. It's the reason we have to hurry and get you to the relative safety of my brother's beach house."

Mack drove and for a while they didn't say anything. Then, "Running away is going to make you look guilty."

"I know, but I couldn't stay, Mack. I had to get out of there."

"The one thing it will also do is alert the killer that his or her plan is in jeopardy. Whoever it is will be looking for you, too." Mack thought about the person who had been on the other end of the phone the night Clifford came after Toni. Had he or she killed the man?

"Don't you see? It had to be Hank!" Toni exclaimed.

"Warren?" Mack shook his head, clearing away his momentary reverie. "We can't be sure he's the one, or if he is, he doesn't have an accomplice. Clifford had a long list of people who could have cheerfully done him in, no problem."

Mack was grateful the beach house garage and backyard were enclosed by a seven-foot-high wooden fence. He guided Toni around it. He could tell she needed to lie down and rest by the way she leaned into him as they walked the few feet to the back door of the beach house.

Mack was also glad his brother was the planner in the family. He had enough food stocked up to feed an army. Mack smiled. With three kids Matt had no choice. He, Rachel and the kids came here two weekends a month, weather and jobs permitting.

"It's a nice place," Toni commented, taking a seat on the comfortable overstuffed couch. "Hopefully I won't be staying here long."

"Yes, hopefully," he said, filling the space beside her. "Now I think you'd better rest for a while. Are you hungry?

"You going to whip up one of your culinary masterpieces?"

"I can be persuaded."

"You can, huh. What does a girl have to do to, ah, persuade you?"

"This." He pulled her into his arms and coaxed a kiss from her lips.

"I must say I like your winning ways, Mr. Jessup."

"I'm glad you do because I intend to let you use the most effective means possible to persuade me. But later." He eased out of her embrace and stood up. "What you need right now is rest," he insisted, comfortably ensconcing Toni on the couch and fluffing up the couch cushion behind her head before leaving the room.

As he prepared a quick but easy meal for them, Mack thought about everyone connected with the case. The embezzlement charges would have to take a backseat to the murder charge. Together he and Toni would have to make a list of all possible suspects and eliminate the ones most unlikely to have done the deed.

CHAPTER FOURTEEN

Mack gave Toni's shoulder a little nudge. When her eyes fluttered open, he smiled. "You looked so peaceful I hated to wake you."

"It's all right." She yawned, then raised up on an elbow. Mack had placed a tray on the coffee table. "You always fix so much food. Before I know it, you'll have me as fat as a cow."

Mack smiled. "In that case I'd have to start fixing tofu, because I like you just the way you are."

Toni made a face at the thought of tofu. "So it's only my body you're interested in. All this time I thought you wanted me because I have this wonderfully intelligent brain."

"You have nothing to worry about on either count, because you have an equal share of beauty and brains. And I, for one, think that's one hell of a dynamite combination."

"You do?" Toni couldn't help noticing the desire inflaming his eyes. "Down, boy, I'm starving."

"Just my luck to have a woman who's starved for only food. Maybe after I've fed you, you'll be more wanton—I mean willing." He grinned wickedly.

He couldn't have her any more willing if he tried, Toni thought. Just being close to him threw her senses into overload. "I said I was starving for food, but I wonder if maybe I shouldn't amend that to include hunger for a certain sexy man." She moved her hand across the front of his jeans.

"Keep that up and our dinner will get cold."

"That's why microwaves were invented."

Later Mack warmed up their dinner and they ate in companionable silence. After clearing away the dishes, Mack returned to the living room.

"Now to get down to business."

Toni sighed. "Yeah. Hank is the obvious one we should start with."

"Bob said he had an alibi, but didn't want to publicly reveal who he was with. That someone must be well known."

"Do you have any idea who it could be?"

"According to the company grapevine, Nina Townsend."

"Nina Townsend! But I thought…"

Mack's brows arched. "You thought what?"

"I thought she and Clifford were having an affair."

"From what I've been able to sort out, Warren is her latest conquest."

Toni smiled. "So that was his ace in the hole."

"Come again?" Mack's eyes narrowed in confusion.

"Hank always hinted that the job of director would fall to him. Now I know how he planned to accomplish it."

Mack laughed. "I see. He was in essence sleeping his way to the top."

"That's funny because it's what he accused me of doing with Clifford. He even had the nerve to put Mr. Townsend on my list of sugar daddies, as he called them."

"It would appear that Nina Townsend was spreading herself a little thin, doesn't it?"

"I wouldn't put anything past that woman. I've often wondered how she got Mr. Townsend to marry her. They're total opposites."

"Opposites do attract, you know. I never got around to questioning her, but I will," he said with a determined look in his eyes. "If Townsend had only let me finish my investigation." But there was no reason why he couldn't continue on his own with a little help from Bob. "Maybe his wife is the reason he didn't want me to. Her amorous involvements with the male employees of the company would have proven embarrassing, to say the least."

"Yeah, I can well imagine it would. It's possible that Nina's affair with Clifford could be motive enough for Hank to kill Clifford."

"Maybe. Hank is, after all, a pretty volatile character. He could have lost his head and killed Clifford in the heat of passion, if he did in fact kill him. But so many things don't add up."

"You're right, they don't. Damn it, Mack." She settled back, disappointed.

"I know how frustrated you must be feeling, baby." He pulled her into his arms, wishing with all his heart he could take that look off her beautiful face and replace it with a smile.

"Oh, Mack." She laid her head on his shoulder.

"There are other people on the list. Maybe one of them did him in. I think that whoever did it should get a medal."

Toni smiled. "Unfortunately, what you think isn't the biggie here. Who's next on the list?"

"Pat Davis."

She raised her head to look at Mack. "Pat!"

"You don't know what he held over her head?"

Her eyes widened. "No."

"It's as if she was holding something back." He let Toni go and eased back against the couch. "First, Clifford promoted her to executive secretary, then promised to promote her husband to mail room manager."

"But Joe never got the position."

"Exactly."

"But—"

"As it turned out, Clifford wanted more from Pat than she was willing to give."

"Surely he didn't expect her to sleep with him!"

"I think he expected it to be the natural conclusion to the bargain."

"But Pat is happily married to Joe."

"Clifford found that out when she refused to do what he wanted."

"How do you know all this?"

"I got it straight from the horse's mouth."

"From Pat!" she said incredulously. "She's always been wary of discussing her personal life. How did you convince her to confide in you?"

Mack smiled. "It's my lethal charm, don't you know?"

"I can believe it. What I don't understand is why he made her executive secretary unless—" She stopped. "You know why, don't you?"

"He wanted her to monitor your activities. He wanted to know what you were doing at all times so he could frame you royally."

"But Pat is my friend."

"He was banking on the fact."

"It's hard for me to believe she would go along with it."

"Oh, he was smart. He convinced her that he was concerned about you overworking. And it was all for the good of the company."

"That doesn't make sense." Toni frowned in bafflement. "You said he wanted to know Pat in the biblical sense."

"He knew what good friends you and Pat were, so he elevated her to a position which suited his purposes. He knew she and Joe were happily married and a wife would do just about anything to help her husband succeed."

"He was emotionally blackmailing her, then?"

"You got it."

"Poor Pat. But when Joe didn't get the promotion, how did he continue to get her to cooperate?"

"He threatened to fire her. The Davises just bought a new house, furniture and a car. They need the income from her job to help pay for those things, not to mention having several children to raise."

"The bastard."

"He was that, all right."

"Was she the one who altered the records?"

"No. I think Warren was the one who sabotaged your work whenever he got the chance. He may not have been alone, either."

"My God. I'm afraid to ask who's next on the list."

"Joe Davis."

"Joe? What does he have to do with the records? He's in the mail room."

"You keep forgetting that his wife works with you every day."

She shook her head. "It still doesn't compute."

"When I questioned Joe, he admitted that Clifford had him by the throat."

"Now I'm beginning to see the light." She paused to reflect on the idea. "Mr. Clifford was using reverse blackmail, with Pat as the object."

"Joe had only to delay sending out envelopes to the different companies when Clifford gave the word."

"I can't see Joe compromising his position that way—ah, Pat is the integral part in this very human equation. I keep forgetting that. But he didn't give Joe the promotion."

"No, he didn't. Put together what he was threatening Pat with, the loss of her job and Joe's, not to mention compromising his integrity, and you have a motive for Joe to kill him."

"I can't believe Joe would do that." She recalled his attitude at times. "I take that back; I can. He loves Pat, and he's fiercely protective of his wife and family. Our esteemed CEO was even more of a bastard than I thought."

"Yeah. That's a nice word for him, actually."

"It's going to be harder to solve this case than we ever imagined, isn't it?"

"Yes. I'm afraid it is."

"What about the mail room manager? Do you think he was involved too?"

"No. I don't think he'd have the guts or the temperament to go along with Clifford on something of this magnitude. Let's go to the next person on the list."

Toni's expression was blank. "Who's left?"

"John Victor Townsend Jr."

"Mr. Townsend!" Her eyebrows rose in stunned disbelief.

"Yes, the head honcho himself. If he knew about his wife's affair, which I'm sure he did, he had more than enough reason to kill the man."

"I'm not sure he did know for certain about the affair."

"Believe me, he knows about all of his wife's affairs, past and present."

"If that's true, then one more affair shouldn't have bothered him overly much."

"It would if it involved stealing money from his company."

"You could be right," she said thoughtfully.

"Then there is Nina Townsend, who was playing Hank and Clifford."

"The woman is married and couldn't have either of her lovers, so why would she risk everything by killing Clifford? She had her cake and was eating it too, apparently."

"I have a plan to flush out the real killer."

Toni smiled. "Good, when do we start?"

"We don't. Bob and I will do what needs to be done."

"But what am I supposed to do in the meantime?"

"You stay safely secluded here."

"Mack."

"Don't thank me," he said, rising to his feet and stretching his arms and legs.

"I didn't leave the hospital to come here and sit around and twiddle my thumbs. I have to do something to save myself."

"If Bob finds out where you are, he'll take you into custody now that you have left his protection."

"Protection! Ha! He was going to arrest me, and you know it."

"Maybe, but he won't see it that way, I promise you. I know Bob."

"The same goes for him about you."

"What do you mean?"

"He knows you as well as you know him. Since you were partners he knows how your mind works. He'll be watching you like a hawk."

"I know. And if I'm with him while he investigates I'll be able to keep a check on what's going on."

A sigh left Toni's throat. "Mack, I'll go crazy here by myself."

"I figured you would, so I've decided to get my sister to come stay with you."

"A babysitter! You've got to be kidding."

"No. I'm not. Mariah will be stimulating company for you."

"Not as stimulating as working to personally clear myself." She crossed her arms over her chest in frustration.

Mack grinned, pulling Toni to her feet and circling his arms around her neck. "There isn't anything you can do at the moment, baby."

"I guess you're right," she agreed reluctantly. "But when there is, promise me you'll let me help."

"I promise," he said, locking his fingers behind her neck, touching his forehead to hers. "I'd better be going. I have to return my brother's van."

"I don't want you to go."

"And I don't want to leave you, baby, but..."

"I know. The longer you stay gone the more suspicious the lieutenant will become."

"Oh, Bob is going to know right away what I've been up to. He just won't know how I managed to pull it off." Mack laughed. "And that's going to bug the hell out of him."

"He's your friend."

"Yeah, he sure is. That's the beauty of this whole thing. Bob is going to be trying to outsmart me at every turn. The challenge is going to prove interesting."

"Men."

"You women love us."

"Yes, we do, don't we?"

"Do you love me, baby?"

Toni swallowed back her declaration of love. It wasn't the right time to tell him. Maybe it never would be, if she were never able to prove her innocence.

"Such a serious look." His eyes pleaded to be let in on her thoughts.

"Not so serious, just thoughtful is all. You'd better go."

"Trying to give me the bum's rush?"

"Not at all, but as you said, Bob awaits."

God, he didn't want to leave her. Mack lowered his head for a parting kiss that changed into a passion-arousing sensation threatening to glue him to the spot. Reluctantly, he ended the kiss and set her away from him. He found he was trembling as much as the woman standing in front of him.

"We have unfinished business, pilgrim," he said in a husky, slightly off kilter John Wayne imitation.

"That's the best I've heard so far."

He grinned at the compliment. "I'd better go." He headed for the door.

"When will I see you again?"

"I don't know, baby. I'll call you."

As Toni watched him leave, loneliness gripped her. It was as though a part of her had walked out the door.

As he headed for his brother's house, Mack felt incomplete. Toni Carlton made him feel whole. From the first moment he saw her she'd affected him like no other woman had since Linda Hutton. But what he felt for Toni was stronger and deeper than that had been. Toni had the power to destroy him. And if she were proven guilty, she'd do the same thing to him professionally, too. He intended to do whatever it took to free her and clear her name because he knew deep in his soul she was innocent.

Mack guided the van into his brother's driveway. A few minutes later he was in Matt's living room. He slipped the keys to the beach house off the ring before handing him the keys to the van.

"I thought seriously about not giving your Jag back."

Mack laughed. "Rides that good, huh?"

"Even better, if that's possible. One day when I can afford it, I'm going to get one for my own personal use."

"If Rachel lets you."

"Oh, she will all right, she loves me."

"I do, do I?" came a soft, feminine voice from the doorway.

"Most definitely, Mrs. Jessup." Matt smiled lovingly at his wife.

"Enough of the mushy stuff, guys, I've gotta go."

"Yeah, the mushy stuff." Eight-year-old Matt Jr. echoed his uncle's words as he scrambled into the room.

Mack walked over to the boy and ruffled his hair. "How's my favorite nephew?"

"Becoming more of a smart aleck with each passing day," Rachel supplied. "Like his uncle," she tacked on.

"Don't be unkind, Rach. I know you love me. I'd like to stay and listen to more of your flattery, but I really have to be going."

"I'll walk you to your car," Matt said, urging Mack toward the front door.

Once they were outside, Matt started questioning his brother.

"You're neck deep in something, aren't you? Mama is right to worry about you, isn't she?"

"One question at a time, counselor. For your information, I know what I'm doing this time."

"I distinctly remember hearing you say the same thing seven years ago."

A strained look came into Mack's face. "That time was different."

"How was it different? Mack, you let your heart rule your head back then. Aren't you doing the same thing this time? Marc told me about you and this Toni Carlton."

"Marc should mind his own damn business," he grumbled.

"You're our brother; we care about you."

"I know that, but there is no need for you to worry about me this time."

"I don't think I could stand it if you reverted back to the way you were after the Linda Hutton fiasco."

"That won't happen with Toni," Mack gritted out.

"How do you know?"

"I just do, that's all. I really need to go see Mama and smooth her ruffled motherly feathers."

"You're not going to tell me what's going on, are you?"

"I can't, Matt."

He heard the hurt intake of breath in Matt's voice when he said, "I can't force you to confide in me."

"It's not that I don't want to. I simply can't at the moment."

"Well, if you find you need to talk to someone, I'll be here."

Mack's expression softened. "I know. Don't think I don't appreciate your concern, because I do."

Mack thought about what he'd said to his brother after he left. He knew in his heart Toni was different. He couldn't put it into words, but he knew it was true.

Mack sat in his car in front of his mother's house for a few minutes before getting out to go inside. His very Spanish mother was a worrier. He'd have to think of a way to placate her until this thing with Toni was resolved. Somehow he had to find the right words.

As he started up the walk, his sister's Jeep turned into the drive. He stopped to watch as she climbed out. When she saw him, she walked over to him. In looks Mariah took after their mother. She had the same black hair and warm chocolate eyes, but that was where the similarity ended. His only sister was a petite, adventurous bundle of keen, quick wit and boundless energy.

"Where are you coming from, pequena?" he asked, fondly pulling her into his arms and hugging her tightly. When he released her, they headed for the front porch.

"You're not going to lay that heavy big brother act on me again, are you?"

"And if I was? Don't sweat it, Riah. I'm glad to see you. I have a favor to ask of you."

"Oh, God. What is it? I'm not going to do your laundry. I love you dearly, big brother, but your one flaw is not one I want to deal with."

"Only one, huh?" He laughed.

"Actually, there are many, but that one was the first to come to mind. So what do you want me to do for you?"

"Can you spare a week or two from your busy schedule?"

Mariah's brows arched curiously. "I'm not that busy at the moment. My boss is on a month's vacation so I'm free to do pretty much what I want until he gets back. Why?"

His sister worked part-time for Ken Worthington, a private detective. She was his girl Friday, or something like that.

"I have a friend who—"

Mariah's eyes lit up like an arcade game. "It's the new woman in your life Marc keeps raving about, isn't it? You want me to keep an eye on her. All right." She stretched the last two words out. "I read about the police finding her at the scene of a murder. Her boss', if I remember correctly. You don't think she did it, do you?"

Mariah never failed to amaze him. She was quick on the uptake. "No, as a matter of fact, I don't."

"I can tell by the way you said it you're gone on her."

"And if I am?"

Before Mariah could answer the porch light came on and the front door opened.

"Are you two going to stay out there all night?" Marianna Jessup inquired, opening the screen door.

"No, Mama," Mack and Mariah answered in unison and walked past their mother into the living room.

"Sit down and talk to your mother," she said to her son. To her daughter she said, "Mariah, go out to the kitchen and get us some coffee. I just made a fresh pot."

"Yes, Mama," she answered and hurried out to the kitchen, leaving her brother to face the music alone.

Mack cleared his throat. "Matt caught up with me and told me you were worried."

She shook her head. "You're so like your Uncle Juan. You both tend to keep things bottled up inside, especially the hurt. Don't worry, I don't intend to lecture you. I just had to see for myself that you were all right. And this girl of yours, when am I going to meet her?"

"Soon, Mama."

"How do you feel about her?"

"Mama."

"All right, keep the knowledge locked in your heart."

"Now, Mama. You'll meet her soon. I promise."

She smiled. "I guess I'll have to be satisfied with that."

He wanted to shout to the whole world that he loved Toni, but right now he had to do everything in his power to save her. And the way things were shaping up, it wasn't going to be easy.

He and his mother and sister sat enjoying their coffee. After a while his mother went to bed, leaving the younger generation, as she called them, alone to talk.

"Riah, can you stay with Toni?"

"I don't see why not. Mama is going to be visiting Uncle Juan and Aunt Rosa for two weeks. They've been begging her to come for a visit almost forever." Mariah laughed. "Our cousin Gina told Mama she needed to get a life."

"She did? She has the nerve of a tightrope walker."

"She has a point, Mack. Mama is still young and attractive. Several gentlemen at the church are interested in her."

"I agree. She needs someone else to worry about and fuss over besides us. You'll be moving out soon." Mack handed her a copy of the key to the beach house.

"Maybe, but not for a while yet. Now, tell me about your girlfriend."

Mack felt completely wiped out by the time he reached his house. He wasn't surprised to see Bob's car parked in front. He'd hoped to avoid him until tomorrow, but he should have known better. Bob was a tenacious cop. Toni's disappearance reflected on him, since she was unofficially his responsibility.

Bob got out of his car and walked across the lawn to where Mack had parked his Jag. "All right, Mack, where have you stashed her?"

"You look as tired as I feel. How about having a drink with an old friend?"

"You're not going to get around this by ignoring my question, Mack."

"You're off duty now, aren't you?"

"All right, have it your way for the moment, but eventually I intend to receive an answer."

Mack unlocked his front door, then stepped aside to admit his friend. Once they were seated on the couch with drinks in hand, Mack turned to Bob.

"Toni's not your killer, Bob. I'd stake my reputation on it."

"That's exactly what you're doing, you know."

"Bob, I have to help clear her."

"Meaning that you want me to let you tag along during the investigation?"

"I can be of help to you as well. You need a partner since you're temporarily without one. I've already talked to almost everyone involved in the embezzlement case. The two cases are too closely related to separate them."

"I figured that much out for myself. You can come with me on one condition, and in one capacity only."

"I know, as an observer."

"Like you're going to go exactly by the book. You never did when you were on the force. A leopard doesn't change his spots."

"That's not precisely true."

"Are we going to start being precise now? Where is she, Mack?"

"In a safe place."

"That's all you're going to tell me, isn't it?"

"It's all I can tell you right now."

"If it turns out she's guilty as sin you're going to have to tell me or I'll have to take you in for obstructing justice, an accomplice after the fact, you name it."

"You're coming across loud and clear, Bob."

"Just so long as we understand each other."

"Oh, we do."

"You have it bad, don't you?"

"I don't know what you're talking about."

"Yes, you do. As one friend to another, walk softly, Mack. Love can be a double-edged razor, as you've learned from past experience."

"Were you also going to say it cuts both ways?"

"Something like that." Bob took a swallow of his drink.

"Don't worry, Bob. As I said before, I hear the warning loud and clear. So when do you officially start the investigation?"

"Tomorrow when we get the preliminary report from the coroner's office."

"Surely there's no question that Clifford died from the gunshot wounds."

"Probably not, but you know we have to go through the entire process."

"There are a lot of people who didn't care for Clifford or the way he did business."

"Including your Ms. Carlton."

"Because she had reason to dislike the man doesn't mean she killed him. I could have done him in."

"You think I haven't thought of that? The day I had to arrest Toni Carlton on embezzlement charges you reacted like a lion standing guard over its mate."

"About Hank Warren's alibi…"

"Until we know the exact time of death we won't know if it'll hold water."

"But he was with Nina Townsend, wasn't he?"

"I can't tell you that either, Mack."

"Your expression tells me all I need to know."

"You're not going to screw up my investigation. Stay away from Warren and the Townsend woman unless I'm there with you to conduct the questioning."

"I never expected to do anything else."

"Yeah, right, and I'm the President of the United States. I'm warning you, Mack. Let me handle it my way."

Mack didn't say anything, just stared out the window and took a deep swallow of his drink. He smiled when he looked at his friend and saw the exasperation on Bob's face. Mack was sure that Bob knew it wouldn't do any good to say anything else to him. Moreover, he deduced that his ex-partner was calculating his next move, and damning him for making it more difficult by refusing to tell him where Toni was.

CHAPTER FIFTEEN

The sound of a key turning in the lock awakened Toni. She had meant to go to sleep in the bedroom, but ended up falling asleep on the couch. She expected it to be Mack, and was surprised to see that it wasn't. This exotic-looking young woman with the black hair and chocolate eyes could only be Mack's sister, Mariah.

"I didn't expect you to get here until tomorrow."

"No time like the present." Mariah lowered her suitcase to the floor and held out her hand. "I'm Mariah Jessup."

Toni clasped the proffered hand. "Toni Carlton." She shook her head, and then smiled to herself.

"Okay, what's the joke?"

"No joke. It's just that you're not like any babysitter I've ever seen."

"Babysitter? Is that what Mack told you I'd be?"

"Well, he didn't actually call you that."

"But he gave you that impression, right? You're a little old to need one, don't you think?" She laughed. "A friendship is more likely. Has my brother told you very much about me?"

"Only that you were interested in criminology and you work for a private detective. He also said you'd be stimulating company while he—"

"Has all the fun? Well, we won't let him get away with it, will we?"

Toni grinned. "I think I'm going to like you."

"Since you're innocent we'll have to help my brother prove it."

"Mack isn't going to like us interfering, you know."

"That's a given. What do you think we should do first?"

"I'm going to need my computer. I can access a certain link to the Townsend's computer files that might prove useful. Townsend's is where I worked until—anyway, I need to gain access into it."

"Is your computer at your apartment?"

"No. Actually, it's at Mack's house."

"Oh, then we don't have a problem. I'll zip right over and get it."

"Lieutenant Barnes is sure to have the house under surveillance, and of course there's Mack to contend with."

Mariah's teeth worried her bottom lip. "You're right, we do have a problem. Don't worry, I'll find a way around it. Just leave the strategy to me."

"Mack's right about you."

"What do you mean?"

"He says you're a natural for investigation. He's thinking of asking you to join him and Marc at Jessup Investigations when you've finished your criminology degree." Mariah smiled. "He really said that?"

"Maybe I shouldn't have said anything."

"I'm glad you did." A big grin spread across her face. "So he's proud of his little sister after all."

Toni yawned. "I think it's time we got some sleep."

"I agree. We'll need all the rest we can get if we're going to go sleuthing."

"Sleuthing, huh? Sounds intriguing."

"It can be, not that the man I work for lets me do much of it. Ken is a chauvinist where the idea of women facing danger is concerned. I thought he was going to have a cow when I told him I was considering joining the police department."

"Are you?"

"Actually no, but I mentioned it to get a reaction from him."

Toni laughed, shaking her head. "You have a bit of the devil in you, just like your brother said, don't you?"

"Maybe a little around the edges."

"I'd say it's more than that. You're not afraid of anything, are you?"

"My mother's wrath. If she finds out what we've been up to there's going to be hell to pay."

"She sounds like a formidable woman."

"Not really. She's one of those people you don't cross, not because of her temper, but because she has a way of looking at you that puts you to shame."

"I see. She sounds like my mother. It must be their Latin attitude toward motherhood."

"Mack told me your mother is Italian." Mariah laughed.

"What is it?"

"I was thinking that since you and I also share a similar Latin heritage we should make a good team."

"Only on this case. I'll stick to stock market analyses, thank you, and leave the sleuthing to you and Mack once this whole thing is cleared up. If it ever is."

"It will be. Mack and I will make sure of that."

"Such confidence."

"A Jessup characteristic, don't you know? Look, Toni, I know how hard this must be for you, but hang in there."

"I'm glad Mack sent you to me. My spirits needed a lift."

"Now, let's get some sleep. I've got some strategy for my subconscious to work out."

Mack had a headache to top all headaches from his overindulgence in drink the night before. And added to that he was unhappy to wake up and find himself alone in his big bed. He wanted Toni beside him, beneath him, or himself beneath her, making love.

He had to stop thinking like this and find evidence to clear her so they could be together. When this whole mess was over, he was going to marry Toni. Together they would fulfill their fantasies.

Right now he had to get past the obstacles standing in the way of that happiness, which wasn't going to be an easy task by any means. He left the bed and headed for the shower. After finishing dressing, he ventured into the kitchen to brew a strong pot of ambition. That was exactly what he was going to need to face the day.

Although Marc could handle the routine paperwork, Mack knew he'd have to go into the office and do the rest. He'd call Bob and see what his schedule was like. With any luck they should be able to come up with something conclusive about the Clifford murder today.

Mack was seated in front of his computer screen concentrating on the Townsend files when his friend Bob entered his office.

"Daphne said I could come right in." He gazed at the Townsend logo emblazoned on the screen. "I thought you'd been taken off the Townsend investigation."

"I was, but I'm just going over the information before returning the disks to Townsend's."

"This is Bob, your ex-partner. If I know you, you're weeding out all the possibilities, looking for mistakes or overlooked facts and misplaced clues."

"Ah, you know me so well. As a matter of fact, that's exactly what I'm doing. So when do we—when do you start questioning all the people involved?"

"I was waiting for you to get around to asking that. The coroner's findings are incomplete right now, but we should have the results of the ballistics tests sometime this morning." He pushed up the sleeve of his jacket and glanced at his watch. "In another hour or so. But in the meantime, I'm going to start with all the people who might have had it in for Clifford."

"I can help you there. Only half the company is suspect. He was that kind of guy." Every time Mack thought about what the man had done to Toni, he wished he were alive so he could kill him.

Mack went over the list of suspects with Bob as he had with Toni. When they finished, he glanced at his friend.

"So what do you think?"

"I'd say you were as thorough as always. This case is loaded with corporate intrigue, not to mention office politics, with a little murder mixed in. Now, the thing is to sort out this mess and slip each piece of the puzzle into place."

"The key is to put them into place, not to force them."

"Mack."

"All right," he groused. "Who do you want to start with?"

Mack noticed the tense, frightened look on Pat Davis's face when he and Bob entered the office.

"Pat, I—Lieutenant Barnes and I would like to talk with you," Mack said in a tone of voice meant to soothe away her apprehension.

"We can use Mr. Clifford's old office. Hank—Mr. Warren, the acting CEO, isn't in yet."

"CEO? When did that happen?" Mack queried.

"Yesterday. He is now acting CEO."

Bob glared a warning at Mack before asserting his authority. "Can you get someone to cover your desk while we talk, Ms. Davis?"

"Yes, of course. We have a temporary assistant until Toni—ah, I'll get Connie to cover the desk," she finished nervously. Pat rose from her seat and walked into Toni's cubicle and returned with Connie.

Mack's mouth tightened in resentment when he saw the petite blonde woman come from Toni's space. He didn't like the idea of someone replacing her. She should be there doing her job, a job she was damned good at, and still would be doing if not for Frank Clifford and his cohort.

Mack and Bob waited for Connie to settle in at Pat's desk before they and Pat went into Clifford's office.

"Have a seat, Ms. Davis," the lieutenant invited once they were inside.

Pat gazed from one to the other before taking a seat.

"Now, Ms. Davis, tell us about your relationship with Frank Clifford, starting from the time prior to your working in this office."

"I worked downstairs as a receptionist when I first came to Townsend's six and a half years ago. I'd worked my way up to junior secretary in personnel when I first had any contact with him. He seemed impressed with me—my work—and asked Mazie, my immediate supervisor, if he could borrow my services. Eventually it led to a promotion to executive secretary to the CEO."

"Why did he pick you, as opposed to others who had been with the company longer?" Bob probed.

"I—I—ah…"

"You can be honest with him, Pat," Mack encouraged.

Bob's eyes narrowed suspiciously and he glanced from Mack to Pat.

"I thought it was because…" She looked embarrassed. "I found out he had a specific reason later."

"A sexual one?"

"Not precisely."

"What?"

"He wanted me to keep an eye on someone on his office staff."

"Who?"

"Toni Carlton," Pat reluctantly replied.

"And did you?"

"I didn't feel right about it because Toni and I are friends."

"But Clifford insisted."

"Yes, he did. He said executive secretary jobs didn't grow on trees and if I wanted to keep mine I'd better do as he said. I was tempted to tell Toni what was going on, but he said my husband was up for the position of mail room manager and if I wanted him to have a fair chance at getting it, I'd better cooperate, so I complied."

Mack's jaw tensed as he listened to the questions Bob put to Pat Davis, but he let things continue without interfering.

"Did he also have personal intentions toward you?"

Pat bit her lip and squirmed restively in her chair.

"You're going to have to tell us the truth. You can do it here or down at the station, whichever you prefer."

Pat sat twisting her hands in her lap for a few moments. Then tears slid down her cheeks. "He—ah—I can't," she sobbed.

Mack covered her hands with his. "Calm down, nobody is going to condemn you. Come on, tell us the truth."

"Well, one of the few nights I ever worked overtime, when Toni was out sick, he—oh God. He—he forced himself on me," she cried.

Mack growled. "Why that dirty son of a—"

Bob cut him off. "Mack, you'd better let me handle this." He sent Pat a compassionate glance. "When did this happen, Ms. Davis?"

"Six—six months ago." She sniffed, gazing at them with wet, red-rimmed eyes.

"Did you report him to the police and file rape charges against him?" Lieutenant Barnes asked.

"No, I couldn't do that."

"Why not, Pat?" Mack probed gently.

"I was afraid. It wasn't because of anything Mr. Clifford threatened to do or say or that I didn't think anyone would believe me."

"Then what was it, Pat?" Mack encouraged.

"It was my husband Joe. I was afraid of what he might do if he found out. He'd have k—" Pat's eyes widened in horror at what she'd started to say.

Mack and Bob traded speculative glances. The more they found out about Frank Clifford, the more he disgusted them.

"Where were you the night he was killed?" Bob asked.

"At home with Joe and the kids watching videos and eating popcorn. Oh, and my mother-in-law joined us."

"And neither you nor your husband left the house?"

"Well, Joe did go out for some beer."

"At what time?"

"I don't remember. Eleven o'clock, I think."

"One last question. Do you know for a fact that Frank Clifford was framing Toni Carlton for embezzlement?"

"Actually, no, but Toni told me he was, and I believe her."

"That'll be all for now, Mrs. Davis."

Pat swiftly left the office, not needing any further encouragement to do so.

"What do you think?" Mack asked, turning to Bob.

"I don't think she had anything to do with the killing."

"Who's next on the list?"

Hank Warren walked in. "What are you doing in my—here? I already gave the police a statement, Lieutenant." He glared at Mack. "What's Jessup doing here?"

"He's here as an observer. I'm glad we ran into you. I have some questions for you."

"I thought I'd answered all of them."

"Why did you give the gun to Ms. Carlton?"

"She told me she didn't want to be the victim of an assault. That was when she decided to take self-defense classes. I gave her my gun when she mentioned her neighborhood had been plagued by a stalker."

"You're lying and you know it, Warren," Mack ground out.

"You'd like to think so, wouldn't you?" he shot back. "I gave her the gun during the time we were—ah, involved."

"She was never involved with an asshole like you."

"Is that what she told you?" Hank laughed. "And you believed her?"

The phone buzzed, snapping the tension. Hank stepped behind the desk and picked up the receiver. "Yes, Pat?" He glanced at Lieutenant Barnes. "It's for you." Then he handed him the phone and glared at Mack.

"Barnes here. Thanks, Sid." He hung up and glanced at Hank. "According to the ballistics report the bullets taken from the body came from your gun, which was fired at point blank range at approximately 11:30 p.m. to 11:40 p.m. the night of the murder, which means that your alibi may or may not be made public."

"Since I was nowhere near the scene of the crime I don't see why it has to be. As I said before, it could cause a lot of problems for the person I was with."

"May I remind you that this is a police investigation, Mr. Warren. We're not concerned with your personal problems. We're answerable to the people of this city. Not reporting all the facts could be miscon-strued to look like we were suppressing evidence."

"I didn't kill him, Lieutenant."

"So you keep saying," Mack added.

"Whatever happened to innocent until proven guilty?"

Lieutenant Barnes took out his notepad. "I want you to tell me your story one more time."

A frustrated growl left Hank's throat. Mack could tell that the other man wasn't anxious to spill his guts in front of him and drew some measure of satisfaction from the man's reluctance. After every-thing Toni had told him, he deserved what he got.

"My lady friend and I—we spent the evening at my apartment in, shall we say, pleasurable pursuits."

"All evening? Can you prove it?"

"The security man at my apartment building saw us come in."

"At what time?"

"Nine-thirty or ten."

"Until when?" Mack questioned.

"Listen, Jessup, I don't have to—"

"Who is this mysterious lady friend of yours?" Mack probed.

Hank vaulted angrily from his chair. "It's none of your damned business, Jessup."

"It was Nina Townsend, wasn't it?" Mack persisted.

Hank glared daggers at Lieutenant Barnes. "No one was supposed to know the identity of the person I was with."

"I made you no promises that it wouldn't become public knowl-edge. So far, the media hasn't gotten wind of it."

"That's not to say they won't." Hank stared venomously at Mack.

"Oh, I won't say anything to them if you cooperate with Lieutenant Barnes."

Bob silenced Mack with a look. "At the moment we only have your word on who you were with, and we will be questioning Mrs. Townsend and the security guard at your apartment building."

As Mack and Bob made to leave, Hank couldn't resist one final dig.

"I have to say that Nina is an improvement over my ex-lover, who happens to be your present one," Hank taunted Mack. "And believe me, I'm in a position to make comparisons."

"Why you..." Mack made a grab for Hank.

Bob restrained him with a police hold. "Let him go, Mack."

"You'd better call your dog off, Lieutenant." Hank sneered.

Bob hurried Mack out of the office.

"Mack, if you can't—"

"I know, Bob. It's just that the guy is a complete bastard. He'd like nothing better than to see Toni go to jail. Then the field would be clear and he could further his aspirations to take over the company."

"You may be right, but beating him to a pulp won't help Toni. In fact, it might hurt her. I know you don't want to do that."

"No, I don't. Damn it, Bob, she's innocent."

"I know you believe that, but it's not up to you to judge. Now let's go down to the mail room and have a talk with Joe Davis."

"How did you talk your sister-in-law into helping us, Mariah?" Toni asked.

"That's my secret. Rachel and the kids are going to be our decoy while we get what you need from the house."

"What if Mack comes home?"

"He won't. Marc said he was busy helping Bob—Lieutenant Barnes—question the Townsend employees. And he has plenty of work to plow through when he gets back to his office. He probably won't get home until late."

"Didn't Marc get suspicious when you questioned him?"

"Marc is a fan of yours. He'll help you all he can."

Toni smiled. "I'm glad to have the approval of the Jessup clan."

"I'd say you are really fortunate that Mack loves you."

"He hasn't said that."

"Not in so many words, maybe, but I can tell that he does. Call it sisterly intuition."

"Rachel and the kids should be at Mack's right about now. Put on your sunglasses and hat."

Toni did as told. "I look like a movie star incognito."

"Doesn't everybody in Southern California?" Mariah said, donning her own sunglasses and hat. "See, we look like twins."

"I should have known you had all your bases covered."

"Always, my dear sister in adventure."

While Rachel Jessup and her kids kept the policeman busy in front of the house, Toni and Mariah hauled Toni's computer equipment out the back and put it into Mariah's Jeep.

Later at the beach house, they set up the computer and Toni transferred her Internet connection to the beach house phone, then hacked into the Townsend computers. She downloaded everything pertaining to the embezzlement case.

"You understand all this stuff?" Mariah asked as Toni scrolled through one screen, then the next.

Toni shot her a confident smile. "Of course, it was my job to..."

"And it will be again."

"Only if I'm cleared of embezzlement, not to mention an impending murder charge."

"We can do it, Toni. Nothing is impossible for a Jessup."

Toni and Mariah retrieved a few interesting records with falsified dates.

"It doesn't prove anything. My late boss had to have kept records of his shady dealings hidden some place, but where? They would have to be at his fingertips for easy access," Toni murmured absently. "He thought he was so clever. He must have made a mistake somewhere, and I'm going to find it."

CHAPTER SIXTEEN

Mack and Bob picked up on something akin to wariness if not outright fear on Joe Davis's face when they entered the mail room and walked over to him.

"You wanted to talk to me?" Joe asked.

"This is Lieutenant Barnes from the L.A.P.D. He has a few questions to ask you concerning Frank Clifford's murder and other things pertaining to the case."

"Why would you want to ask me anything about that, Lieutenant?"

"According to what your wife told us, the night of the murder you went out for beer. Where did you go? And what time did you get back?"

Mack could tell how badly the man wanted to avoid answering Bob's questions. It made Mack wonder if he had something to hide. How was he connected to the crime when the gun belonged to Hank Warren, who supposedly had given it to Toni? Toni had told him she'd never seen the gun before that night. Even if she'd had the gun, why would she have given it to Joe Davis?

"I left the house to go to the Liquor Emporium on Overland at about eleven o'clock," Joe answered.

"What time did you get back home?" Bob asked.

"Ah, 11:15 or 11:30. The video *Rocky II* was playing in the VCR when I walked into the family room."

"Do you think they'll remember seeing you at the liquor store?"

"I—I don't know. If you're trying to lay this murder on me, forget it. I didn't kill the bas—Clifford."

"You somehow found out what he'd done to your wife, didn't you, Joe?" Mack probed.

"I don't know what you mean, Jessup."

"I think you do. Tell us the truth," Mack urged him strongly.

Joe was silent for a moment before answering. "Yes, I found out what that son of a bitch had done to my wife. I admit that I wanted to take him apart with my bare hands, but I didn't shoot him."

"You want us to believe that someone beat you to it?" Mack asked. "Joe, every man is protective of his woman. Some carry it to extremes."

"You mean murder. I swear I didn't go that one step too far, although…"

"Although what?" inquired the lieutenant.

"The urge to kill him was so strong I could almost taste it."

The lieutenant cleared his throat. "Suppose I told you more than one set of prints was found on the gun. What would you say then?"

Mack noticed that beads of sweat had popped out on Joe's forehead and above his upper lip. He had a gut feeling he was holding back something vital to the case. Mack knew he couldn't afford to let anyone off the hook. Too much was at stake.

"How did you find out, Joe?"

"A few months ago Pat suddenly turned nervous and moody, yelling at the kids and bitching at me, which isn't at all like her. She's usually even-tempered and calm. Then she started having nightmares. One night she woke up screaming."

"And?" Mack put his hand on Joe's shoulder and squeezed it in a gesture of empathy.

"For some time our love life was nearly non-existent. Whenever I asked her why, she'd burst into tears. I knew something was very wrong, but I couldn't get her to tell me about it."

"So you grew frustrated." Mack saw the warning glare Bob shot him, which said in no uncertain terms that he should back off and let him handle it.

With ill grace Mack complied and eased away from the man and walked over to the window.

"Frustrated? Mad as hell is more like it. At first I thought Pat was having an affair—then I thought no, she wouldn't do that. She loved me and the kids. Then a bill from the Women's Clinic came in the mail confirming that the result of her AIDS test was negative."

"Then what did you do?" the lieutenant asked.

Joe sighed heavily. "I confronted her with it. She tried to blow me off by saying it was a routine part of her checkup. I didn't believe her, and I told her so."

"And?"

"One night during one of her nightmares it all came pouring out—what Clifford had done to her and how he was forcing her to help him because of me."

"Then what did you do?" Bob prompted.

"Nothing."

"You find out a man raped your wife and you do nothing! Come on, Davis."

"In my mind I—"

"You what?"

"I took him apart, limb from limb."

Mack watched the look of frustrated rage on Joe's face. As much as Joe hated Clifford, he was sure Davis hadn't killed the man.

"What about the gun?" Bob asked.

"One day while I was waiting for Pat to come out of the ladies' room, before leaving the office to go home, I noticed her desk drawer wasn't closed all the way. I saw something shiny, metallic, and pulled the drawer out. It was a handgun, a .22 automatic.

"I was stunned. How had my gentle wife, who couldn't stand to look at a gun, much less possess one, come by such a weapon? It occurred to me that she had it for protection against Clifford, or maybe that she was waiting to kill him for what he'd done to her. I took the gun and stuck it in my jacket pocket. Knowing what she'd gone through and how she might possibly be planning to remedy the situation was the last straw. I intended to confront Clifford and have it out with him, job or no job.

"But first I wanted to talk to my wife and find out where she got the gun. I never got around to doing it. I waited a few days, but she seemed not to notice that it was missing so I figured it wasn't hers. But I wondered whose it was and what it was doing in her drawer. After finding out what Clifford had done, I was adamant that Pat not work overtime, whether Toni was there or not. Her look of relief was so profound it made me want to kill the bastard even more."

"You had the gun all this time?"

"Yes, I hid it in the garage. I have a lockbox I keep my tools in. I was going to get rid of the thing, but after a while I forgot it was there, or maybe blocked it out.

"When he threatened to fire Pat and then me, it was all I could do not to take him apart. Pat was scared and pleaded with me not to go after the bastard. She said if I did it would wreck our lives, and I should think of the children. I should have done what my instincts urged me to do from the start, but I didn't. Instead I went along with Clifford's plans. Believe me, I was only biding my time until..."

"Until?"

Joe didn't answer. He didn't have to. Mack had heard the barely suppressed violence in the man's voice. He turned away from the window and looked at Joe. "Did Pat ever voluntarily say anything to you about the gun?"

"No."

"How did the gun get from your lockbox to Clifford's apartment?" Bob prompted.

"Pat was on edge the night of the murder. I hated seeing her like that. I just lost it and took the gun out of the lockbox and went to see Clifford, but I didn't shoot him. We argued and he said some things about my wife. When I took the gun out of my pocket, he threw something that knocked it out of my hand. Then he grabbed the gun and threatened to shoot me with it if I didn't leave, so I left. He was very much alive when I left his condo."

Bob finished writing in his notepad. "That'll be all for now."

"Meaning you intend to question me some more at a later date?"

"You can go back to work."

Joe didn't hesitate; he quickly left the room.

Bob arched a brow. "What do you make of what he said?"

"I believe him," Mack said thoughtfully.

"That leaves Warren and…"

"Toni. I know. Remember, Bob, they're not the only ones involved in this case."

"I haven't forgotten."

"Toni?" Mariah called out to her new friend's back.

"Hmm."

"You've been at it for hours. It's time to take a break, as in eating dinner."

"You go ahead, I'm not finished yet."

Toni had felt that she was onto something several times, but nothing had come of it either time. She finally got up from the computer in defeat and went back into the living room and sank down on the couch in frustration.

Mariah smiled encouragingly at Toni. "I've made one of those fifteen minute stroganoff meals Rachel has in the freezer. It isn't up to Mack's standards, but it's not too bad, if I say so myself."

"Anything you make is fine, Mariah. I'm not interested in food right now. I've got to come up with something, and quick."

"I'll help you all I can. You know that."

Toni smiled. "Yes, I do. But there doesn't seem to be anything either of us can do at the moment."

The two ate dinner and were in the process of cleaning up the kitchen when the phone rang. Toni glanced anxiously at Mariah. They knew who was on the other end, and neither was looking forward to being read the riot act.

Taking a deep breath, Toni picked up the receiver. "Hello."

"Toni, what in the hell are you and Mariah up to? I come home to find all your computer equipment gone."

"Mack, I can explain."

"Let me speak with my sister," he said sharply.

"But Mack—"

"Now!"

Toni had never heard Mack use that tone of voice when speaking to her. There was no doubt he was furious. She handed the receiver to Mariah.

"All right, Mack, let's get this over with. I know you're angry, but we—"

"Angry! Angry doesn't begin to describe what I'm feeling right now." He reached for a calming breath. "You're playing amateur detective again, aren't you, Mariah? I want you to stop it right now. This is a murder investigation, for Christ's sake. You both could get hurt or worse."

"Now you're exaggerating, Mack. We only picked up Toni's computer. I don't see why you're going off like this."

"Don't you? Well, let me spell it out for you, Miss Jessica Fletcher. The crux of this investigation is centered on the corporate intrigues going on at Townsend's. Most of the evidence against Toni is hidden somewhere inside the Townsend computer system. The person in league with Clifford probably killed him. You can be damn sure they'll be monitoring the company computer and if they are and you've…" He let his voice trail away.

"I see what you mean. Toni might have alerted him or her by hacking into the system."

"Not only that, it's against the law. A jail term is what you'll get if you're caught. Now, let me speak to Toni."

Mariah hunched her shoulders and handed the receiver back to Toni.

"Now Mack, don't take it all out on Mariah, she only—"

"I know very well what my sister was trying to do." Concern made his voice sound harsh. "I don't want anything to happen to you, Toni."

"I know you care, Mack."

"It's more than that, Toni. Listen, I can't say what I want to over the phone. As it is, I'm having to use the pay phone at the supermarket so the police can't trace the call. The battery on my cell phone is shot or I would have used it. I'll be out to see you later. Take care."

"Mack—I'll be waiting." She hung up.

"Though I hate to admit it, my brother has a point. Whoever killed Frank Clifford could know or suspect that you're onto them because of the cyberspace trail you might have left behind."

"I hadn't considered that." Toni's brows rose thoughtfully. "Whoever logs in on the system does leave a trail and it is logged in on the hard drive. You're right, I may just have given myself away."

Mack called Matt and had him drop by his house.

"Okay, Mack, what's up?" Matt asked after entering his brother's living room and closing the door.

"I'm going to need your help again."

Mack traded clothes with his brother. He counted on the fact that they resembled each other closely and left the house in his brother's van. He took a few detours to be on the safe side before heading for the beach house.

Toni heard footsteps crunch on the sand seconds after the van pulled up alongside the beach house. Her heart started beating faster at the thought of seeing Mack again. Even though she knew he would be angry with her, she still wanted to see him. She and Mariah waited in the living room for him to come inside.

Mack never failed to notice everything about Toni whenever his eyes lighted on her. He'd been angry when he discovered what she and his sister were up to. But now…He couldn't help softening at the wary look in her eyes.

"Well, have you found out anything useful?"

"I wish." Toni let out a defeated sigh. "No, I haven't been able to find out anything, important or otherwise. I'm beginning to think no such evidence exists."

"It exists, all right. People like Frank Clifford can't resist letting someone know how clever and powerful they are. Somewhere there is proof and someone who is well aware of what it could mean for them should anyone discover the truth, which brings me to the reason for my visit."

"Now, Mack," Mariah began in her most finessing voice.

"Stop right there, young lady. I brought you here to offer companionship to the woman—for Toni."

Disappointment washed over Toni when Mack chose not to reveal his feelings, but someday she was going to get him to say those three precious words: I love you.

"Toni can tell you just how seriously I've taken my, ah, assignment." Mariah giggled.

Mack shot her an assessing glance. He was used to his sister's double-talk and he wasn't about to let her get away with it this time.

"You're an excitement and danger junkie, Riah. Well, you're not going to get me to agree to let you do any more sleuthing."

"Mack," she pouted.

"I mean it, Mariah. You and Toni have put your safety in jeopardy. What if Bob had seen you today? You know he has someone watching my house. Oh, and Matt told me that you even involved Rachel and the kids."

Mariah had the grace to blush guiltily at that revelation. "Only indirectly."

"Mariah."

"All right, but it worked, you'll have to admit."

"What am I going to do with you?"

"Hire me when I've finished my degree."

Mack glanced at Toni.

She hunched her shoulders. "I couldn't help it, Mack. I had to tell her."

"She's never going to let up on me now, you know that, don't you? Maybe by the time she finishes her criminology degree she'll have learned something about caution."

"I resent that," Mariah retorted. "I'm always cautious."

"Yeah, right."

"Mack, I've got a few errands to run. Are you going to be here for a while?" Mariah asked.

"Just make sure it's not anything dangerous, okay?"

Mariah flashed him a conceding smile. "All right, big brother." With that she grabbed her purse and headed for the door.

After she'd gone, Mack turned to Toni. "There may be hope for that girl yet."

"I'm enjoying her, Mack. How's the investigation coming?"

"So far not so good. First, I want a more affectionate greeting from you now that we're alone."

"Oh, Mack," she said, letting her lips instinctively home in on his.

"Baby, I've missed you so much."

Her mouth curved into a passion-arousing smile. "It's only been a matter of days since you've last seen me."

"It's not the same as waking up to you by my side, seeing you every single day, making love to you every night."

"You're right. It's been torture for me being away from you."

"I can't wait to see you cleared of these ridiculous charges so we can get on with our lives."

Toni laid her head against his chest. It wasn't what she longed to hear, but she was sure it wouldn't be long before he admitted that he loved her.

Toni led Mack to her bedroom.

CHAPTER SEVENTEEN

Several hours had passed and Mack had just walked back into the living room, contemplating leaving the beach house, when Mariah returned. He saw the knowing grin on her face and felt the urge to put her across his knee and spank her butt.

"Not a single word, Riah."

"What is there to say? You've been comforting your lady." She flashed him another mischievous grin. "Where is the love of your life, by the way?"

"In the bathroom." Mack walked over to the floor to ceiling window and gazed out over the moon-silvered ocean. "Nothing I do seems to help."

"Maybe not at this moment, but you're going to save Toni. I have every confidence in you, my brother."

"But how am I going to accomplish this miracle?"

Mariah squeezed his shoulder. "You're a genius, you'll find a way. Tell me, what does Bob have?"

"Not a hell of a lot, but enough to muddy the water. We're going to have to do some careful sorting through. Toni said she'd never seen Hank Warren's gun until that night. I found out the gun had been in her friend Pat Davis's office desk drawer at Townsend's, where Joe found it and took it. What am I supposed to make of that? I believe Toni." He absently dragged his fingers through his hair. "None of this makes any sense. I need some serious answers to my questions."

"Have you asked Toni about it?"

"No, not yet."

"Why?"

"I don't want her to think I don't trust her. Her integrity has already been questioned because of the embezzlement charges lodged against her."

"I see what you mean." Mariah arched her brows in commiseration. "You do have a problem, but you'll solve it. You're good."

"Thanks, pequena." He hugged her tight.

"A mutual admiration society. Is it an exclusive club or can anyone join?" Toni queried from the doorway.

"Only certain people are allowed in." Mack walked over to her and pulled her into his arms and just held her. "And you happen to be a charter member."

Toni closed her eyes, reveling in his warmth. "I needed to hear that."

"If you two are going to—"

"Behave, little sister," Mack warned. "We need to get something straight before I leave." He guided Toni over to the couch.

"What?" Toni arched questioning brows.

"Like what you and Mariah will and will not do together or independently."

"Mack, we were only trying to help."

"I want to keep you and my sister safe."

"We won't do anything stupid."

"Toni and I—" Mariah began.

"I want your promise that you won't do anything without running it by me first."

"Suppose we can't get in touch with you when we need to?"

"Contact Marc. One of us will be available to offer advice."

"We won't purposely do anything that will endanger Toni's life, Mack," Mariah conceded finally.

He looked into Toni's eyes. "Do I have your word?"

"Yes."

He beamed a loving smile on her. "I don't know when I'll see you again. I've got to get the van back to Matt. He's waiting for me. I'll keep in touch." He kissed Toni, hugged his sister and then he was gone.

Toni turned to Mariah. "How are we going to do any sleuthing now that we've agreed not to do anything without telling him?"

"Never underestimate Mariah Jessup," Mariah answered. "There is a lot we can do without purposely endangering either one of us."

"You're one crafty fox, Mariah."

"The word is vixen for the female of the species. Mack told me something I think you should know." Mariah outlined what Mack had revealed to her.

Toni frowned. "Why would Joe Davis say that he had found the gun in a desk drawer at Townsend's unless it was true? The only way Pat could have gotten the gun was for Hank to have given it to her. Why would he do that and then turn around and say he'd given it to me? You don't suppose she and Hank were ever—close?"

"If you want an answer to your question you're going to have to ask her."

"You're right. It's exactly what I intend to do in the morning."

"Have you been in touch with Toni Carlton, Mack?" Bob pointedly asked his friend the next morning when Mack opened his front door to him. "As if I need to ask," Bob added.

Mack hesitated before speaking. "You know I have. Come on in. You have one of your men following me at all times. I'm sure he reported that I made a call at the pay phone outside the supermarket?"

"Mack—" Bob began, stepping into the living room and shutting the door.

Mack held up his hand. "I know what you're going to say."

"I don't have to repeat my views, you know them already. I hope you didn't reveal anything you shouldn't?"

"Look, Bob, I—"

"Forget it. You're not going to tell me anyway. You really aren't helping by keeping her whereabouts a secret. Eventually she'll have to come out of hiding."

"I know, but not just yet. Her life could be in real danger if the killer finds out where she is."

"You keep assuming that she isn't the killer."

"I know she isn't. I don't want to go there with you."

"Neither do I." Bob's smile turned incredulous. "How you can be so loyal where women are concerned after what happened with Linda Hutton, I'll never know. Changing the subject, we need to have another talk with Pat Davis and Hank Warren about the gun after what we've learned from Joe Davis."

"That's the first sensible thing you've said this morning. And don't forget about Warren's alibi."

"I haven't forgotten."

"Have a cup of coffee with me before we go?"

"Sure, why not." Bob followed Mack into the kitchen.

"Hello, Pat?" Toni said, twirling her finger in the phone cord.

"Toni! Where are you? The police are looking for you."

"I know all that. Can you talk?"

"Yes. Hank is out of the office."

"Hank? Why would it matter if he—"

"He's the new acting CEO until an official vote to decide whether to make him permanent is taken. Didn't Mack tell you?"

"No, I guess he forgot." She intended to take it up with him the next time she spoke with him. "Mack said Joe told him he found the gun in your desk a while back."

"I know."

"How did you come by the gun?"

"I saw it in your desk drawer."

"You couldn't have!"

"But I did. It's exactly where I got it."

"That's impossible. Hank never gave it to me. As if I'd accept anything from him. I wouldn't spit on him if he was on fire and he knows it, so why would I accept anything he had to offer?"

"I don't know. All I know is that's where I found the gun."

"Are you sure? Or did he give it to you because—"

"Don't say it, Toni. I love my husband and I don't have affairs."

"I know you don't. I'm sorry. When did you take the gun from my desk?"

"A few months ago when…"

"When what?"

"I can't talk about it over the phone."

"It has something to do with our late boss, doesn't it? Did he try to come on to you? Is that it?"

"Toni, please, I can't—" A sob tore from Pat's throat.

"What's the matter? Are you crying? Oh, my God! Did he—"

"I can't talk anymore."

"Pat, don't hang up." The line went dead.

"What happened?" Mariah asked.

"She hung up on me."

"Why?"

"I can't tell you. I've got to talk to her in person. She usually takes a coffee break at the Coffee House across the street from Townsend's."

Mariah's eyes widened. "You're not thinking of going there, are you?"

Toni looked at her watch, grabbed her purse, sunglasses and hat and headed out the door. "We'll have to hurry."

Mariah followed. "Do you think it's a good idea to go over there in broad daylight?"

"No. But since I don't have my car we'll have to go in yours."

"Are you sure the woman is in?" Mack asked Bob.

"According to the housekeeper, when I called earlier, Mrs. Townsend should be in all morning, considering that she rarely rises before ten o'clock."

They walked up to the front door of the Townsend mansion and Bob pressed the doorbell. It was a few minutes before the housekeeper answered.

"Yes, may I help you?"

Bob took out his badge. "I'm Lieutenant Robert Barnes, L.A.P.D. I called earlier. Is Mrs. Nina Townsend in?"

"Yes, she is. Won't you come in?"

Mack took in the size and ambiance of the house as they followed the housekeeper into the living room. There had to be at least nine bedrooms, and everything about the place had the flavor of wealth stamped on it. He glanced at Bob and smiled. He could see that his ex-partner was experiencing the same uncomfortable feeling he was.

The housekeeper cleared her throat. "I will let Mrs. Townsend know you are here."

Mack slowly circled the room. Paintings by well-known contemporary artists and reproductions of the great masters covered the walls. Whoever decorated the house had been flaunting their wealth; everything was expensive, almost garishly so.

"My housekeeper said you wanted to see me." When Nina Townsend's heavily made up eyes lit on Mack, she smiled, batting her lashes at him. "Are you Lieutenant Barnes?" she said in a husky female-appreciating-male voice.

"No, I am," Bob answered.

Nina shifted her attention in his direction. That flirtatious demeanor did not alter as she sensuously moved away from the doorway and sauntered into the room. Her smile widened to encompass both men.

She wet her bright red lips with her tongue. "To what do I owe this visit from two such handsome hunks of the law?"

Mack could understand how Hank Warren and Frank Clifford, any man for that matter, might be attracted to this sensual creature. She literally oozed sensuality. And immediately the image of finger-mussed brassy blonde hair, rumpled satin sheets and wild, hot sex came to mind. The woman was sexual dynamite.

He thought about her husband. If two people were ever opposites it had to be J. V. Townsend Jr. and this woman. He remembered Toni saying something to that effect. Now that he'd met Nina Townsend he agreed with her. Mack glanced at Bob and guessed what he was thinking.

"Mrs. Townsend," Bob began, "I'll be handling the questioning. Mackinsey Jessup is joining us as an unofficial observer."

"I could have sworn you were both—I mean I thought he—Never mind. What is it you want to ask me?"

"If you'll have a seat, I'll be glad to enlighten you."

Her eyes still on Mack, Nina seated herself on the couch, making sure the short red and white dress she wore displayed her slim legs to advantage. Mack shot her an assessing gaze and took a seat across from the couch to study her.

Bob took out his notepad and joined Nina on the couch. "I was given to understand that on the evening of November 25th you were in the company of one Hank Warren at his apartment between the hours of 9:30 and midnight."

"Who told you that, honey—Lieutenant?"

Bob flipped back through his notepad. "Hank Warren said the two of you were, ah, involved."

"Well, he lied," she snapped. "I left his place at eleven. We had business to take care of and afterward we—I mean after it was concluded—I went home."

Mack's eyes narrowed at the provocative way she fidgeted with the hem of her dress, which seemed to rise higher with every movement of her body, exposing even more of her slender brown thighs. Remembering how she had sauntered into the room, Mack stuck to his earlier observation that the lady, and he thought of the term loosely in connection with her, was sexual dynamite.

Bob wrote something on his notepad, then glanced at Nina. "Mrs. Townsend, could you elaborate on the business the two of you conducted?"

Nina's face went blank for a moment. Then her wide sensual mouth relaxed into a smile. "It was confidential, hon—Lieutenant." She shifted her gaze to Mack, flashing him a come-hither smile.

Mack's lips quirked into a derisive smile and he beamed the full force of his contempt on her. Her smile faded and she tossed her head indignantly and focused her attention on Bob. Mack smiled in earnest and remained silent, letting Bob conduct the questioning without interfering.

"Where did you go after leaving Warren's apartment?"

Nina's eyes widened and she nervously circled her lips with her tongue. The housekeeper entered with a silver coffee pot, three bone-china cups and a crystal plate of finger cakes.

"I thought you might like some coffee," the housekeeper announced.

"Thank you, Cara, I did forget to offer these gentlemen refreshments. You can put the tray on the table. Then you can get los—I mean, return to your other duties."

The housekeeper did as she was told, but the obvious resentment she felt at her employer's rude dismissal was evident. Mack could tell that the housekeeper couldn't stand Nina Townsend. He wondered if there was some specific reason why Cara felt that way.

Nina leaned forward, causing her breasts to jiggle and jut forward. "Would you care for some coffee, Lieutenant Barnes? Oh, and you, too, of course, Mr. Jessup."

"None for me, thanks." Mack sat back in his seat to resume his silent study of the mistress of the house.

"Thank you," Bob said. "I'll take mine black."

"Please, honey, call me Nina," she said after she'd poured the coffee and set the pot back on the tray. "How about one of these finger cakes?"

"No, thank you." Bob repeated his earlier question.

She pouted for a moment, then reluctantly answered. "I came back home."

"What time was that?"

"Lieutenant, I really don't see why you're asking me all these questions."

"The coroner placed the time of Frank Clifford's death between 11:15 and midnight."

"I was in bed asleep before midnight."

"Can anyone corroborate this? The housekeeper? Your husband?"

"My husband was out of town on business and Cara was in her quarters doing I don't know what. Sleeping, I guess."

"Then there is no one to back up your story that you came in before midnight?"

"I don't need one. I had nothing to do with Frank's death."

Bob stuck his notepad back in his pocket. "No one is accusing you of anything, at least not yet." He stood up and straightened his jacket. Mack followed suit. "We'll be going now, Mrs. Townsend. I'll probably be questioning you again, so please keep yourself available."

"You can't keep coming here like this. What will the neighbors think? What will the publicity do to my rep—I mean, the Townsend name?"

"I have to inform you that there will be no way of keeping your involvement in this case a secret."

"Why should my name even be mentioned, Lieutenant, since I wasn't the one who killed Frank?"

"If you didn't do it, then you don't have anything to worry about, do you, Nina?" Mack said with a hard, taunting smile.

Minutes later, seated in the police car, Bob turned to Mack. "I know what you were up to in there. I warn you, Mack, I won't tolerate any interference with my investigation. I could tell by the way you were looking at Nina Townsend you've already planned to question her when I'm not with you. If you—"

"Relax, Bob."

"Relax? How can I?"

"I haven't done anything yet."

"Yet, that's the operative word." Bob started the car and pulled out of the semi-circular drive.

CHAPTER EIGHTEEN

As Toni and Mariah entered the Coffee House across from the Townsend building, Toni spotted Pat Davis sitting in a booth near a side window. She let out a relieved sigh at finding her alone and slid into the seat opposite her.

Pat looked up in surprise. "Toni! What are you doing here?"

"I had to talk to you, see you face to face. Why did you hang up on me?"

Pat seemed to panic and made to get up, but Mariah eased into the empty seat next to her, effectively aborting her escape. Pat shifted her gaze back to Toni.

"Look, Pat, I'm not here to harass you. I need to know the answers to a few questions. Like, how did you know the gun was in my desk?"

"I didn't know. Finding it there was a shock."

"Why were you searching through the drawers?"

"I needed a staple puller and I couldn't find mine, and since you were out of the office, I couldn't ask you if I could borrow yours. When I opened your desk drawer, I discovered the gun."

"When precisely did you find it?"

"Six months ago."

"That long ago? Why did you take it?"

Pat lowered her head, gazing intently into her coffee cup as though hoping she would find the answer in its liquid black depths. The waitress arrived and asked Toni and Mariah if they wanted to order.

"Two coffees, please," Mariah answered for them both.

Toni kept her face averted until the waitress had gone.

"All right." Toni placed her hand over Pat's. "Tell me about it."

"Mr. Clifford had—he had—"

"Already forced himself on you? I guessed as much. Why in heaven's name didn't you go to the police, Pat?"

"I couldn't do that."

"Why not? Was it because of Joe?"

"He wasn't the only reason."

"You did eventually tell him what happened, didn't you?"

"Not exactly. You know what Joe is like. He would have killed…" Pat's eyes bulged with fear. "He didn't do it, Toni."

"Calm down, Pat, I didn't say that he did. Can you tell me what happened that night?"

"The one day you were off sick, he, Mr. Clifford, maneuvered me into staying late, saying he had to have certain reports to take to San Francisco that night. He had to have those reports all right," she said bitterly, tears sliding down her cheeks. She quickly wiped them away.

Toni felt that she'd gone as far as she could, and didn't want to traumatize Pat any further with memories of the attack.

"How did you find out the gun was Hank's?"

"Your Mackinsey Jessup and that police lieutenant questioned Joe about it yesterday. They told him it was registered to Hank Warren and it was found at the scene of the murder. He said Hank claimed that he'd given it to you months ago for protection."

"And you actually believed that?"

"Well, I…" Her voice faded.

"You know how much I loathe the man. How could you think that?"

"I don't know." She gestured with her hands. "I guess I wasn't thinking."

"Why did they happen to question Joe about the gun in the first place? I don't get the connection."

"That was my fault. When they asked me where we were at a certain time on the night of November 25th, I told them we were at home watching videos with the kids."

"But why would—"

"I told them that Joe had gone out for some beer. They wanted to know where he went, what time he left and what time he got back."

"I see."

"He wasn't going to tell them anything, but Lieutenant Barnes asked him what if he told him his fingerprints were on the gun. Joe broke down and told them where he'd gotten it. You see, he'd had it for months."

"When did you tell your husband about the rape?"

"I didn't exactly tell him. I started having nightmares about that night and I guess I must have cried out something in my sleep. Naturally Joe wanted to take him apart when he realized what he'd done to me."

"How did you manage to keep Joe from doing it?"

"Believe me, it wasn't easy, but we both needed to keep our jobs. We've kind of over-extended ourselves. Joe knew he couldn't afford the luxury of losing his job, not to mention his freedom, if he did anything to the man. The bastard knew he had us between a rock and a hard place.

"I hated him. He needed killing after what he'd done to me. When I saw the gun in your desk drawer something inside me snapped, and on impulse I took it. I don't know if I intended to kill him or use it to scare him if he tried anything else. I just don't know. In the end I justified taking the gun by convincing myself that I needed it more than you did. When you didn't seem to notice that the gun was missing, I decided to keep it.

"Then it disappeared from my desk. After that Joe became adamant that I never be alone with Mr. Clifford or work overtime if I could help it. I know you probably thought it was all for Joe's benefit, but it wasn't."

"You didn't kill him, did you, Pat?"

"No. But I'm not sorry that somebody did what I didn't have the guts to do. No. I didn't kill the bastard and neither did Joe." She glanced intently at Toni. "You do believe me?"

"Yes, but, Pat, I didn't kill him either. Maybe it was Hank or…"

"Or who?"

"I can't say. It would only be guesswork on my part."

Toni could tell Pat wasn't completely convinced.

Just then Mariah spotted a cop walking through the door and signaled to Toni.

"I've got to be going, Pat. If neither you, Joe nor Hank is the murderer, I've got to find the real killer." Toni rose casually from her seat and she and Mariah left through the side entrance leading out to the parking lot.

Mariah started the Jeep. "That was a close one. I don't think the policeman recognized you."

"Me either. At least I hope he didn't."

As Bob pulled the squad car up to the curb in front of the Townsend building, Mack caught a glimpse of two familiar looking young women leaving through the side entrance of the Coffee House. His breathing suddenly constricted; it was Toni and Mariah! What were they doing there? The answer to his question walked out the front entrance. When Pat Davis saw him, she glanced nervously at the Coffee House parking lot.

Evidently he hadn't made himself clear. It looked like he would have to have another little heart-to-heart talk with the dynamic duo. Mack got out of the car and met Pat Davis as she reached the curb of the Townsend building. Bob sat in the car for a moment, watching as his friend approached Pat Davis before finally leaving the car to join them.

"How was your coffee break, Pat?" Mack inquired.

"Same as usual."

"Really? Did you run into anyone interesting?"

Pat flinched.

Mack noticed the way Bob was looking at him and he smiled. He was sure Bob suspected that he was holding out on him and didn't like it one bit. Mack felt a lecture coming on, and knew that Bob was waiting for just the right time to deliver it.

Pat didn't answer Mack's question. Once inside the building she headed for the bank of elevators. He reached out to hold the door open. Then he and Bob stepped inside, one on either side of her.

As Mack and Bob left the Townsend building Bob asked, "Where do you suppose Warren went? According to Connie Parker, his personal assistant, he should have been in his office."

"I don't know, but you can be sure of one thing. The man is devious. I'd go so far as to say dangerous. If I'm any judge of people, Nina Townsend didn't waste any time calling him after we left her house. I'm beginning to wonder if they weren't in on the killing together."

"It would seem that a certain amount of circumstantial evidence is pointing in quite a few directions. Don't you think it was strange that Warren didn't leave word that he was leaving the office or when he'd be back?"

"Yes, I do. After questioning the Davises further, I believe their story. It looks like Warren's perfect alibi isn't going to fly."

"He's not the only one involved. We've yet to question Mr. Townsend himself. His secretary says he's due back in the office tomorrow afternoon. He just returned from a business trip in Seattle."

"I want to be with you when you question him."

"Mack, I don't think you—"

"Bob."

"I thought I'd try. Let me drop you off at your house so you can pick up your car."

All afternoon and well into the evening Toni went over every piece of information again and again.

"There has to be something."

"What did you say, Toni?" Mariah walked over to where Toni sat hunched over her computer.

"Oh, nothing, just talking to myself."

"You'd better watch that. You know what they say."

"Don't worry, I'm not crazy. I haven't started answering back."

Mariah glanced at her watch. "I want to check on my mother. She came back home early from visiting with my Uncle Juan. She was supposed to spend two weeks at his house. I called my uncle to find out why she had cut her visit short, but he couldn't tell me anything. I hope she's not sick. She didn't sound like herself when I called her earlier. I'll be back in a couple of hours if she doesn't need me."

"Stay with her as long as you need to, Mariah. I'm not some helpless little baby, you know. I am capable of fending for myself."

"I know you are, but I hate leaving you here alone."

"Go!"

With reluctance, Mariah picked up her purse to leave.

"Maybe I should call Mack."

"No, Mariah. I'll be all right. Really."

"You're sure?"

"Yes, silly, now go."

Hearing Mariah talk about her mother made Toni think about her own, and how much she missed both her parents.

After an hour Toni called it quits on the computer and walked over to the phone. As she prepared to punch in her parents' number, she thought she heard a noise and her heart raced. She listened again for the noise, but didn't hear anything."Mom—yes. Mom! Can't you call me Toni? I know you think it doesn't sound feminine. Is Daddy there? Yes. I miss you, too, Daddy. I don't know when I'll be able to come visit. Is retirement agreeing with you and Mama? That's good. I'll try. There was a mix up about that. No, it isn't serious. I'm not their thief, and I'll prove it to them. No, no, you don't need to put off your trip. Yes, I want you to go. Okay. Yes, Mom. I love you too. Bye."

"How touching."

"Hank!" Toni whirled around and said in a strangled voice, "How did you get in here?"

"I coaxed a window open."

"How did you find out I was here?"

"I saw you and that luscious female you were with entering the Coffee House from my office window. I'd know that sexy little body of yours anywhere. You were trying to pump Pat Davis for information, weren't you? I figured the two of you must have had a nice talk. Since I wanted to know where you'd disappeared to, I got in my car and waited for you to come out. Then I followed you."

"Why didn't you call the police? I would have thought that it was an opportunity you couldn't pass up. "

"What? And spoil my chance to sample what you've been giving Jessup, and probably Clifford too? Afterward I'll take pleasure in turning you in."

"You must be out of your mind," she said, backing away. "I hate your guts. I'd rather cozy up to a boa constrictor."

"You acid-tongued little bitch, I'm not giving you a choice. I'm going to make you pay for that insult, and all the other rotten things you've ever said to and about me." He made a grab for her.

Toni tried to escape him, but he caught her. She struggled, kicking and swinging her hands and elbows, trying to disable him the way she had learned to do in her self-defense class, but he knew how to block her, and used his brute strength to subdue her.

He grinned triumphantly. "I've waited a long time for this, you haughty bitch. Thought I wasn't good enough for you, didn't you?" When he tried to punish her with his overpowering kisses, Toni jerked her head away.

"Looks like you're going to have to wait a while longer, Warren," Mack said from the doorway, his tone soft yet deadly.

Recognizing the threat in Mack's stance, Hank relaxed his grip on Toni.

"Get your hands off her, Warren." Mack advanced toward them.

"You're not going to stop me from turning this little thieving murderer over to the police."

Toni twisted out of Hank's grip. Mack grabbed him, punched him in the face and then drove his fist into his stomach, forcing him to drop to his knees. Mack pulled his fist back to hit him again.

"That's enough, Mack, let him go," came Bob's firm voice as he entered the room.

Mack hesitated, debating whether to hit Hank again, then released his quarry and went to Toni. "Baby, are you all right?"

"I'm fine, he didn't hurt me."

"I suggest we all take a ride to the station." Bob glanced from Toni to Mack, then to Hank. "We can do this voluntarily or we can do it the hard way. If you want it official I can read you your rights and cuff you. Which is it going to be?" When there was no sign of resistance, he called for assistance with transport. Within minutes they were all on the way to the station.

Mack and Toni climbed into the backseat of the squad car.

"I could kill Warren for what he tried to do to you," Mack ground out.

"So could I. He has to be the one who killed Frank Clifford."

"It seems likely. I hope Bob arrests him because I won't be responsible—"

"Forget about him. He's not worth going to jail over."

"I know you're right, it's just that—"

"Believe me, I know how you feel. There have been many times in the past when I've wanted to do the same thing. What do you think will happen now, Mack?"

"I don't know, baby. We'll have to wait and see."

"How did you happen to arrive at the beach house, as they say, 'in the nick of time'?"

"I saw you and Mariah leaving the Coffee House. I intended to ream you both up one side and down the other for ignoring my advice concerning your safety."

"We didn't ignore it. I didn't leave Mariah any choice other than to do as I said."

"And you expect me to buy that? Look," he took her hands in his, "I care about you and I don't want anything to happen to you, all right?"

"I know, but we weren't in any danger."

"Not then, as far as you knew. Warren must have seen you from his office window. That must have been the reason he left his office in such a hurry. Bob and I had intended to question him."

"You're right. He did see us from his window. He told me so, which reminds me. Why didn't you tell me he had been made the temporary CEO?"

"I meant to."

"He's been angling for the top seat, and it looks like he finally got his wish."

"It'll be a temporary position if he's convicted of murder."

"If he's convicted? That's a pretty big if."

"You didn't do it, and Warren's alibi doesn't hold water if Nina Townsend is to be believed. I think there will be an arrest soon."

"I hope he's the one arrested, not me."

"The guilty person will be exposed, one way or another."

"I want to believe that."

"Then do," he said, drawing her closer to his heart.

CHAPTER NINETEEN

"About your sudden departure from the hospital," Bob said to Toni. He eased a lean hip onto the end of his desk at the station.

"I had to get out of there, the walls were closing in on me."

"But that's not the only reason you left, is it?"

"Bob, Toni's had enough for one night. It's nearly midnight. She wasn't trying to escape. If she had she'd have been long gone by now."

"And you would have no doubt helped her. Mack, may I remind you that this is a murder investigation? I could hold Toni as a material witness. I thought protective custody would ensure her safety during the investigation."

"You can't tell me you weren't seriously considering detaining me on a more substantial charge, can you?"

"I don't know what would have happened after I questioned you."

"Come on, Bob, be straight with us," Mack said in an annoyed voice. "You were as certain as Toni and I were that you were going to arrest her."

"We'll never know now. She left the hospital before I could do anything."

"What now, Bob?" Mack asked.

"The way it looks there's a chance a judge will say Toni and Hank Warren and possibly Mrs. Townsend were in some way in collusion on the killing. He may suggest detaining Warren and Toni and bringing Mrs. Townsend in for questioning."

"Bob—"

"I won't detain Toni, pending the findings from the coroner's office. We should know something conclusive on cause of death by tomorrow afternoon at the latest. Until then, you can take Toni to your house. Returning to the beach house isn't a good idea. I'll have someone drive you back to get your car."

"You're going to continue posting your men at my house, I take it?"

"I have to, Mack, you know that." Bob glanced at Toni, offering her an apology. "I'm sorry."

"I'm no better off than if I was in jail."

"What can I tell you?" Bob hunched his shoulders.

"Nothing," Toni answered tiredly.

"After what you've been through, I agree with Mack that you should go home. If you want to file assault charges against Hank Warren you can."

"I do."

"Then follow me. I know, you'll want to come with her, Mack."

"You got that right."

When Toni and Mack arrived at his house, she turned to him and smiled. "I'm glad you came to the beach house when you did."

"Me too. By the way, where's my sister? She was supposed to be with you."

"She called your uncle earlier and found out that your mother had cut short her visit with them. After talking with your mother, Mariah was worried that she might not be feeling well or that something was wrong."

"I'd better call and find out what's going on. I don't want Mariah going to the beach house alone."

Mack reached for the phone to call his mother. As he spoke, Toni noted the concern in his face. He was a magnificent specimen of manhood and as sexy as all get out. In other words, as Pat had once said about him, he was a hunk. She knew he cared about her, but did he actually love her? She knew he desired her, but desire wasn't love. They were good in bed, but being compatible physically didn't insure that it was love. Toni didn't want to think Mack had only fallen into lust when she had fallen in love.

"Share the load."

"What?" Toni said, jolted out of her momentary reverie.

"There's something heavy preying on your mind, and I don't think it has anything to do with the situation you're in."

"How's your mother?"

Mack grinned. "Changing the subject? All right, you're obviously not ready to tell me what's bothering you. My mother is fine. She just wanted to get back home to have a certain Latin gentleman call on her, according to what Mariah said."

"From what I've heard about your mother, she deserves a good man in her life."

"I see that Mariah's been flapping her gums again." He laughed. "The man who marries her will have his hands full."

"He'll have someone special."

"Like I have."

"Mack—"

"I happen to love you very much, Antonia Carlton."

Toni's heart leapt into her throat at Mack's declaration. She'd hoped for this.

"Aren't you going to say anything, sweet Toni?"

"I love you, Mack, with all my heart."

"I knew that."

"You did? When did you realize that you loved me?"

"From the moment you opened your eyes after you'd fainted in my office."

"But you never said—"

"I was waiting for the right moment, but it never came and now—"

"I'll probably go to prison."

"No, you won't," he said vehemently.

"Mack, how do we know that?"

"You're Innocent of both charges, and we're going to prove it."

Toni took his hand in hers. "Mariah was right."

"About what?"

"She said I was lucky that I had you in my corner."

"I always knew that sister of mine had a good head on her shoulders. Now," he said pulling Toni to her feet, "I'd like to celebrate."

"And how do you propose doing that."

"By having a love festival."

Toni frowned in confusion. "A what?"

"Festival. And I don't mean with food."

"Then what?" She flashed him her most innocent smile.

"Come on and let me show you."

Mack lifted Toni into his arms and carried her into his bedroom. He slowly undressed her, taking in every nuance of her softly curving body.

"You're beautiful, Toni."

"I'm glad you think so." She gasped when his fingers found her nipple and traced a circle around the aureole.

"I love you," he said softly and kissed her deeply.

When she felt Mack's hand sear a path down her abdomen and onto her thigh, Toni thought that her legs would collapse and she eased his hand away. And with trembling fingers she helped Mack out of his clothes. At last he stood magnificently naked before her. A sigh left her lips at the sight of him.

"I want you, Mack, and I can't wait," Toni said, her voice husky with passion.

"As I want you. And you don't have to wait, baby."

Mack lifted her onto the bed and joined her. He worshiped her body with his hands, his mouth, his mind and his heart.

Toni did the same, reveling in the taste of his mouth and the touch of his fingers on her flesh. She moaned her pleasure when he moved to unite them.

Mack found himself losing control and spiraling into oblivion, taking Toni with him.

Later, as they lay in each other's arms, Toni noticed how quiet Mack had become.

"What is it?"

"You've restored me," he said in an awed voice.

"Restored you? How?"

"I never thought I'd fall again."

"In love, you mean?" She snuggled closer.

A look of tender love came into his eyes. "Yes." He kissed her forehead. "Seven years ago I thought I'd fallen in love. Her name was Linda Hutton. She was involved in one of the cases I was working on, and she used my feelings for her to get me to help her escape punishment."

"Is she the reason you left the police department?"

"Yes. You see, I convinced the D. A. that she wasn't an integral part of a scam to swindle old people out of their property, that she was merely an unwitting accomplice. You can't know how badly I felt when I found out she had been lying to me, using me all along. I vowed to never trust another woman. My sister and mother and Rachel being the only exceptions.

"I couldn't face anyone I knew for a long time. As an officer of the law it was my job to protect and serve the people. Instead I let them, and myself, down." Mack paused, reaching inside himself to compose his emotions. "I resigned from the department and got a degree in finance, specializing in financial investigations. Then I opened my own business."

"Where do I stand in your scheme of things?"

"You're now at the top of my list of trusted women, Toni."

"Oh, Mack. You don't know what it means to me to hear you say that. I won't betray your trust. I am innocent, you know."

"I believe you are."

She lovingly caressed his cheek. "I also have a confession to make. You've restored my faith in love. Before I met you I had no one special in my life. I purposely let my work become my panacea. It worked pretty well most of the time, but there were times when I longed for that special closeness my parents share. I wanted to one day have what they have. I knew I'd recognize that special kind of love once I found it. And I vowed to never let it get away from me. I have that with you, Mackinsey Jessup."

His warm affectionate smile enveloped her in his spell.

"I guess that means that you don't need further proof?"

She ran her finger down his throat to his chest. "Oh, I don't know. If it means that you're going to make love to me, please, by all means, show me more proof."

"I will, as much and as many times as you want me to."

Toni and Mack were having breakfast the next morning when Bob arrived. Toni couldn't help tensing up at the sight of him. It was a morning similar to this one that the good lieutenant had come to arrest her on embezzlement charges.

Mack picked up on Toni's uneasy vibes. He wanted once and for all to clear the woman he loved. It shredded his heart to see the look of dread in her eyes when she saw Bob.

"You ready, Mack?" Bob asked.

"In a minute. I have to call Marc, then say good-bye to my lady."

Bob shot him a knowing smile, then turned to go back into the living room.

After hanging up with his brother, Mack pulled Toni into his arms and kissed her. He gazed into her eyes. "You be good while I'm gone and get some rest. No more amateur sleuthing without me. Understand?"

"I understand, but will Mariah?"

Mack grinned. "Her boss is due back soon. He'll keep her occupied."

"I wouldn't count on it," Bob said wryly from the doorway.

Knowing his sister as well as he did, Mack had to agree with Bob. When had she turned into such an independent woman? It wasn't so long ago that she was wearing two long ponytails and being a royal pain in the butt. Now she was this strikingly attractive, intelligent woman. Where had the years gone?

Mack glanced back at the house as he and Bob reached the street. He didn't want to leave Toni. What he wanted to do was stay here and make love to her all day.

"Let's go, Romeo," Bob teased.

"You'll get yours one day, my skeptical friend, and believe me, I can hardly wait."

"Watching you is enough to keep me on the alert."

"If you find the right woman you won't feel that way."

"I don't think such a woman exists, at least not for me. Now, come on. I'd like you to come with me to the crime lab. We have a resident genius who is unbelievably astute in his methods of deduction."

Mack had never met a more thorough criminology specialist than Paul Norman. The man checked every piece of evidence with more than a fine-toothed comb. He examined the evidence down to the most minute details. Mack agreed with Bob's assessment of the man's talents. If even the slightest inconsistency existed, he believed the man would find it.

By the time Mack and Bob left the crime lab it was afternoon. Bob called Townsend's to see if Townsend was back in his office. Mack really didn't see what they would accomplish by questioning him about the murder. According to his wife and his secretary, Townsend had been booked on a flight to Seattle at the time the murder had taken place and he had just returned from his trip today. But maybe it was worth a shot.

Mack could tell that Townsend was not exactly pleased to see him. Oh, he was cordial enough when he asked them to take a seat in his office. The man probably thought he'd seen the last of Mackinsey Jessup after removing him from the embezzlement case.

Mack was still puzzled about his dismissal. It made him wonder if the man hadn't somehow used him to cover up something. He hated being used. Could Townsend have possibly been the person on the other end of the line the night he met Toni? But why would he steal from his own company?

"My secretary said you wanted to ask me some questions about the unfortunate death of my CEO. I don't know what I can tell you. I've only just returned from a business trip, as I'm sure you already know."

"How much do you know about your wife's association with Frank Clifford?" Bob asked.

"You mean her affair with him?" He winced. "My wife is not known for her discretion, as I'm sure you've found out. I've known about her relationship with Clifford for quite some time."

"And you've done nothing?" Mack interjected, incredulity spiking his voice. "Somehow I find that hard to believe,"

Townsend grimaced wearily as he glanced at Mack. "What would you have me do, Mr. Jessup?"

"Get angry, put a stop to it, divorce her, something."

The older man smiled wryly. "And are you suggesting that I took steps to remedy the situation?"

"Did you, Mr. Townsend?" the lieutenant asked.

"I know she's had more than a few lovers and will probably continue to have more."

"Mr. Townsend, you want us to believe that you didn't care that your wife was sleeping around?"

"You wouldn't understand if I tried to explain it to you, Lieutenant."

"Try me."

"I realized what kind of woman Nina was shortly after our marriage, but I loved her anyway. My father and everyone we knew said I should get rid of her. What they failed to realize was that I loved her and would take her on any terms I could have her."

Mack could relate to the man on that level. Hadn't he himself also been obsessed with a woman to the exclusion of everything and everyone else? Could he condemn Townsend for succumbing to the same weakness? Mack felt sorry for him.

"Getting back to the night of the murder..." Bob cleared his throat. "What time did you leave on your business trip, Mr. Townsend? I need to know the flight number and when the plane arrived in Seattle."

"That doesn't pose any problem for me. The plane left at 10:30 P.M. November 25th and landed three hours later in Seattle."

"I didn't think Townsend would be of much help to us," Mack said wearily as they left Townsend's. "That leaves Hank Warren and Nina Townsend."

"And Toni Carlton, Mack."

"No, it doesn't. She's not your killer."

"You need to keep things in perspective. It doesn't look good for Toni."

"I know that, but—"

"But you believe in her innocence. I know, I've heard it all before. But, Mack, you've got to be prepared for the possibility that she may be lying."

"I'll never believe that. I'll find a way to clear her. You'll see."

Mack saw the expression on Bob's face and knew he wanted to say more, but he resisted the impulse.

CHAPTER TWENTY

When Mack got home that evening he found Toni in her bedroom, standing in front of the window looking out. From the doorway he stood watching her, wondering what was going through her head. She obviously hadn't heard him enter the house.

His Toni was so beautiful and she loved him as much as he loved her. Frustration tore at him. He had to find the person who helped Frank Clifford frame her and who also, in all likelihood, killed the man. If he didn't, the woman he loved would be lost to him.

"How long have you been home?" Toni asked, turning around.

Mack blinked, pulling himself out of his distressing reverie. "Only a few minutes. You were so deep in thought, I guess you didn't hear me."

"You're right, I didn't. I've been thinking. There must be something I've overlooked."

"You've gone through all the records over and over again."

"Still, there has to be something." She walked over to the dresser and picked up her purse and rummaged through it.

"Toni? What are you doing?"

"Looking for my keys. I have to get my computer from the beach house."

"I'll take you."

Two hours later Mack helped Toni set up her computer in the guest bedroom.

"What now?"

"I don't know, Mack. I keep thinking if I go over this enough times I'll find the answer."

"If you don't find it, it won't be because you haven't tried."

Toni hacked into the Townsend computer, but found she could not bring up the business program. She probably had Hank to thank for changing the access code since he had taken over as CEO. Of all the rotten luck.

It suddenly occurred to Toni that what she sought might not be in the business program at all. She'd been focusing her attention on that particular feature, going on the assumption that her former boss had hidden the evidence of his scheming there.

Mack watched Toni's face and saw the moment her expression changed. "Toni, what is it?"

"I don't know, but I'm going to run a listing of all the companies Townsend uses as exchange centers to circulate bonds and securities to other cities, states and countries. Knowing Frank Clifford, he was too smart to run the risk of having all the money he'd stolen confiscated. He would have been very careful. Why didn't I think of this before?"

"Think of what? You're not making any sense."

"I will in a minute. Be patient with me a while longer."

He watched her bring up the various companies. Several hours passed as he watched Toni scan the listings.

"How many names are on this thing?"

"Hundreds, even thousands, I should imagine." Toni smiled. "You should have some idea. Mr. Townsend did hire you to find the thief."

She was right, he had been hired to do just that. "Because there were so many I only concentrated on the files that had been tampered with, leading to lost funds, or those that seemed to follow the initial pattern established by the thief. Townsend took me off the case before I could complete my investigation. You know that."

"How close were you to exposing the real thief?"

"I don't know. I continued studying the files after Townsend took me off the case. You see, I'd made extra copies to examine and—"

As Toni glanced up at Mack, she saw him arch his brow and stare at nothing, as though recalling to mind something important he'd forgotten until that moment.

"You remember something?"

"I may be able to help you narrow your search." He left the room and returned a few minutes later with two disks. He put them on the desk.

"What's on them?"

He sat down on the bed. "That's what we're going to find out."

She looked disheartened after bringing up the search screen on the first of the two disks. "Mack, at the rate we can scan them it could take days."

"Maybe not, I'd gotten as far as the M's." He pointed out where he'd stopped. "I'll call Marc and tell him I'll be late coming in to the office."

"You don't have to do that."

He rose from the bed and stepped over to her chair and placed his hands on her shoulders and massaged them. "I know I don't, baby." He kissed her neck. "I want to. All right?"

She flashed him a devastating smile. "All right," she said softly, covering his hand with hers.

For the next few hours they searched the disks without finding anything out of the ordinary.

Toni sighed wearily. "Sifting through this is like reading an unabridged copy of *The Never-Ending Story* in superscript."

"Wasn't it you who told me patience has its rewards?"

"Don't remind me."

"Come on, let's start on the T's"

Toni glared at the screen. There was still a lot of information to scan. Mack had finally had to leave and go to his office. She glanced at the clock on the nightstand. It was almost six o'clock. Mack would be home soon. She'd hoped to be able to tell him something positive for a change.

"Don't look so depressed," Mack said from the doorway, and did a rendition of "Smile, Darn Ya, Smile."

"Al Jolson?" Toni laughed "You're a certifiable nut case, Mackinsey Jessup."

"I cheered you up, didn't I?"

"You did that, all right." Her laughter died and a serious look replaced it. "I haven't had any luck at all with this, Mack."

"You're not giving up, are you?"

"No."

"Good. Don't. After dinner I'll help you."

It was close to midnight when Toni finished studying the companies that commonly traded securities. She'd checked the warrants, units and mutual funds index Mack had provided. Still nothing. She took a breather, then returned to the computer to run the options listing. These were the companies known by the layman. She came across a company she hadn't heard of, ValueCorp International, and punched issue description, expiration month, the strike price and the letter. The cursor blinked, "Please wait!" Then the words "Confidential—password required" flashed on the screen. To leave this listing engage escape key."

"I think I've found the dummy corporation, Mack."

"How can you be sure?"

"It's locked up tighter than Fort Knox. Have you ever heard of ValueCorp International?"

"No, but there is one way to check on its authenticity."

"The address. It's located in Santa Clarita." Toni frowned and repeated, "Santa Clarita? There's nothing there that I know of."

"Why didn't anyone think of checking ValueCorp International before?"

"It isn't one I was assigned to work on."

"Who handled it, then?"

"Probably Clifford. Or Hank, I suppose."

Their eyes met in mutual realization that it could be Hank.

Mack hated to crush her hopes of being exonerated on the embezzlement charges, but he couldn't let her lose sight of the realities involved.

"Don't get your hopes up that Warren is the one who killed Clifford and was the partner helping him steal from the company by framing you, because it doesn't necessarily follow."

"I know you're right, Mack, but—" He held her close. "I know, baby."

"What do we do next?"

"First thing in the morning I'm going to check out a few possibilities. Now, my love, you're coming with me."

"And where are you taking me?"

"I'll give you three guesses."

Toni barely had time to shut down her computer before Mack was shuffling her out of the room and down the hall to his.

"Mack, the handsome Lieutenant Barnes is here to see you," Daphne cheerfully blared over the intercom the next morning.

"One of these days, Daffy...Send him in."

Mack could tell by the set look on his friend's face he had something to tell him that he wasn't going to like.

"To what do I owe this visit?"

"The coroner has finished his findings."

Mack braced himself. "And?"

"The cause of death was not from the gunshot wounds, although the loss of blood from the shooting probably expedited his death."

"All right, Bob, let's have it. Tell me why you came here. You could have told me that over the phone."

Bob's mouth quirked into a wry smile. "Still sharp as a razor's edge, aren't you, Mack? The indomitable Mack attack."

Mack laughed at the name his colleagues had pinned on him when he was on the police force. "Did you expect my brain to atrophy because I'm no longer with the department? What was the real cause of death?"

"You remember Paul Norman from the crime lab?"

Mack nodded.

"He matched up the findings from the coroner's office with the DNA report, using a special computer program he'd written. He found trace patterns that closely resemble those of a cardioplegic drug."

"Cardioplegic drug?"

"A drug often used to freeze the heart during surgery. In small doses it can be given as a medication for certain heart conditions."

"Go on."

"Clifford died from a heart attack, not the gunshot. I checked with his doctor and found out he didn't have a heart condition and had never been prescribed a cardioplegic drug."

"Are you saying this cardioplegic drug acted like a poison in his system and gave him a heart attack? My next question is, why did you come all the way over here to tell me this?"

"If I were you, I'd get Toni a good criminal attorney."

"Why are you doing this?"

"Come on, Mack. The fact that her father is a doctor, not just any doctor, but a heart surgeon, did not escape our investigation."

"He's retired, Bob. The bottom line: Are you going to arrest Toni?"

"I haven't been ordered to do that—yet. The information we have so far isn't enough to arrest her."

"That's not to say that you won't find something else that could at a later date, right?"

"Mack, I—"

"Let's not pussyfoot around. You think it'll come to that, don't you?"

"Look, Mack, you're an ex-cop. You know as well as I do that an overzealous D.A. could take this and run with it. I just thought I should warn you."

"I'm sorry, Bob. I appreciate you coming here, man. What do you think will happen now?"

"A more thorough investigation will be conducted on all the suspects. Now that it's been narrowed down to probable method, that changes a few things."

"You already have probable motive and opportunity, now possibly method, where Toni is concerned. What you need to find out next is whether any of the other suspects had access to the drug." Mack knew that he needed to question Toni's father about the drug before the police did. By telling him about the drug now, his friend had given him time to do it. He realized what a good friend he had in Bob. "I appreciate this, Bob."

Bob grinned. "That's what friends are for. Hey, I've got to be getting back to the station."

"When do you think you'll be—"

"You've got till this afternoon. It's all the time I can give you, Mack. After that…"

"I understand. And thanks, man."

"No problem." Bob turned and left the office.

Mack searched through the Townsend files and found the number for Toni's father.

CHAPTER TWENTY-ONE

Toni was past frustration in trying to find the password to get into the confidential information file of ValueCorp International. She was sure that her boss had implicated his accomplice in it. He had been a cruel, devious man, one who wouldn't hesitate to blackmail a partner who wanted out of his scheme. Frank Clifford had been greedy and arrogant enough to want all he could get, and on his own terms.

Toni replayed what had happened the night she'd inadvertently stumbled onto his plan to frame her. If she hadn't left her keys...Keys. To incriminate her, he'd planted a key to connect her to the safety deposit box that contained a few disks of accounts. He'd put that key on her ring. He'd held her keys as a scare tactic to press his advantage. Knowing him, he'd want someone to know how clever he'd been.

Keys! Could he possibly have made that the password?

Toni returned to her computer and hacked into Townsend's. She brought up the listing of companies and accessed the ValueCorp International file. "Confidential—password required" blinked on the screen. When Toni typed in the word keys the screen flashed, and then the ValueCorp company logo came up. In parentheses Placentia Holding Company appeared with a post office box and a phone number.

Toni copied down the phone number, then picked up the phone and punched in the number.

"Placentia Holding Company. May I take a message?"

"I'd like to speak with the president?"

"Sorry, we're just a message answering service."

"Then who would I—"

"I'm sorry, ma'am, I can't help you."

Toni hung up. Placentia Holding Company was only a front. She had to find out who Clifford's partner was. The information had to be out in plain sight in case his partner tried to double-cross him. She was sure he would have prepared for possible betrayal. Whoever the partner was, he or she held the key to clearing Toni.

Mack left the office early so he could break the news to Toni about the coroner's findings. He couldn't reach her father to ask if she'd had access to the drug prior to Clifford's demise. He knew in his gut the woman he loved wasn't guilty of murder, pre-meditated or any other kind, but that wasn't enough for the law. He would have to ask her where her parents were.

He found Toni sitting in a chair, gazing at the computer screen.

"Have you found anything?" he asked.

"Mack! I've just discovered the password to get into ValueCorp's confidential file."

He wondered why she looked less than pleased by the revelation. "And?"

"It's owned by Placentia Holding Company, which is probably just a front for the real owner. We'll have to go through the tedious process of finding the real owner because the only address we have is a post office box, and the only phone number belongs to an answering service."

"It's a good thing businesses have to be registered with the International Stock Exchange. There may be more transferal companies listed, but invariably the paper trail will lead to whoever set it up, be it Clifford or his partner. I'll get Marc to do the cyberspace leg work on this. We should know the name of the legal owner or owners of Placentia Holding Company pretty quickly." Mack phoned his brother and gave him the particulars. Now all they had to do was wait. In the meantime he had other things he needed to discuss with Toni.

"You had something you wanted to say to me, Mack?"

"Bob came to see me this morning. Frank Clifford didn't die from gunshot wounds, as we all assumed. He died from an overdose of a cardioplegic drug."

"How is that possible? As far as I know he didn't suffer from any heart problems."

"How did you know what kind of drug that is?"

"When I was in college, during summer vacations, I helped my father out in his office at the naval base. I learned a lot about heart ailments and heart surgery."

"When was the last time you visited him there?"

"Three or four months ago. I helped him clear out his office when he retired from the navy. I don't understand why you're asking me all these questions."

"Do the letters M, M, O mean anything to you?"

"No, they don't." She observed him with curiosity. "Mack, what are you trying to tell me?"

"They stand for method, motive and opportunity." Mack waited for his words to sink in.

"I never took any cardioplegic drugs from my father's office," she said, offended.

"Don't get your back up. I know that and you know that, but—"

"The law might not believe I passed up the opportunity to use the drug to do my dirty work."

Mack drew her into his arms. "I wish I could tell you not to worry and that everything will be all right." He didn't want to suggest that she consult a criminal attorney, but he was beginning to think she was going to need one.

"But you can't, can you? Oh, Mack." She laid her head against his chest.

He stroked her hair. "I know. Where are your parents now?"

She raised her head. "They're in Italy visiting my mother's family. I had to do quite a selling job to convince them that I'd be all right while they were gone and that the charges against me were a mistake."

"This could be all cleared up before they get back."

"I can only hope you're right, Mack. The last postcard I got from them said they were visiting a great aunt who lived in a small village in the hills surrounding Tuscany."

"Don't sweat it. You look hungry. I'll bet you haven't eaten all day. Come on out to the kitchen, pilgrim, and watch while I rustle us up some grub."

Toni laughed. "All right, Duke. I am starved. What have you got in mind?"

"I'll let you choose."

"And help, too. How generous of you."

"Come on, woman."

"You're so primitive. I'm not sure I like that."

"You know you do." He flicked his eyebrows à la Tom Selleck. Toni shook her head, then taking his hand, led him out of the bedroom to the kitchen.

Mack and Toni were finishing their dinner of stir-fried chicken when the phone rang.

Their eyes met.

Mack swallowed a forkful of chicken, then wiped his mouth with a napkin. "I'll get it." He rose from his chair and walked over to the kitchen phone. "Yes? What did you find out, Marc? I see."

Toni watched Mack cradle the receiver. "What did Marc find out?"

"According to the International Stock Exchange, the company is owned by an investment group."

"Which probably means that we'll never be able to track down the actual owner's name. Damn Frank Clifford. He's ruining my life from the grave!"

"What we have to do now is chase down the names of the group members."

"Sure. He no doubt took care of that too. Come on, Mack. I was so sure this would lead us to the accomplice. Instead, this information could make it impossible for me to clear myself."

It twisted his guts to see that anguished expression on Toni's face. How much more of this could she take? He was sure there would be much more to come. "This only shows how thoroughly Clifford planned his scam."

"Millions of dollars are involved. Even if you were the owner of the company it doesn't prove that you stole the stocks, bonds and securities from Townsend. In order to prove anything illegal was going on, the D.A.'s office would need physical evidence. So far they've been unable to come up with anything they could use in court. It looks as if the bonds and securities have vanished off the market without a trace."

"Good old Frank certainly did his homework."

"Not necessarily. He considered himself a smart man. He probably hid them in some foreign bank, planning to convert them to cash when the heat died down."

"But where, Mack? The man is dead so we can't ask him, not that he would tell us if he were alive."

"Would he have hidden the location in the computer, the way he did ValueCorp International?"

"With him anything was possible. Where will it all end, Mack? What am I going to lose besides my career?"

"You're scared and I don't blame you, but we'll find out the truth, Toni. I won't rest until we do."

"I love you."

"And I love you."

"I can't figure out who you're imitating this time."

"I'm not imitating anyone, Toni my love," he said softly, "just being myself."

"Glad to hear it, because I love you just the way you are."

THE PERFECT FRAME

The next morning Mack and Marcus ran a complete check on ValueCorp and discovered other holding companies that were also subsidiaries of Placentia.

"This guy Clifford was a real slimeball, Mack. He didn't mess around. Look at this list of holding companies connected to ValueCorp. Those securities are long gone. It's going to take one hell of a lot of checking to track them down, if we ever can."

"Placentia isn't the true owner of ValueCorp International. Evidently Clifford was only using it as a cover-up. There's more to this than we know. If only I'd been able to find this out while I was investigating the thefts," Mack said, feeling impotent with frustration.

"You wouldn't have found out anything except what Clifford wanted you to."

"I should have done something to stop him."

"You didn't know, Mack, so quit beating yourself up about it. All right?"

"If I'd gone with my instincts about Toni's innocence earlier—"

"Even if you had, you wouldn't have necessarily been able to prevent any of this from happening to her. You'd better tell Bob what you've found before he finds out from another source."

"I know you're right."

"I'm going to my office and let you get on with it."

Mack decided to wait until he had something more substantial before contacting Bob. He had time. What he'd found out so far hadn't helped Toni; it had only clouded the issue, making things appear worse than they actually were.

Clifford had to have made a mistake somewhere. Even a diabolical mind like his wasn't infallible. Maybe the answer he sought was in Clifford's personal files. And right now those files were under Hank Warren's control. He wished that Warren's name had been found on the title proclaiming him as the owner. It would have helped clear Toni.

He didn't want to deal with Warren directly. But there was Pat Davis, a woman who had one of the best reasons in the world to hate Frank Clifford's guts and every reason to help her friend. There didn't seen to be any love lost between Pat and Hank Warren either. Yes, she was the logical one to help him. He picked up the phone.

"Pat, this is Mackinsey Jessup."

"Yes?"

Mack heard the wariness in her voice. "There is something you can do for Toni."

"What? I'll do whatever I can. I still consider her my friend."

"I know you do, Pat. You can help by finding out who okayed the release of securities through ValueCorp International. A file on the company should be in the CEO's office."

Pat gasped. "What about Hank?"

"He can only do something if he finds out. You know his schedule."

"But his PA—"

Mack didn't give her time to think of any more excuses not to help him. "Did you really mean what you said about wanting to clear Toni?"

"Of course, but—"

"Then do this for her."

"You're putting me on the spot."

"I know I'm asking a lot, Pat, but Toni is worth the risk, don't you think?"

She took so long to answer, Mack thought she wouldn't cooperate. Then he heard a resigned sigh.

"I'll do it, Mack. If I find out anything I'll let you know."

"Thanks, Pat."

Several evenings later Mack watched Toni leave the couch and head out to the kitchen. When she returned ten minutes later, he stopped watching football and observed as she brought in another bowl of popcorn. "We didn't really need any more popcorn, baby. What's bothering you?

"I'm going crazy, Mack. This waiting for the axe to fall is killing me. All I have to do all day is think about my predicament."

He took the popcorn from her hand and set it on the coffee table, pulled her down on the couch, nestling her in his embrace.

"With any luck that may not be the case for long."

She glanced up at him. "Have there been new developments you haven't told me about?"

"No, not that I'm aware of."

"But you said—"

"I know what I said. Maybe I shouldn't have—"

The phone rang. Mack picked up the receiver. "Yes, Pat. Damn! Thanks anyway."

"What was that all about?"

"I asked Pat to look through the files in Clifford's office to see if she could find any information on ValueCorp International."

Her nerves tightened like a coiled spring. "And?"

"Warren caught her before she could see what was in the ValueCorp file. He took it from her and threw her out of his office."

"What do you think is in there? Never mind. I checked Clifford's files myself and didn't find anything. You remember, the day you came into the office to check on me?" She cocked her head to one side. "But then we didn't know about ValueCorp International."

"Clifford may have planted something incriminating against you in there."

"And now Hank has it. Mack, what else did Pat say?"

"That she was sorry."

"I don't blame her. It seems that Frank Clifford has outwitted us again, as he has every step of the way. Now we have to deal with Hank, a man who hates me enough to do anything in his power to destroy me. Especially since I pressed charges against him. What should we do?"

"See my brother Matt as soon as possible. No telling what's in that file. Or any doubt as to what Warren will do now that he has it."

Mack held Toni close, and glancing down at the top of her dark head, he brushed his chin against the silky-softness of her hair. With each thing that surfaced, it pushed Toni further into the blackness of the tunnel. Would they find the light at the end in time to pull her out to safety?

If all these circumstantial facts were ever fused together to form a whole, he shuddered to think what would happen. He closed his eyes on the possibility of losing Toni. He couldn't lose her now.

Mack eased from the bed. After making sure he hadn't awakened Toni, he left the bedroom and went out to the kitchen. As he mixed nutmeg with milk and sugar and put the pan on the stove, he tried to logically sort through the situation. Who was manipulating things now that Clifford was dead?

"Mack, what are you doing up? It's the middle of the night." Toni yawned sleepily from the kitchen doorway.

"I might ask you the same question." His male equipment hardened at the sight of her sleep-flushed face and passion-tangled hair. She had on only her nightshirt, and the heat from her body had caused it to cling provocatively to every swell and curve.

Toni smiled. "I missed a certain big warm body."

She watched as Mack turned off the fire under the milk. He was one sexy hunk of man. She gasped inwardly at the way his pajama bottoms rode so low on his hips. He was so fine. Her nipples tightened and peaked against her nightshirt.

"A big warm body, huh? Is that all I am to you, woman?"

She purposely chose not to answer that question. He knew he meant more to her than that.

"Toni."

She circled her arms around his waist. "You're my life, Mackinsey Jessup."

"As you are mine, Toni Carlton." He caressed her cheek with his knuckles. "And don't you forget it."

"Oh, Mack." She moved her cheek against his hand.

"I know, love, I feel the same way." He bent his head and moved his lips over hers. The kiss was slow, thorough and though devouringly potent, also tender.

Her voice turned husky as she said, "What are we going to do about it?"

"What did you have in mind?"

She eased her fingers across his sex. "You think you're going to need that warm milk?"

His breath caught in his throat, then grew ragged. "Not any more. I think you're all the sleep-inducing agent I'm ever going to need."

She took his hand and brushed a kiss across the sensitive back. "I was hoping you'd say that."

The throbbing in his groin was almost painful now. "I'm your slave." He groaned.

She tugged at his hand. "Come, slave, and do the bidding of your monarch."

"Your wish is my command, oh queen."

CHAPTER TWENTY-TWO

"I think we need to have a meeting right away. This morning, if possible, Matt."

Toni chewed the inside of her cheek as she listened to Mack's phone conversation.

"Great. We'll be there. Thanks, Matt."

"What did he say?" Toni asked anxiously.

"We'll meet with him in about twenty minutes in his office. He has to be in court at eleven." Mack noticed her anguished expression. "Don't look like that."

"Like what?"

"Going to see Matt is just a necessary precaution."

"I know. Considering the speed with which things are moving, it looks like I'm seriously going to need your brother's expertise."

"I don't want to hear you talk like that."

"I'm sorry, Mack. I guess this is really beginning to get to me."

His smile was filled with love when he said, "You're only human. A situation like this would get to anybody. What you have to do is think positive and stay focused."

"You're right. I've been duly pumped up. Thank you, kind sir."

"My pleasure, ma'am," he drawled in his best Tommy Lee Jones imitation. "Now I think we'd better get a move on."

"I'm glad you came to see me," Matt said after listening to Toni and his brother. "You say this Warren character might possibly have in his possession something potentially volatile to use against Toni, Mack?"

"Yes," he answered worriedly. "We don't have any idea what's in that folder. I think he'll turn it over to the police just to hurt Toni and completely discredit her."

"Then we should be prepared for a call from Bob."

Mack had seen the way Toni tensed when Matt mentioned his friend's name. He knew she was remembering the last time Bob had arrested her. And the time before that when he'd had her under 'protective custody' in the hospital. "It seems inevitable, since he's the one who suggested we talk to you."

"Toni, is there anything else that I need to know?" Matt asked.

"No, nothing."

"I'll try to find out what I can." Matt glanced at his watch. "I've got to be in court in fifteen minutes. As soon as I know anything I'll call you." He looked at Toni. "You're still staying at Mack's, I take it?"

"Yes, she is," Mack answered and moved to usher Toni out of Matt's office.

Toni flashed Matt a smile of thanks as they left.

"What are you thinking, Toni?" Mack asked as he drove them back to his house.

"About what could be in that file, and why Bob hasn't contacted you about it."

"I was wondering the same thing—unless there's nothing incriminating in it, or Warren hasn't gone to him with it yet."

"He wouldn't pass up the chance to make me look guilty. Do you really believe there's anything in it that could implicate me?"

"I don't know. I guess we'll have to wait and see. I know it's not a very comforting thought."

"No. It isn't."

After dropping Toni off at his house, Mack decided to pay a visit to the police station.

"Mack!" Bob looked surprised when he walked in.

"I thought you'd be coming to see me, so I came to you first."

"We tried contacting Toni's father. And as you no doubt know, he's out of the country and we weren't able to talk with him because, in the tiny village where he and his wife are visiting, the telephone service leaves a lot to be desired. It may be days before he gets the message. Do you know when they're expected back?"

"I have no idea, a few weeks maybe."

"You want any coffee?" Bob asked. When Mack refused, he poured himself a cup and walked over to his desk and sat down. He pulled out a worksheet and cleared his throat.

"We have four people we are seriously considering as suspects who could have killed Frank Clifford. They all have reasons for killing the man. At first it was assumed that he died from gunshot wounds, but it was later discovered that he had died from an overdose of heart medication. The thing is, he didn't have a heart condition.

"Now let's go through a simple process of elimination. J. V. Townsend Jr., who is the president of Townsend's, happened to be out of town the night of the murder. That would seem to discount his involvement. The interesting thing about him is that he knew about his wife's affairs, and specifically the one she'd had with Frank Clifford. Although Clifford worked for Townsend, he didn't fire him, which is hard to believe.

"Next we have Nina Townsend, who is married to J. V. Townsend Jr., but is having an affair with Hank Warren who, like Frank Clifford, works for her husband's company. She'd also had an affair with Clifford. She claims to have been with Hank at his apartment at the time the murder was committed. The question is, how could she have gotten hold of the drug that killed Clifford?

"The third suspect, Hank Warren, works for Townsend's and was Frank Clifford's PA. Hank is vying for a promotion and is probably sleeping with the president's wife in hope of using that to his advantage. The question is, did Clifford find out about the affair between Hank and Nina? Did he use it as leverage over Hank? This could be a possible motive for Hank killing Clifford. But did Hank have access to the drug?

"The last suspect, Toni Carlton, who also works at Townsend's and claims to have overheard Frank Clifford plotting to frame her for embezzlement, thus ruining the career she prizes. Toni's father is a heart surgeon and she had access to the drug that killed Frank Clifford. She was found at the murder scene, along with a gun. She has no memory of the killing. The facts strongly point to her as the killer.

"Did she shoot him or did she poison him? Or both? Still, there is something here that doesn't add up."

"You're hunting for something that will prove conclusively who the killer is and you can't find it, right?"

Bob smiled and put the worksheet back in his desk drawer. "Why did you really come here, Mack?"

"I told you—"

"I know what you told me, and I don't buy it. You came to pump me for information. What do you want to know?"

The intercom buzzed before Mack could answer, and Bob picked up the phone.

"Yes. Send him in."

Grinning like a Cheshire cat, Hank Warren appeared in the open doorway. Underneath his arm he carried a file folder. "Jessup," he said pleasantly. "You decided to go to the police first, huh?"

"Why are you here, Warren?" Bob asked impatiently.

"I have something you might find interesting, Lieutenant. It concerns a mutual friend of mine and Jessup's and a company named ValueCorp International." He handed the folder to Bob.

Mack gritted his teeth. It was all he could do to keep from strangling the man.

"If looks could kill, hey Jessup?" Hank taunted.

"Don't push it, Warren," Mack snarled.

"Should I consider it as another one of your threats?"

"Have a seat, Warren, while I examine this," Bob instructed.

"I have to get back to the office, Lieutenant. If you need to ask me anything, I'll be there until six o'clock. After that you can find me at home." With one last triumphant smirk for Mack's benefit, he moved to leave the room.

Mack started after him, but restrained himself when he saw the challenge in Hank's eyes when he glanced back at him. The bastard was waiting for him to do something stupid. When he realized Mack wasn't going to rise to the bait, he left in a huff.

"You're finally learning to restrain that Latin-African temper of yours," Bob said in mock astonishment.

Mack ignored the jibe. "What have you got?"

"I think you have some idea what's in this folder. You came here to see if I already had it, didn't you? And if you could find out what it might have to do with a certain lady."

Mack stood taut, waiting for Bob to confirm his worst fears.

"You knew about ValueCorp International before you came here. You don't have to answer. I can see it in your face. You really should have told me about this, Mack."

"Are you going to tell me what's in it?"

"It's evidence, Mack. Only Toni's lawyer will be privy to the information contained in here."

"Matt will be in touch with you sometime today."

"I could haul you in here for suppressing information."

"Are you considering doing that, Bob?"

"No. But I warn you, Mack, I won't hesitate to come after you if I find out you've been attempting to obstruct justice."

"I wouldn't expect anything less from you, Bob."

"As long as we understand each other."

"We do." Mack knew his friend would do just as he said because he'd done so in the past. The thought revived the old pain of Linda Hutton's betrayal and his subsequent resignation from the police force.

Mack decided to go in to his office. But after only a few minutes, he found that he couldn't concentrate. He swiveled his chair around and gazed out the window.

"Need a friend?"

Mack swung his chair around and gave his brother a cursory smile.

"Your enthusiasm is staggering."

"I'm sorry, Marc. I have a lot on my mind."

"Lean on me, brother."

Mack laughed. "Like the song? I should have followed your advice."

"Am I hearing you right? My brother, the revered Mackinsey Jessup, considers his lowly associate's advice to be worth something!"

"Marc."

"What happened, Mack? Did Bob find out about ValueCorp International before you got around to telling him?"

"You guessed it."

"It's not like you to play the procrastinator, big brother. Is what's in there as damaging as we feared?"

"I don't know. Hank Warren produced the file on ValueCorp International. I have a feeling that there is definitely something incriminating in it because Bob wouldn't tell me anything. He'll only share the information with Toni's lawyer."

"And does she have one?"

"Matt."

Marc shrugged his shoulders. "Oh, then she's in good hands."

"The best. I needed to hear that. You do have your uses, don't you, baby brother?"

"Mack."

"Excuse me, my young apprentice." He grinned. "Is that better?"

Marc nodded his approval and smiled. Then his expression turned serious. "Things aren't looking too good for Toni, are they?"

Mack sighed. "Not at the moment."

"Be optimistic. Something will happen to turn things around."

"I hope so. I can't lose her, Marc."

As he sat on the love seat next to Toni in his living room observing his brother, Mack couldn't contain his impatience any longer. "What did you find out, Matt?"

His brother took another swallow of his coffee. "You still make the best cup of coffee in the family."

Mack rose from his seat. "Cut the bull, Matt."

Matt's eyes never left Toni's face. "Distribution papers were in the file."

Mack frowned. "What does that mean?"

"I'll tell you, Mack." Toni rose from the couch and walked over to the window. "As you know, when a sum of money or securities are withdrawn from a fund or, in this case, a holding company, and used by the beneficiary, in this case me, there are papers showing a pattern of liquidation. What it means is since I am technically the registered owner, the trail leads to me. Right, Matt?" she continued, not waiting for him to confirm it.

"I thought my stumbling onto the access code was a stroke of luck and I had uncovered Mr. Frank Clifford's plan. But it wasn't by accident; he meant for me to discover it. He evidently had disposed of just enough of the negotiable securities through this holding company and its subsidiaries that I supposedly own to incriminate me."

Toni turned away from the window to face them. "It was obviously one of the many signs he told me would surface before I was eventually convicted and sentenced to jail for embezzlement of company funds."

Mack didn't like the way Toni sounded. Her manner was emotionless, detached. She was tuning him out, keeping him from sharing her pain, not letting him help arrest her fears.

"He did it one better, though, don't you think? He inadvertently outdid himself by conveniently getting murdered and leaving me to suffer the consequences. Isn't that a joke?" She laughed.

"Toni—"

"Don't worry, Mack, I'm not cracking up. I'm too damned angry to let that happen. I intend to fight this any way I can. I refuse to let that monster win."

Mack walked toward her and took her in his arms. "That's my girl. For a moment I thought—"

"I know what you thought."

"Now can we please sit down and discuss this calmly?" Matt suggested. "I have a few questions that need answers."

Toni sat down beside Mack. "All right, Matt. What do you want to know?"

Matt took a file from his briefcase that had all the information he'd managed to get from the police and coroner's offices. "We know Frank Clifford didn't die from gunshot wounds, as was first believed. The coroner's report confirms this. He died from an overdose of a cardioplegic drug. He was not a heart patient, so how this substance got into his blood, and who put it there, is the real mystery.

"Toni's father is a retired heart surgeon. The possibility that she may have gained access to this drug prior to the murder is in question. We need to go over the night of the murder. Tell me everything you can remember, Toni. It says in the police report that you sustained a head injury and had to be taken to the hospital."

"That's true."

Matt switched on a tape recorder. "Start with when you decided to go see Clifford."

When she'd finished, Matt wrote down some things on his legal pad.

"You don't remember what happened after entering Clifford's apartment?"

"There are blanks I can't account for. The first thing I recall is hearing sirens and loud voices. It was as though I awakened on a movie set, and all the lights suddenly flashed on and the cameras started rolling and the action began to unfold. It all seemed so unreal. Frank Clifford lay dead on the floor, his chest covered with blood."

Matt arched a brow. "What about the gun?"

A distant searching look came into her eyes. It was as though what she sought was just beyond her reach, too elusive to grasp. "I don't know how it got there."

"And you haven't remembered anything else about what happened?"

She shook her head. "Not really, only bits and pieces that don't make any sense or connect."

Matt studied the police report. "In essence fifteen to thirty minutes can't be accounted for."

"That's about the size of it."

Matt frowned. "The time element could very well be the determining factor in this case since we're dealing with drug poisoning as well as a shooting."

"Couldn't Hank Warren or Nina Townsend have done it just as easily?" Toni asked.

"I intend to look into all the possibilities." Matt glanced at Mack. "Helping to run down those possibilities should give my brother plenty to do."

CHAPTER TWENTY-THREE

"What have you found out about Nina Townsend, Marc?" Mack asked his brother the next morning at his office.

"That she isn't the ditsy woman she'd have everyone believe. Mr. Townsend met her in the hospital when his father had a heart attack six years ago. And get this, she was working as a nurse's aide."

"And Townsend fell head over heels in love and married her. He tried to reform her, kind of like Professor Higgins did with Eliza Doolittle in My Fair Lady."

"But with no fairytale ending."

"It wasn't long before she started playing around on him," Mack said bitterly.

"Man, I know you were burned badly, but—"

"It's in the past, Marc," he tersely interrupted.

Marc frowned. "Is it? Have you really got all the pain and betrayal out of your system? Feelings are feelings, Mack. Can they truly be forgotten on demand? I don't think so."

"I've learned to put them in perspective."

"And if this miracle really did happen you have Toni to thank, right?"

"Yes, she's shown me a side of relationships I no longer believed existed." He cleared his throat. "Now, about Nina Townsend. Would she have knowledge of the drug you mentioned?"

"Yes, she would, considering that the cardiac floor was where she was assigned as a nurse's aide. It makes her as much a serious suspect as Toni."

Mack's brows furrowed in curiosity. "How did you find this out?"

"I talked with the Townsends' maid, Cara Benitez. I think she has a thing for her boss. She was more than a little eager to reveal all she knew about her employer."

Mack rubbed his chin between his thumb and forefinger. "I picked up on her dislike of Nina Townsend when Bob and I paid a visit to the mansion. You know what this means, don't you?"

"I know what it could mean."

"Maybe I should give Bob a call."

"Maybe it's Matt you should call first."

Mack glanced at his brother as if seeing him for the first time. "When did you become so smart?"

"I have you for a teacher. Don't you think it was inevitable that some of your best qualities would eventually rub off on me?"

Mack shook his head at the Jessup arrogance he saw gleaming on his brother's face.

Just as he reached for the phone to call Matt, it buzzed, and he picked it up.

"Matt! I was just going to call you."

"I need to see you and Toni in my office right away."

Mack's face molded into an alarmed frown. "What is it, Matt?"

"I can't explain it over the phone. I will when you get here."

"Matt, I—" He heard the dial tone. Mack snatched the phone away from his ear as though it were a snake that had sunk its fangs into him. A chilling foreboding slithered down his spine. He thought about Toni and all she'd gone through, and knew it was only the tip of the proverbial iceberg. He knew he couldn't shield her from whatever it was his brother had to tell them, but God, how he wished he could.

"I take it there's a break in the case?" Marc inquired.

"Yes, evidently," Mack answered grimly and rose from his chair, heading for the door. "Have Daffy organize my desk. The two of you can finish up."

"Consider it done."

As they drove in silence to Matt's office, Mack shot quick glances at Toni from the corner of his eye, wondering what was going through her head. Her expression had remained blank since he'd picked her up from the house to take her to Matt's office.

"The news doesn't necessarily have to be bad, Toni."

"I know what you're trying to do, Mack, but how can you expect me to believe that?"

"We don't know anything yet."

"How did Matt sound when he told you to bring me to his office?"

Mack hesitated.

"See, you have to admit that he didn't sound very optimistic."

"Here we are," he said, relieved to call a halt to the discussion. He didn't want to answer her because what she said mirrored his own feelings much too closely.

Matt met them personally at the door and ushered them into his office. His secretary had left for the day, he explained.

"All right, Matt," Mack said after he and Toni had taken a seat. "Let's have it."

"Cardioplegic drugs are commonly used by many heart surgeons during surgery to immobilize the heart."

"We already know that," Mack said impatiently. "I don't see—"

"Let me finish. It's also used in small doses by heart patients."

"Okay, Matt. Where are you going with this?" Mack groused.

"According to the crime lab's expert, Paul Norman, it takes from fifteen to thirty minutes for the drug Cyclocardia to be absorbed into the blood. It leaves behind chemical traces."

Mack plowed his fingers through his hair. "So?"

"Because of the time it takes the drug to circulate through the system to cause death and dissolve leaving only a trace is crucial. If Toni doesn't remember whether she got there before or after the shooting, you know what a D.A. could make out of that."

"Damn."

"Exactly, I couldn't have put it better myself."

"And we thought nothing else damning could possibly surface," Toni said quietly.

Matt grimaced. "That's not all."

Toni tensed, preparing herself to hear the worst.

"Norman has found identical chemical trace patterns in the DNA report of another person."

"Another person?" Mack shook his head. "What other person?" His brother had really lost him now.

"J. V. Townsend Sr."

"What?" Toni's eyes widened in shock. "But he died of natural causes from a stroke and a massive heart attack."

"Evidently not. According to Paul Norman—"

"I'm sick of hearing that guy's name," Mack growled.

"Mack, J. V. Townsend Sr. was evidently taking Cyclocardia for his heart. Paul Norman calculated the probable complications if a patient ingested more than his or her usual dosage. He discovered that it could simulate the symptoms of a massive heart attack and/or stroke."

"What are you trying to tell us, Matt?" Toni calmly asked.

"Townsend literally died in your arms, Toni. You were found cradling his head in your lap and later kneeling next to Clifford's body. Do I need to go on?"

"How did this Paul Norman discover the drug was a medication that Townsend took?" she asked.

"He got the information from both his doctor and the coroner's office. According to him, he studied Clifford's DNA report and realized that it resembled another DNA report he'd seen. Then he recalled where he'd seen it: Townsend's. And from there he—"

"Put two and two together," Mack muttered. "Which means that someone knew what an overdose could do to both Townsend, considering his heart condition, and Clifford, who didn't have one. This same someone knew how to adjust the dosages to fit their purpose. That takes a more than ordinary knowledge of the drug."

Matt took up the theme. "And since they both were Toni's bosses and she was having problems with both, and her father happens to be a heart surgeon, and she worked for him at one time, and her two bosses just happened to die within months of each other… Circumstantial though it may be, it's the kind of evidence the D. A.'s office will use to get a conviction against Toni. And add to that the embezzlement charges—do I need to elaborate?"

Toni said quietly. "No, you don't. What do you think will happen now?"

"Because Nina Townsend lived in the same house as her father-in-law she had access to his medication. She could have easily killed him and Clifford with it," Mack pointed out. "She had also been a nurse's aide in a cardiac unit."

"You're right there," Matt confirmed. "As I said before, those crucial fifteen to thirty minutes will most likely determine who is officially charged with committing the murders."

"You think it could be me!" Toni gasped.

"I'm not saying that. Any number of people could have done it. Which one is anybody's guess. We'll have to wait and see what the D.A.'s office will do next."

They didn't have long to wait, for almost as soon as Toni and Mack had arrived at his house and sat down to drink their coffee, the doorbell rang. Mack opened the door to see his friend. Bob entered the living room with a grim look on his face. Toni was sitting on the couch. The lieutenant walked toward her. Mack followed.

Bob turned to his friend. "I'm sorry, Mack." He cleared his throat and looked at Toni. "Antonia Carlton, I'm arresting you on suspicion of the murders of one Frank Clifford on November 25th and John Victor Townsend Sr. on August 6th."

Toni's cup rattled. She put it down and rose stiffly to her feet, listening in stunned disbelief as Mack's friend read her her rights.

When he'd finished she said simply, "I didn't kill Frank Clifford or Mr. Townsend, Bob."

"It's not for me to determine that, Toni. I'm only doing my job. Believe me, I don't like this any better than you do."

"Bob—" Mack's voice cracked.

"Mack, I can't tell you any more. You'd better call Matt." He turned to Toni. "If you come quietly, you'll make it easier on everyone. I'd hate to have to cuff you."

Toni looked to Mack. The plea in her frightened brown eyes tore at his heart and sliced his guts into ribbons.

He caressed her cheek. "Don't worry, baby. I'm coming right behind you, as soon as I call Matt."

"Mack, you're—" Bob started to object.

"I'm coming, Bob," Mack said flatly, leaving the lingering impression that he would do something rash if his friend objected.

Matt arrived at the police station minutes after Toni and Mack. He talked to Bob, then asked to be left alone with his client.

"If you think I'm going anywhere, forget it," Mack challenged his brother.

"Mack, I think you should—" Toni began.

"Don't make me have to escort you out of here." Bob's expression turned steely with intent as he and Mack exchanged glances.

Toni smiled at Mack and squeezed his hand. "Please. I'll be all right. If Matt feels that he needs to talk to me alone I'm sure he has a good reason for doing so."

"He better have." Mack glared at his brother, his look promising retribution. He then exited the room with Bob.

After going over everything, Toni cast a wistful glance at Matt. "Is there a chance a judge will grant me bail?"

"I'm not very optimistic about that. If a judge should grant you bail, it will probably be out of reach. But I'll do all I can for you, Toni. Now I have to confront my brother. Believe me, I'd rather face down an arena full of saber-toothed tigers and rattlesnakes."

Toni smiled wryly. "He can be a pretty formidable character, can't he?"

Matt returned the smile. "I see you know him well."

"I love him well," she said softly.

"Damn it, Matt," Mack roared once he and his brother arrived at Mack's house. "Why did you insist on talking to her alone? Did you tell her something you didn't want me to hear?"

"Of course I didn't. Will you please calm down? Cursing at me won't change anything. It certainly won't get Toni out of jail. We're going to have to work hard toward that end. You're the investigator in the family. And if you ever needed to use your expertise, now is the time, my brother."

"It's hard for me right now. All right? The woman I love is in jail for something she didn't do. And all I seem able to do is stand around and do nothing."

"All the more reason for you to pull yourself together and do what you've been trained to do."

"I know you're right, but the idea of leaving her in that place…"

Matt put a hand on his brother's shoulder and squeezed. "I can only imagine what you're going through. If it were Rachel, believe me, no way in hell would I be able to stay calm, rational and objective."

"When do you think you can get Toni a hearing?"

"I'm pushing for tomorrow morning, but the court calendar is jammed."

"What about Warren and the Townsend woman and what we know about her background?"

"Bob says he'll hand the information over to the D.A.'s office and bring her in for questioning. As for Warren, they can't prove anything against him, though he's still a person of interest in the investigation. Right now their main focus is on Toni. To them she has the strongest motive for committing the murders."

"Matt, Warren hated Frank Clifford's guts as much as anyone. And as for Nina Townsend, she could have been bored with Clifford and convinced Warren to help her take him out."

"That's all guesswork and may or may not be true, but we can't prove it. If you're going to save Toni, I believe you've got your work cut out for you."

After his brother had gone, Mack paced back and forth in his study, wracking his brain for answers. There was something so patently strange about this whole situation. If he could only find the glue to make this puzzle stick together.

Those critical fifteen to thirty minutes kept coming back to batter his mind without letup. They were the key, if he could only find the lock that it fit into.

CHAPTER TWENTY-FOUR

The tense, uncomfortable look that came into the Townsend housekeeper's face when she opened the door to Mack the next morning put him on the alert.

"Mrs. Townsend is asleep, Mr. Jessup," she informed him.

"I've come to talk to you, Cara. That is your name, isn't it?"

"Yes, sir." A look of wary curiosity suffused her face. "Why would you want to speak to me?"

Mack hadn't noticed the last time he was there how pronounced Cara's Spanish accent was. He cleared his throat. "Several things about the night Frank Clifford was murdered keep bothering me, and I thought you might be able to clear them up for me."

"If I can. I do not see how I can help you."

Mack smiled. "You would be surprised at what you know that you don't think you know. May I come in?" She opened the door. "Of course," she said, running her palms down the sides of her uniform before leading him into a nearby sitting room. "Can I get you some coffee?"

"No, thanks. You're a live-in housekeeper, aren't you, Cara?"

"Yes, sir."

"Mrs. Townsend said she came in well before midnight on the night of November 25th. Can you substantiate her claim?"

Mack noticed how the woman nervously bit into her lip and refused to look him in the eye. She was definitely hiding something. But what?

"I really do not remember the exact time she came in, Mr. Jessup. You see, I was half asleep."

"You didn't happen to glance at a bedside clock or anything when you heard her come in?"

"I do not remember. I—I…" Her voice faltered.

Ever tenacious, Mack plowed on. "Approximately what time did you get to sleep?"

"Eleven-thirty, I think."

"You were in your quarters at midnight then, right?"

She fidgeted with her hands. "Yes, sir."

The way she was acting alarmed Mack, and he couldn't say why he felt that way. It was as though she were attempting to keep from revealing something to him with her vague answers and her refusal to look directly at him.

"Did Mrs. Townsend ever come down and have breakfast with her husband?"

"Sometimes when he went into the office late. Why would you want to know this?"

"How about with her father-in-law?"

Her eyes widened. "Mr. Jessup, I do not—"

"Well, did she, Cara?" he asked, pointedly interrupting her.

"Yes, a few times when she came down he was having his morning coffee."

"Can you remember the last time?"

"No, sir, I cannot. Please, I—"

"Could it have been the morning he died?"

Cara's eyes seemed to grow even larger. Mack noticed the pulse fluttering in her throat.

"What are you trying to get her to tell you about me, Mr. Jessup?" Nina Townsend asked from the doorway.

"Mrs. Townsend." Mack smiled engagingly. "Maybe you can help us."

"I doubt that. What are you doing here, Mr. Jessup?" She demanded.

"Maybe I came to see you."

Nina smiled coyly. "You can leave, Cara. Oh, wait. Get me some coffee. Would you like some, Mr. Jessup?"

"All right."

"Bring a cup for our guest."

Mack watched the housekeeper, taking in her attempt to control her obvious dislike of Nina Townsend as she left the room.

"You're a very attractive man, Mr. Jessup," Nina purred. "Why are you checking up on my daily schedule? Did you have something, ah, in mind?" Her look was provocative.

Mack mentally gritted his teeth at the syrupy-sexy tone in her voice, the sensual movement of her body as she sauntered toward him. "You'd be interested if I did?"

"If I could believe it's what you really came here for."

"What other reason could I possibly have?"

"Oh, I don't know. To help your little girlfriend out of the trouble she's in, for one. I heard on the radio that she's been arrested on suspicion of murder. Maybe you can fill in a few of the details for me."

Mack realized how right his brother had been about this woman not being the dumb blonde she pretended.

"Well, Mr. Jessup?"

"I think I'll pass on the coffee after all. I have to go to my office. And by the way, I wouldn't begin to feel smug if I were you."

"And why shouldn't I? I'm not the one the police have in custody."

"Keep in mind they've arrested the wrong person."

Her brows arched in surprise. "And you think I'm the right one?" She laughed.

Mack shrugged his shoulders before leaving the room.

"I was on the right track, Matt, I'm sure of it," Mack exclaimed minutes after storming into his brother's office.

"How can you be sure the housekeeper remembered?"

"If you'd seen the look on her face you would have understood."

"Mack, you sure you're not over-projecting?"

"No way, Matt. My gut instinct tells me that Cara is more involved in this than she wants us to know. I've got to figure a way to get her to admit it."

"You have to be careful not to harass her."

"I know that, Matt. I'm not stupid. If what I have in mind works, I won't have to do anything."

Matt frowned. "What do you have in mind?"

Had she let her ambition bring her to this? Toni asked herself as she sat on the cot in her jail cell. She shared the cell with two rough-looking women. She hadn't killed anyone or stolen from Townsend's, and yet here she was in jail among criminals! Oh, God, how she wished...

What? her conscience taunted. *You were out of here? Dream on. The police and the D.A.'s office believe they have the guilty party: you. Why would they look any further?*

She heard the approach of the jail matron.

"All right, Carlton, follow me."

"What?"

"Follow me."

Were they letting her out? Her heart rate sped up when she was shown into a consultation room. Matt was waiting for her.

"Matt, what—"

He smiled. "Sit down, Toni."

She eased into the chair across from him.

"New information has surfaced."

Her mouth went dry and she laved her lips with her tongue. "What kind of information?"

"Let's just say it's enough to warrant releasing you."

Toni frowned. "But I thought—"

"You'll be getting out in a matter of hours."

"Matt, I don't understand. What about the embezzlement charges?"

"That isn't our main concern right now. Look, I'll explain everything once you're released. I promise."

As Toni was leaving the police station with Matt and Mack, a policeman was leading Nina Townsend inside.

"Mack, is she the one who killed Mr. Townsend and Frank Clifford?"

"The police think she might have killed her father-in-law after finding out she had morning coffee with him on the day he died. They think it's possible that she got some of his medication and slipped it into his coffee before he left for the office. If Townsend took his regular dose at the office, coupled with what he'd had at home, it would have been enough to cause a massive heart attack and/or stroke."

"But what about Frank Clifford?"

"She could have found a bottle of Townsend's medicine and dropped some into Clifford's coffee. As for her alibi, according to the housekeeper it had to be sometime around midnight when she got home. She isn't sure if it was before or after."

"Her poor husband. After all he's been through with her, and now to find out she might have killed his father…"

"Especially after claiming that he loved her so much he was willing to overlook her many affairs just to keep her. He probably won't waste any time getting her a good criminal attorney."

"You sound so unsympathetic to his problem, Mack."

"I've been there, done that."

"Oh, Mack."

"It's all right, Toni." He smiled, squeezing her hand. "You've helped me get over her."

"You sure?"

He kissed her. "I'm positive."

"I still can't remember what happened during those missing minutes," Toni said once she, Mack and Matt were all seated in Mack's living room.

"The killer doesn't know that," Mack answered.

"But isn't Nina Townsend the guilty party?"

"I don't believe she did it," he said, his expression thoughtful. "But if she did, she would have needed help."

"But, Mack—" She shot Matt a pleading glance. "Matt? Would one of you please explain what's going on?"

"We're going to arrange for certain people to find out that you are beginning to remember what happened that night."

"You know I haven't." She shook her head in confusion. "How can you arrange it?"

"Baby, leave it to us," Mack answered gently. "We have to flush out Nina's accomplice, if she has one. Or entrap the one who really committed the murders. Now do you see what direction we're going with this?"

"I'm beginning to. It's the only way to uncover the truth."

"You're going to move back into your apartment."

"But won't that seem strange, since I've been living at Mack's so long?"

"Not necessarily. We could let it slip that the relationship between you and Mack has cooled and you've decided to move back into your own place."

Toni cast a loving glance at Mack. "They would be dead wrong about that."

Mack returned the look with a smile. "Yes, they would."

A few days later when Mack stepped into the elevator at the Townsend building, Hank Warren, J. V. Townsend Jr. and Pat Davis were on it. He couldn't have asked for a more perfect setting, or audience, for his performance.

"Mack, how is Toni?" Pat asked. "I've meant to call her after I heard she'd been released and Nina was arrested." She glanced uncomfortably at Townsend and cleared her throat as the elevator moved down to the next floor.

"She's doing fine, I guess."

"You guess? Aren't you and she—I mean, she has been staying at your house."

"Not anymore."

"Since when?"

"Since she decided to move back into her own apartment." He made his voice sound as though it hurt to admit it to anyone. "Before she moved back she was beginning to remember things about the night of the murder."

"Do you think she'll remember everything?"

"Eventually. It's only a matter of time."

The elevator door opened and several other people got on.

"Did you and Toni have a fight? If you did, just give it time and you'll make up."

Mack shifted uncomfortably. "I don't think so. She—we've decided to end our relationship." He purposely looked away so he could observe the satisfied smirk on Hank Warren's face at his revelation. Mack felt like smashing his fist into it, but restrained himself. Barely.

The door opened on the street level to let some of the passengers off. As the elevator went down to the parking level, Mack studied the players in this scenario. Pat looked thoughtful as she moved in the direction of her car, where her husband stood waiting.

Townsend walked over to his car, his expression unreadable.

Mack wondered if he had even been listening to what was being said. He seemed to be in his own world.

The look on Hank Warren's face was anything but blank.

"So she finally wised up and kicked you to the curb, huh, Jessup, now that she doesn't need you anymore. Right?"

Mack's jaw twitched. "I wouldn't say anything else if I were you, Warren. It's not too late for you to join Nina. I think you and she are involved in the murders. And some way, somehow I'm going to prove it."

A sneer twisted Hank's facial features. "You can't prove something that isn't true, Jessup. We both know it was your, ah, ex-lover who really did the dirty deeds," he said before striding to his car.

The man was so cool and self-assured it made Mack's insides riot. Soon he would know the truth. So would everyone else.

CHAPTER TWENTY-FIVE

It felt strange being in her apartment again, Toni thought. It definitely didn't feel like home anymore. Mack and Marc had helped move her things back the day before. She wondered if Mack's plan would work.

Just as she measured out some coffee for the coffee maker, she heard the downstairs door buzzer.

She punched the com button. "Yes." Silence. "Is anyone there?" Still no answer. She shrugged her shoulders. It was probably someone who had the wrong apartment. All this waiting was getting to her. Mack could be all wrong and they wouldn't find the real culprit. Toni didn't want to believe that. The question was who they would catch in their trap, and when.

The phone rang.

"Toni."

A relieved smile spread across her face. "Mack."

"How's it going, baby?"

"I don't know. When do you think someone will make a move?"

"It shouldn't be long now. At least I'm hoping it won't."

"Suppose you're wrong and they don't take the bait."

"You can't think like that. You have to think positive, remember."

"I know, I'm sorry. It's just that all this waiting is nerve wracking."

"Believe me, I understand. Bob has a man posted across the street. You have the signal beeper if anyone tries to break in, don't you?"

"Yes."

"Hang in there, kid."

"Bogart?"

"I'll have to practice another one."

"You mean you actually practice?"

"Of course I do. Woman, you wound me to the quick. How else do you think I got so good? Good night, kid."

"Good night, you nut."

"Now is that any way to talk to the man who loves you?"

She curled her finger in the phone cord. "I do love you, Mack."

"I know."

"Han Solo?"

"No, Mackinsey Jessup. I love you, Toni."

The next morning Toni went downstairs to the laundry room. As she turned on the washer, she heard the door close and swung her head around. Comprehension dawned when she saw who was standing there with a gun in her hand and her back against the door.

"You! I would never have expected..." Toni blurted.

"It was all a trick." The woman moved away from the door and toward Toni. "You didn't really remember what happened."

"No. All I remember is that somebody hit me over the head. It was you, wasn't it? You shot Mr. Clifford, didn't you?"

"I had to."

"Why?"

"He was a disgusting man and earned the right to die as he did. He and Mrs. Townsend deserved each other."

"What are you planning to do?"

"I don't know now."

"What had you planned to do with me before?"

She pointed the gun at Toni. "Shut up and let me think."

The door opened and in walked Lieutenant Barnes. Mack followed him inside

"Put the gun down, Ms. Benitez. We heard everything. You can't get away, policemen are stationed outside. I'll take that," he said, holding out his hand for the gun.

"How did you guess it was me that shot Mr. Clifford?" Cara directed her question to Mack, but handed the gun to the lieutenant.

"You were too vague about the time you heard Mrs. Townsend come in. I figured it was because you had barely made it into the house before she did. I was right, wasn't I?"

"Yes." Cara let out a weary sigh. "I followed her to Mr. Clifford's condo. And when she left, I went in to talk to the bastard."

"Why would you do that?" Toni asked, puzzled.

"To convince him to take that bitch and leave John in peace. I knew you did not steal that money. I heard her telling him on the phone one night how they would get away with shifting the blame on you."

"So Nina was his partner."

"Yes, I think so."

"You're not sure?" Mack asked.

"It had to be Mr. Clifford. I did overhear her talking to him. Who else could it have been?"

"Yes, who else indeed?" A frown bracketed Mack's mouth.

"I still don't understand why you would care so much, unless—" Toni began.

"It was because of your boss, Townsend Jr. Wasn't it, Miss Benitez?" Mack asked.

"You're in love with Mr. Townsend!" Toni said, awed by the revelation.

"We all have our fantasies, our dreams," Cara answered. "Mr. Clifford insisted that I have a drink with him. When he turned his back to get it, I saw the perfect opportunity to escape, but he saw me and grabbed me. I saw the gun beneath a magazine on the coffee table and I reached for it. We fought for the gun and it went off. He pushed me away and clutched his chest. He was very angry and came after me. I shot him again."

"Did you kill John Townsend Sr.?"

Cara bowered her head and answered. "Yes."

"But why?" Toni asked. "What did he ever do to you?"

"He was so mean and so cruel to his son. He tried to make him look small because he is not this ruthless business animal he himself was. Every time I heard him berating John like that, I wanted to kill him. I care for John so much. His father knew this. He told me once that even though his daughter-in-law was a slut, at least she was a cut above being a lowly Mexican housekeeper with a green card. You have no idea how much I hated that old man."

Bob cleared his throat. "Are you ready to go down to the station, Ms. Benitez?"

"As ready as I will ever be, I guess." She said the last with a resigned sigh.

Toni watched in stunned silence as Bob led Cara Benitez away. "I think she really loves Mr. Townsend."

"So do I," Mack replied.

"Why are you looking like that?"

"Like what?"

"Like you walked out in the middle of a movie and are annoyed because you didn't see it from the beginning. It's over, Mack."

"I think Bob will be making an additional arrest," he said, drawing her into his arms. Let's go back upstairs to your place." He put an arm around her shoulders and started walking.

"Why should we want to do that?" Toni said mischievously.

Mack stopped walking and brought her in front of him and kissed her. The contact, as always, was so electric, and so exciting.

Mack groaned, not wanting to ever let her go. "This isn't the proper place for me to make love to you. I can't wait for you to move back in with me."

"Who says I'm going to? Living alone has a certain appeal."

"What kind of appeal?"

"Well, I—"

"I'm all ears." He waited. "See, you can't think of a reason because you know it doesn't exist."

"Oh, shut up."

"You're right. Action speaks louder than words. We can go to my place if you'd rather."

"That's all right. My place is closer."

At the sound of the telephone ringing early the next morning, Mack swam through layers of sleep to wake up and answer it.

"Who could be calling so early?" he grumbled, reaching for the receiver. "Yeah?" He sat bolt upright in the bed, waking Toni.

She frowned. "Who is it?"

"Shh. We'll be there as soon as we can. All right."

"Mack!"

"Get dressed."

"Aren't you going to explain?"

"Later. Hurry up and get dressed."

Mack drove in silence. Toni glanced at him, her eyes full of questions.

"Mack, where are we going?"

"To the police station."

"The police station!" But why unless…Toni wanted to insist that he tell her now, but seeing the set look on Mack's face, she resisted the urge to pursue it further. What was going on? Why were they on the way to the police station?

Mack pulled his car into the parking lot. He and Toni entered the building and headed for Lieutenant Barnes' office. Bob was waiting by the door and signaled them inside.

What was going on? Toni wondered. Mr. Townsend, Hank Warren, Nina and Cara Benitez were present.

"Mr. Townsend! I don't understand." Toni shot the lieutenant a baffled look.

"Have a seat. All will be made clear to you." Bob indicated two empty chairs around his desk for her and Mack.

"I demand to know what this is all about," Hank snapped.

"Coffee anyone?" the lieutenant offered.

"I'll have some." Townsend cleared his throat.

"Anyone else? No? Well, I guess we can get started then. I know you're all anxious to know why you're here."

"You arrested Cara. Since she's the killer," Nina pouted, "why can't I go?"

"We need answers to a few questions first."

"What questions?" Toni wanted to know.

"Patience, my dear Watson," Mack interjected.

"It's elementary," Toni answered absently. "Mack!"

He laughed. "Sherlock Holmes is one of my better imitations, don't you agree, Mr. Townsend?"

"Father said you were astute beyond the realm of normal investigation. It appears that he was right, doesn't it?"

Toni was bewildered. "Mack, I don't understand any of this."

Townsend quirked an eyebrow. "How did you guess, Jessup?"

"Your alibi for the night of the murder was too pat. But the thing that really put me onto you was your besotted husband act in the face of your wife's many affairs. I fell for that at first because of a past relationship I had that went sour. I sympathized with you up to a point. But when your wife was arrested on suspicion of killing your father and you appeared to be so forgiving and loving, it made me wonder. That long-suffering-love-in-the-face-of-everything act just didn't wash. It made me question your feelings for your father.

"I knew when I took the job you weren't anywhere near your father's equal as far as running the business is concerned. How did you find out your wife was in on the scheme to steal from Townsend Investments?"

He looked at Cara Benitez and smiled. "It was Cara. Nina had invited Hank Warren to our house when I was away on a business trip. She overheard my wife talking to Warren about their plans. To Nina, Cara was just a lowly housekeeper, a nobody, someone beneath her notice. With Nina it was always about money. So how better than to sleep with both Clifford and Warren, ensuring that she would get it either way the wind blew." He turned to his wife. "That is what you did, isn't it, Nina, my dear faithful, devoted wife?"

Nina squirmed in her chair and had the grace to look away.

"You knowingly let it continue!" Toni gasped in disbelief.

"For a time, until I was ready with plans of my own. She'd been drawing money from ValueCorp International for months using Ms. Carlton's name. You see, I found out Nina was part owner with Warren. Every time I laid down a clue that pointed to Clifford as the thief and Warren as his partner, either Clifford or Warren managed to outmaneuver me. I had the files reflect that Nina was the real owner of the holding companies."

"But it isn't what the file—" Hank stopped when he realized he was incriminating himself.

"Oh, Clifford changed it when he changed the password. I thought I could stay one jump ahead of him. But I was wrong. He was in charge all the way. He had my wife and my company exactly where he wanted them."

"Why did you make Hank CEO?" Toni asked.

"I had planned to reveal his duplicity with the ValueCorp file, but he got hold of it and changed the information. Because Clifford had been so clever in covering his tracks, it made it more difficult to spring my trap. The file only appeared again when you figured out the password. It was too late by then. I was stuck with him."

Toni glanced at a silent Cara. "She may have shot Clifford," she turned to Townsend, "but you killed him and your own father, didn't you, Mr. Townsend?"

Townsend swallowed and then coughed, covering his mouth. "Actually Cara didn't shoot Clifford, I did. I'll explain later. She was only trying to protect me. Now as for my father, from the time I was a little boy, my father told me I'd never be the man he was because I didn't have what it takes. He never failed to impress on me that I didn't have any guts. He was wrong about that, you know. I was determined to prove I had the brains to outwit him and make a life for myself apart from him and his company.

"He laughed at me. And when I told him I wanted to be a doctor, he looked at me as though I had lost my mind. He totally disregarded my desire to practice medicine. He saw to it that I didn't get into medical school. Finally I buckled and gave in to his will and majored in finance and administration.

"I hated it with a passion and he knew it, but he didn't care as long as he had someone to take over the reins when he stepped down." Townsend laughed again. "Stepped back is a more accurate description.

"Then I met my wife, Nina. I was enchanted by her sexuality for a time. My father tried to convince me not to marry her. I got a perverse pleasure out of going against him by marrying beneath a Townsend. Of course he never passed up an opportunity to parade his knowledge of her affairs before me. He thought to shame and humiliate me into getting rid of her. It just made me dig my heels in deeper."

"You hated your father that much?" Toni asked, shocked that he had ruined his life for revenge.

Townsend smiled and got up to pour himself another cup of coffee. "Oh, yes, I hated him all right. I decided to give him a dose of his own medicine, so to speak."

"You gave him more than one dose, though, didn't you, Townsend?" Mack prompted.

"You're quite right, Jessup. I knew he would take his medication at the office. I knew his routine by heart. So I slipped several of his pills into the morning coffee he always drank before he left for the office."

"So it wasn't Cara who put the pills into the coffee."

"No. I tried to convince her that it wasn't a fatal dose, but of course, she wouldn't believe me." He looked fondly at her. "She knows me too well, don't you, my Cara bonita?"

"John, I—"

"I don't understand why Cara didn't try to stop—" Toni began, but then figured out the reason. "It's because she's in love with you."

"We've been involved for over a year. My father walked in on us one night, as a matter of fact." Townsend gritted his teeth. "You know, he had the nerve to say she wasn't good enough for me after I told him that I loved her and intended to divorce Nina and marry her.

"My father threatened to ruin me if I divorced Nina, even though he knew the kind of slut she was."

Nina gasped.

He laughed at her. "Father said it was my punishment. I'd made my bed and I would damn well have to lie in it with you."

"But you continued your affair with Cara, didn't you?" Mack probed.

"Believe it or not, I love her, Jessup." He sighed wearily. "Do you have everything you need, Lieutenant?"

Bob nodded.

"You've been taking this all down, Lieutenant?" Townsend inquired.

"Every word, Mr. Townsend."

"Would you like to ask me some more questions?"

Toni sat there in momentary shock. Recovering quickly , she said, "The day Mr. Townsend died he tried to tell me how wrong he had been about something. He knew he was dying and he said he was sorry. At the time I didn't understand why he said those words. I realize now that he was sorry he had driven his own son to kill him."

Townsend laughed. "My father never regretted a decision in his life. He was always right and everyone else was wrong. Whether you knew it or not, he had great respect for you, Ms. Carlton. He said you were the kind of woman I should have married."

"You're wrong, he—"

"No. I wasn't wrong. He was going to make you a proposition the day he died."

"What kind of proposition?"

"He was going to make you director, and then eventually the first woman CEO of Townsend's. He said you had guts and ambition."

"What?"

"Frank Clifford suspected it after talking with my father. He knew he was on the way out. That's why he started setting you up in earnest. I let him because it was—"

"A way of getting back at your father," Mack finished.

"Very good, Jessup. When I decided to hire you, I was sure you would uncover Clifford's master plan." He glanced at Toni. "The one thing I hadn't counted on was that Jessup would fall for you, Ms. Carlton."

"What made you kill Clifford, and how did you manage it?" Lieutenant Barnes asked. "You were booked on Flight 233 to Seattle the night of the murder."

"You're right, I was."

"I checked and you picked up the ticket on time."

"Someone picked up the ticket, but it wasn't me. I met and talked to a man who needed to catch that particular flight to connect with one scheduled to leave Seattle early the next morning. So we traded tickets.

"His flight didn't leave until midnight. I knew that Nina and Warren intended to see Clifford so they could get their share of the money from the sale of the securities. They were going to meet at Clifford's apartment at ten. But the slut had to have her young stud service her first." He glared at Hank. "It gave me all the time I needed. When I went to see Clifford, it was with a purpose in mind."

"You intended to kill him and make it look like he had a massive heart attack." Mack supplied.

"I didn't know that Cara had overheard Nina talking to Warren about stealing from the company, and thought it was Clifford and would go there and confront him. I had a drink with the bastard."

"That was when you conveniently dropped a few of the pills into his glass, didn't you?"

"Dissolved in alcohol or something hot the drug breaks down faster. I knew he would be dead within thirty minutes. I looked out the window and saw Nina and Warren getting out of the car. I told Clifford I had to go, and then quickly left out the back way to where my car was parked. Clifford had a smug smile on his face when I left him. He knew I wouldn't say anything about his part in embezzling the securities because he thought I was in love with my wife. He thought I would want to avoid the scandal."

"Little did he know that you literally couldn't wait to be rid of her."

"Right, Jessup. I drove around to the front, and parked a little ways up the block. I wanted to make sure that Nina and Warren were still there because I intended to call the police. As I started to punch in the number to the police station, I saw Nina and Warren leave the building. As I watched them get into the car, I saw my plan for them go down the drain. I was getting ready to leave when I saw Cara heading up the walkway. I got out of my car and followed her inside. The door to Clifford's place was ajar and I heard him talking to Cara and waving a gun at her. She picked up a vase and threw at him and he dropped the gun. As Cara was reaching for it, I burst into the room and took it from her. I told Cara to go. She didn't want to, but I insisted. Clifford came at me and we struggled with the gun and it went off."

Townsend glared at Mack. "You really suckered me in with that ploy about Ms. Carlton's memory returning. I confided what you told me to Cara." Townsend glanced at Toni. "I had intended to take care of you somehow, but Cara was one step ahead of me and got caught in your trap. I couldn't let her pay for what I had done." His speech began to slur.

Awareness struck Mack and he grabbed the cup of coffee out of Townsend's hand. "Bob, call the paramedics."

"You're too late this time, Jessup." Townsend smiled triumphantly.

"Mack! He didn't—" Toni cried.

"There's nothing we can do. He's taken a massive dose of Cyclocardia. Haven't you, Townsend?"

"It's over for me, but Cara has a chance. And so do you, Ms. Carlton." He shifted his gaze to Nina's shocked face. "The only thing I regret is that I won't be taking you with me, you bitch." Townsend began to choke. "Don't look so horrified, Ms. Carlton. We all have to go some-time."

The choking stopped and Townsend slid to the floor. He was dead before he touched it.

EPILOGUE

"Mr. Townsend's cousin will be taking over the company," Toni said to Mack as they relaxed in his living room several weeks later.

"Where will that leave you?"

"The board decided to abide by the senior Townsend's wish to make me a director, and then when I've gained enough experience, CEO. Once Hank's name came out as one of the owners of ValueCorp International, that ended his term as CEO."

"Marc ferreted out the truth about how he changed the report to implicate you. The embezzlement charge against Warren is one that will stick. He's going to jail."

"What about Cara? I feel so sorry for her."

"According to Matt, she won't have to do any time. Townsend's confession ensured that."

"What will she do now?"

"Townsend made sure she was financially set for life."

"I still find it hard to believe that he actually killed his own father."

"Hate makes people do things totally out of character. Or maybe it draws out a person's true colors."

"All I want to think about right now is you, Mr. Jessup."

"Sounds good to me."

"No imitation?"

"Not this time. I intend to enjoy being myself, the lover, future husband and father to the seven kids I plan for you to present me with."

"So all you want to do is keep me barefoot and pregnant. And I said you didn't have one chauvinist bone in your body."

"Gotcha."

Toni slipped her arms around his neck. "I've got you, Mackinsey Jessup, right where I want you."

He kissed her, then raised his mouth from hers and gazed into her eyes and said, "Right where I want to be forever. I wouldn't have it any other way."

ABOUT THE AUTHOR

Beverly Clark is one of Genesis' original Indigo authors. Her previous titles include *Yesterday is Gone, A Love to Cherish, The Price of Love* and *Bound by Love.* Beverly was born in Oklahoma and now resides in Southern California. She has extensively written for national publications, including over 100 short story romances for Sterling/MacFadden Magazines.

Coming in March from Genesis Press...

SWEET SENSATIONS

BY

GWYNETH BOLTON

PROLOGUE

"Superwoman"
That's right, I turn 'em out
You know my style
Rack 'em, stack 'em
Watch my money pile
Turn 'em out, that's the name of this tune
Chick so fly, make all the dudes swoon
Gear so fresh, all the girls throw shade
They mad and stuff 'cause they know I'm paid...

With the music blasting in her SUV, Deidre couldn't help singing along. She didn't usually ride down the street pumping her own music, but then every night wasn't like the night she'd just experienced. She'd had a chance to make things right and had blown it, big time. Listening to the remake of her past hit and singing along with it had an almost soothing effect.

THE PERFECT FRAME

Deidre "Sweet Dee" James had just gotten off of the plane from Miami where she'd performed for the first time in eleven years. The performance had gone well. After years away from hip-hop, it amazed her that she was still able to grab a microphone and rock a crowd with such ease. There were other parts of the evening that she could have done without, however, and they all had to do with running into her ex, Fredrick "Flex" Towns III.

Seeing him up close and in the flesh again after all that time had shaken her more than she'd thought it would. Seeing him with a young hoochie mama bothered her more than she cared to admit. It had been all she could do to maintain her smile and cool demeanor with her insides churning and her heart pumping furiously. He looked good. The years had certainly been kind to him. She told herself that she shouldn't get jealous of the fact that he had moved on. Things had ended for them a long time ago and she was the one who'd called it off. But telling herself and making her heart listen were two very different things. The fact was that Flex Towns would always touch the deepest part of her. Coming back into the limelight had been a mistake, a big mistake. The only thing she could do to salvage things was dive back into her reclusive life and hope that none of her students at the community college had seen her performing on the *Source Awards*.

She should have known better than to participate. Turning the volume down several notches when she pulled onto her street, she sighed. Back in Minneapolis where she belonged, she was going to put Flex Towns, Sweet Dee, and her past behind her, for good this time.

It's for the best. You can't change the past. Everything happens for a reason. You made your bed, now lie in it. The series of clichés ran through her mind, and not one of them made her feel any better.

She drove down the alley in back of her home, pushed the button for her detached garage, parked and got out. It was nice to be back to a life of relative obscurity. Deidre opened the door to the cottage-style home she shared with her ten-year-old daughter.

254

It wasn't elaborate, but it was home. The white stucco house with green shutters and trim had caught her eye five years ago when she got tired of renting and wanted a more secure home for her child. Although it was small with only two bedrooms, one and a half baths, dining room, living room, den, and eat-in kitchen, the hardwood floors and built-in bookshelves had stolen her heart. The older home made her feel cozy and safe and she needed to feel that. "Mommy, I missed you so much." Her beautiful brown-skinned child with deep-chocolate eyes ran into her arms and gave her a giant hug. Kayla had on her pajamas and a night-scarf around her braided hair, but the vibrant smile and expectant glow in her eyes showed that she was nowhere near ready for sleep. "Kayla, what are you still doing up?" Deidre hugged Kayla and tried to put a sternness that she didn't feel into her voice. Holding her child in her arms made it hard for her to feel anything but joy.

Seeing her made Deidre realize all the more why she was no longer involved with the life she'd left behind. Besides how dangerous the world of hip-hop had become, she would miss Kayla terribly if she had to go on the road all the time. "Grandma said I could stay up and watch you perform with Lil' Niece and Sexy T on the *Source Awards*. Then she said I could wait up for you because I wanted to tell you how great you were. You looked so pretty, Mommy. I can't wait until I'm a big rap star like Lil' Niece!" Deidre looked up and caught Lana James's eye. Since retiring from her job as a high school English teacher, Lana came from New Jersey to visit them more than she stayed home. The doting grandmother knew full well that Deidre didn't like Kayla listening to Lil' Niece and Sexy T.

Looking at Lana James was for Deidre almost like peering into a mirror and seeing how she might look in the future. She and the older woman shared the same golden-honey complexion, the same light brown eyes with flecks of gold that looked like tiger-eye stones, and the same sandy-brown hair with almost blonde highlights. Although Lana was a few inches shorter and a couple of sizes bigger than Deidre's size eight, the resemblance between mother and daughter was striking.

Deidre gave her mother an irritated stare. "Mom, it's so late. You know it's past her bedtime." *And you know she has no business watching a hip-hop awards show,* she added in her thoughts.

Deidre didn't even let her child listen to her own old rap recordings from the nineties. Kayla and her friend Lily thought they were going to be the first little girl rappers to make it big. As far as Deidre was concerned, her child would never be a rapper. If she did become one, it would be as an adult. "The child wanted to see her mother perform, and I wanted to see my baby perform also. Besides, she doesn't have school tomorrow. You were great, by the way." Lana walked over and gave Deidre a hug. "Thanks, Mom, but you know I don't want Kayla listening to some of that stuff. She shouldn't even be listening to 'Turn 'em Out.' " It was hard trying to raise a girl who clearly loved hip-hop culture and rap music as much as she had when she was growing up. Deidre had never thought she would turn into the moral police and criticize the culture and the music, but some of the things she heard on the radio made her cringe. She did her best to filter and control what Kayla was allowed to listen to. Lana waved her arm dismissively and shrugged. "Please, she's going hear it with her friends or outside anyway. I say listen to it with her and then talk with her about it." Deidre shook her head and thought, *This from the lady who wouldn't let me listen to Run DMC in the house. Good grief.* It never ceased to amaze her how laid back Lana had become now that Deidre was the one trying to raise a child. Then she smiled and patted her own daughter on the head.

She was more than happy to stick to her life as Deidre James, single mother and community college writing instructor and leave Sweet Dee behind. It really was for the best. Deidre sighed. "Okay, young lady, you got a chance to stay up way past your bedtime, but now it's time for you to go to sleep. Go to your room and I'll be right there to tuck you in."Kayla pouted and put on a pleading face. "Oh, but I wanted to stay up hear all about the famous people you saw tonight."

"I'll tell you later. Bed. Now."

"Oh, okay." Kayla gave her grandmother a hug and a kiss. "Thanks for letting me stay up, Grandmommy." "You're welcome, sweetie pie, you're welcome. Thanks for keeping me company." Lana smiled and held Kayla extra tightly.

Deidre shook her head as she placed her hand on her daughter's back and walked her to her bedroom. Turning, Deidre found her mother staring at her. Although the expression on Lana's face said she wanted to talk, talking was the last thing Deidre wanted to do. She'd had her chance to talk with Flex and had let it pass. Rehashing the night's events with Lana wouldn't change a thing. Hoping that Lana would put off her inquisition until the morning, Deidre yawned and stretched. "It's late, Mom. Shouldn't you be hitting the sack also?" "Well, I was just wondering if you saw Flex tonight. Did you get a chance to talk with him?" Lana James simply leaned against the wall.

I knew she wanted to talk about that. Maybe I should try getting a job as one of those telephone psychics, Deidre thought wryly. She'd really hoped that the woman would have the decency to wait until the morning to try to squeeze her for information."Oh, I saw Flex with one of his hoochies and I said hello and goodbye. That was the extent of anything I had to say to him." She feigned nonchalance, but inside she was feeling things that she couldn't name.

Really, she thought, *what was I going to say to the man? Hey, Flex, listen. You remember when we were in love all those years ago and I broke it off? Well there's something I've been meaning to tell you...*

Flex was not the same man she'd left all those years ago. In fact he hadn't been the same man since she'd left him. She'd lost track of all the beautiful models she'd seen him with in magazines and on television since he went from Flex the deejay for The Real Deal to Flex, super producer and record label owner. A man of money and power, his life held all the trappings that went along with it. Sure that he had long since removed her or anything she might have meant to him from his heart, Deidre turned to face her mother.Lana's eyes held the unspoken questions that mother and daughter had argued over and disagreed about for a while and Deidre was in no mood to go there.Deidre shrugged. "Mom, things are fine the way they are. I've left that life behind me. Attending that awards show tonight just let me know that I made the right decision leaving that madness.""But—" The elder James woman was about to sing the same tune about Flex but Deidre didn't want to hear it. "Trust me, Mom, everything is for the best." She'd told herself that so much that she almost believed it. The truth was, she didn't know. That was a part of the problem. She didn't know, and she didn't have the guts to find out for sure.Lana shot Deidre an all too knowing look, the kind that made her feel as if she were fourteen again and had just been caught lying about cutting school to hang out at the mall.

"Is it really for the best, or are you making it easy for your-self?"Leaning against the closet door, Deidre let out a sigh. "Ma, I don't want to talk about this now. Please, let's just agree to disagree and give it a rest." "Deidre, every man is not like your father. Even he is not the same man he used to be. You can't keep running away because you're scared that you're going to end up like us—"

Lana's eyes took on a sad expression that pierced Deidre's heart. She had to stop the conversation before they ended up bringing out old skeletons that Deidre was determined should stay in the closet. She couldn't do it, not after just seeing Flex again. "Mom, I said I don't want to talk about this. Please, go to bed. I'm fine. Kayla's fine. She has us. We're all she needs. I'm going to bed."Deidre peeped into her daughter's room. Kayla was fast asleep. It hadn't taken her long at all to drift off. Kayla was her heart and Deidre didn't want to lose her. It was too late to tell

Flex—too late to start up that particular drama again. She had gotten herself out of that life and she just had to make sure that she stayed out. Things were going to be fine. She'd taken care of herself and her child for ten years and she would continue to do so.

THE PERFECT FRAME

2007 Publication Schedule

January

Corporate Seduction
A.C. Arthur
ISBN-13: 978-1-58571-238-0
ISBN-10: 1-58571-238-8
$9.95

A Taste of Temptation
Reneé Alexis
ISBN-13: 978-1-58571-207-6
ISBN-10: 1-58571-207-8
$9.95

February

The Perfect Frame
Beverly Clark
ISBN-13: 978-1-58571-240-3
ISBN-10: 1-58571-240-X
$9.95

Ebony Angel
Deatri King-Bey
ISBN-13: 978-1-58571-239-7
ISBN-10: 1-58571-239-6
$9.95

March

Sweet Sensations
Gwendolyn Bolton
ISBN-13: 978-1-58571-206-9
ISBN-10: 1-58571-206-X
$9.95

Crush
Crystal Hubbard
ISBN-13: 978-1-58571-243-4
ISBN-10: 1-58571-243-4
$9.95

April

Secret Thunder
Annetta P. Lee
ISBN-13: 978-1-58571-204-5
ISBN-10: 1-58571-204-3
$9.95

Blood Seduction
J.M. Jeffries
ISBN-13: 978-1-58571-237-3
ISBN-10: 1-58571-237-X
$9.95

May

Lies Too Long
Pamela Ridley
ISBN-13: 978-1-58571-246-5
ISBN-10: 1-58571-246-9
$13.95

Two Sides to Every Story
Dyanne Davis
ISBN-13: 978-1-58571-248-9
ISBN-10: 1-58571-248-5
$9.95

June

One of These Days
Michele Sudler
ISBN-13: 978-1-58571-249-6
ISBN-10: 1-58571-249-3
$9.95

Who's That Lady
Andrea Jackson
ISBN-13: 978-1-58571-190-1
ISBN-10: 1-58571-190-X
$9.95

2007 Publication Schedule (continued)

July

Heart of the Phoenix
A.C. Arthur
ISBN-13: 978-1-58571-242-7
ISBN-10: 1-58571-242-6
$9.95

Do Over
Jaci Kenney
ISBN-13: 978-1-58571-241-0
ISBN-10: 1-58571-241-8
$9.95

It's Not Over Yet
J.J. Michael
ISBN-13: 978-1-58571-245-8
ISBN-10: 1-58571-245-0
$9.95

August

The Fires Within
Beverly Clark
ISBN-13: 978-1-58571-244-1
ISBN-10: 1-58571-244-2
$9.95

Stolen Kisses
Dominiqua Douglas
ISBN-13: 978-1-58571-247-2
ISBN-10: 1-58571-247-7
$9.95

September

Small Whispers
Annetta P. Lee
ISBN-13: 978-158571-251-9
ISBN-10: 1-58571-251-5
$6.99

Always You
Crystal Hubbard
ISBN-13: 978-158571-252-6
ISBN-10: 1-58571-252-3
$6.99

October

Not His Type
Chamein Canton
ISBN-13: 978-158571-253-3
ISBN-10: 1-58571-253-1
$6.99

Many Shades of Gray
Dyanne Davis
ISBN-13: 978-158571-254-0
ISBN-10: 1-58571-254-X
$6.99

November

When I'm With You
LaConnie Taylor-Jones
ISBN-13: 978-158571-250-2
ISBN-10: 1-58571-250-7
$6.99

The Mission
Pamela Leigh Starr
ISBN-13: 978-158571-255-7
ISBN-10: 1-58571-255-8
$6.99

December

One in A Million
Barbara Keaton
ISBN-13: 978-158571-257-1
ISBN-10: 1-58571-257-4
$6.99

The Foursome
Celya Bowers
ISBN-13: 978-158571-256-4
ISBN-10: 1-58571-256-6
$6.99

Other Genesis Press, Inc. Titles

A Dangerous Deception	J.M. Jeffries	$8.95
A Dangerous Love	J.M. Jeffries	$8.95
A Dangerous Obsession	J.M. Jeffries	$8.95
A Dangerous Woman	J.M. Jeffries	$9.95
A Dead Man Speaks	Lisa Jones Johnson	$12.95
A Drummer's Beat to Mend	Kei Swanson	$9.95
A Happy Life	Charlotte Harris	$9.95
A Heart's Awakening	Veronica Parker	$9.95
A Lark on the Wing	Phyliss Hamilton	$9.95
A Love of Her Own	Cheris F. Hodges	$9.95
A Love to Cherish	Beverly Clark	$8.95
A Lover's Legacy	Veronica Parker	$9.95
A Pefect Place to Pray	I.L. Goodwin	$12.95
A Risk of Rain	Dar Tomlinson	$8.95
A Twist of Fate	Beverly Clark	$8.95
A Will to Love	Angie Daniels	$9.95
Acquisitions	Kimberley White	$8.95
Across	Carol Payne	$12.95
After the Vows	Leslie Esdaile	$10.95
(Summer Anthology)	T.T. Henderson	
	Jacqueline Thomas	
Again My Love	Kayla Perrin	$10.95
Against the Wind	Gwynne Forster	$8.95
All I Ask	Barbara Keaton	$8.95
Ambrosia	T.T. Henderson	$8.95
An Unfinished Love Affair	Barbara Keaton	$8.95
And Then Came You	Dorothy Elizabeth Love	$8.95
Angel's Paradise	Janice Angelique	$9.95
At Last	Lisa G. Riley	$8.95
Best of Friends	Natalie Dunbar	$8.95
Between Tears	Pamela Ridley	$12.95
Beyond the Rapture	Beverly Clark	$9.95
Blaze	Barbara Keaton	$9.95

Other Genesis Press, Inc. Titles (continued)

Blood Lust	J. M. Jeffries	$9.95
Bodyguard	Andrea Jackson	$9.95
Boss of Me	Diana Nyad	$8.95
Bound by Love	Beverly Clark	$8.95
Breeze	Robin Hampton Allen	$10.95
Broken	Dar Tomlinson	$24.95
The Business of Love	Cheris Hodges	$9.95
By Design	Barbara Keaton	$8.95
Cajun Heat	Charlene Berry	$8.95
Careless Whispers	Rochelle Alers	$8.95
Cats & Other Tales	Marilyn Wagner	$8.95
Caught in a Trap	Andre Michelle	$8.95
Caught Up In the Rapture	Lisa G. Riley	$9.95
Cautious Heart	Cheris F Hodges	$8.95
Caught Up	Deatri King Bey	$12.95
Chances	Pamela Leigh Starr	$8.95
Cherish the Flame	Beverly Clark	$8.95
Class Reunion	Irma Jenkins/John Brown	$12.95
Code Name: Diva	J.M. Jeffries	$9.95
Conquering Dr. Wexler's Heart	Kimberley White	$9.95
Cricket's Serenade	Carolita Blythe	$12.95
Crossing Paths, Tempting Memories	Dorothy Elizabeth Love	$9.95
Cupid	Barbara Keaton	$9.95
Cypress Whisperings	Phyllis Hamilton	$8.95
Dark Embrace	Crystal Wilson Harris	$8.95
Dark Storm Rising	Chinelu Moore	$10.95
Daughter of the Wind	Joan Xian	$8.95
Deadly Sacrifice	Jack Kean	$22.95
Designer Passion	Dar Tomlinson	$8.95
Dreamtective	Liz Swados	$5.95
Ebony Butterfly II	Delilah Dawson	$14.95
Ebony Eyes	Kei Swanson	$9.95

Other Genesis Press, Inc. Titles (continued)

Echoes of Yesterday	Beverly Clark	$9.95
Eden's Garden	Elizabeth Rose	$8.95
Enchanted Desire	Wanda Y. Thomas	$9.95
Everlastin' Love	Gay G. Gunn	$8.95
Everlasting Moments	Dorothy Elizabeth Love	$8.95
Everything and More	Sinclair Lebeau	$8.95
Everything but Love	Natalie Dunbar	$8.95
Eve's Prescription	Edwina Martin Arnold	$8.95
Falling	Natalie Dunbar	$9.95
Fate	Pamela Leigh Starr	$8.95
Finding Isabella	A.J. Garrotto	$8.95
Forbidden Quest	Dar Tomlinson	$10.95
Forever Love	Wanda Thomas	$8.95
From the Ashes	Kathleen Suzanne	$8.95
	Jeanne Sumerix	
Gentle Yearning	Rochelle Alers	$10.95
Glory of Love	Sinclair LeBeau	$10.95
Go Gentle into that Good Night	Malcom Boyd	$12.95
Goldengroove	Mary Beth Craft	$16.95
Groove, Bang, and Jive	Steve Cannon	$8.99
Hand in Glove	Andrea Jackson	$9.95
Hard to Love	Kimberley White	$9.95
Hart & Soul	Angie Daniels	$8.95
Havana Sunrise	Kymberly Hunt	$9.95
Heartbeat	Stephanie Bedwell-Grime	$8.95
Hearts Remember	M. Loui Quezada	$8.95
Hidden Memories	Robin Allen	$10.95
Higher Ground	Leah Latimer	$19.95
Hitler, the War, and the Pope	Ronald Rychiak	$26.95
How to Write a Romance	Kathryn Falk	$18.95
I Married a Reclining Chair	Lisa M. Fuhs	$8.95
I'm Gonna Make You Love Me	Gwyneth Bolton	$9.95
Indigo After Dark Vol. I	Nia Dixon/Angelique	$10.95

Other Genesis Press, Inc. Titles (continued)

Indigo After Dark Vol. II	Dolores Bundy/Cole Riley	$10.95
Indigo After Dark Vol. III	Montana Blue/Coco Morena	$10.95
Indigo After Dark Vol. IV	Cassandra Colt/	$14.95
	Diana Richeaux	
Indigo After Dark Vol. V	Delilah Dawson	$14.95
Icie	Pamela Leigh Starr	$8.95
I'll Be Your Shelter	Giselle Carmichael	$8.95
I'll Paint a Sun	A.J. Garrotto	$9.95
Illusions	Pamela Leigh Starr	$8.95
Indiscretions	Donna Hill	$8.95
Intentional Mistakes	Michele Sudler	$9.95
Interlude	Donna Hill	$8.95
Intimate Intentions	Angie Daniels	$8.95
Ironic	Pamela Leigh Starr	$9.95
Jolie's Surrender	Edwina Martin-Arnold	$8.95
Kiss or Keep	Debra Phillips	$8.95
Lace	Giselle Carmichael	$9.95
Last Train to Memphis	Elsa Cook	$12.95
Lasting Valor	Ken Olsen	$24.95
Let's Get It On	Dyanne Davis	$9.95
Let Us Prey	Hunter Lundy	$25.95
Life Is Never As It Seems	J.J. Michael	$12.95
Lighter Shade of Brown	Vicki Andrews	$8.95
Love Always	Mildred E. Riley	$10.95
Love Doesn't Come Easy	Charlyne Dickerson	$8.95
Love in High Gear	Charlotte Roy	$9.95
Love Lasts Forever	Dominiqua Douglas	$9.95
Love Me Carefully	A.C. Arthur	$9.95
Love Unveiled	Gloria Greene	$10.95
Love's Deception	Charlene Berry	$10.95
Love's Destiny	M. Loui Quezada	$8.95
Mae's Promise	Melody Walcott	$8.95
Magnolia Sunset	Giselle Carmichael	$8.95

Other Genesis Press, Inc. Titles (continued)

Matters of Life and Death	Lesego Malepe, Ph.D.	$15.95
Meant to Be	Jeanne Sumerix	$8.95
Midnight Clear	Leslie Esdaile	$10.95
(Anthology)	Gwynne Forster	
	Carmen Green	
	Monica Jackson	
Midnight Magic	Gwynne Forster	$8.95
Midnight Peril	Vicki Andrews	$10.95
Misconceptions	Pamela Leigh Starr	$9.95
Misty Blue	Dyanne Davis	$9.95
Montgomery's Children	Richard Perry	$14.95
My Buffalo Soldier	Barbara B. K. Reeves	$8.95
Naked Soul	Gwynne Forster	$8.95
Next to Last Chance	Louisa Dixon	$24.95
Nights Over Egypt	Barbara Keaton	$9.95
No Apologies	Seressia Glass	$8.95
No Commitment Required	Seressia Glass	$8.95
No Ordinary Love	Angela Weaver	$9.95
No Regrets	Mildred E. Riley	$8.95
Notes When Summer Ends	Beverly Lauderdale	$12.95
Nowhere to Run	Gay G. Gunn	$10.95
O Bed! O Breakfast!	Rob Kuehnle	$14.95
Object of His Desire	A. C. Arthur	$8.95
Office Policy	A. C. Arthur	$9.95
Once in a Blue Moon	Dorianne Cole	$9.95
One Day at a Time	Bella McFarland	$8.95
Only You	Crystal Hubbard	$9.95
Outside Chance	Louisa Dixon	$24.95
Passion	T.T. Henderson	$10.95
Passion's Blood	Cherif Fortin	$22.95
Passion's Journey	Wanda Thomas	$8.95
Past Promises	Jahmel West	$8.95
Path of Fire	T.T. Henderson	$8.95

Other Genesis Press, Inc. Titles (continued)

Path of Thorns	Annetta P. Lee	$9.95
Peace Be Still	Colette Haywood	$12.95
Picture Perfect	Reon Carter	$8.95
Playing for Keeps	Stephanie Salinas	$8.95
Pride & Joi	Gay G. Gunn	$8.95
Promises to Keep	Alicia Wiggins	$8.95
Quiet Storm	Donna Hill	$10.95
Reckless Surrender	Rochelle Alers	$6.95
Red Polka Dot in a World of Plaid	Varian Johnson	$12.95
Rehoboth Road	Anita Ballard-Jones	$12.95
Reluctant Captive	Joyce Jackson	$8.95
Rendezvous with Fate	Jeanne Sumerix	$8.95
Revelations	Cheris F. Hodges	$8.95
Rise of the Phoenix	Kenneth Whetstone	$12.95
Rivers of the Soul	Leslie Esdaile	$8.95
Rock Star	Rosyln Hardy Holcomb	$9.95
Rocky Mountain Romance	Kathleen Suzanne	$8.95
Rooms of the Heart	Donna Hill	$8.95
Rough on Rats and Tough on Cats	Chris Parker	$12.95
Scent of Rain	Annetta P. Lee	$9.95
Second Chances at Love	Cheris Hodges	$9.95
Secret Library Vol. 1	Nina Sheridan	$18.95
Secret Library Vol. 2	Cassandra Colt	$8.95
Shades of Brown	Denise Becker	$8.95
Shades of Desire	Monica White	$8.95
Shadows in the Moonlight	Jeanne Sumerix	$8.95
Sin	Crystal Rhodes	$8.95
Sin and Surrender	J.M. Jeffries	$9.95
Sinful Intentions	Crystal Rhodes	$12.95
So Amazing	Sinclair LeBeau	$8.95
Somebody's Someone	Sinclair LeBeau	$8.95

THE PERFECT FRAME

Other Genesis Press, Inc. Titles (continued)

Someone to Love	Alicia Wiggins	$8.95
Song in the Park	Martin Brant	$15.95
Soul Eyes	Wayne L. Wilson	$12.95
Soul to Soul	Donna Hill	$8.95
Southern Comfort	J.M. Jeffries	$8.95
Still the Storm	Sharon Robinson	$8.95
Still Waters Run Deep	Leslie Esdaile	$8.95
Stories to Excite You	Anna Forrest/Divine	$14.95
Subtle Secrets	Wanda Y. Thomas	$8.95
Suddenly You	Crystal Hubbard	$9.95
Sweet Repercussions	Kimberley White	$9.95
Sweet Tomorrows	Kimberly White	$8.95
Taken by You	Dorothy Elizabeth Love	$9.95
Tattooed Tears	T. T. Henderson	$8.95
The Color Line	Lizzette Grayson Carter	$9.95
The Color of Trouble	Dyanne Davis	$8.95
The Disappearance of Allison Jones	Kayla Perrin	$5.95
The Honey Dipper's Legacy	Pannell-Allen	$14.95
The Joker's Love Tune	Sidney Rickman	$15.95
The Little Pretender	Barbara Cartland	$10.95
The Love We Had	Natalie Dunbar	$8.95
The Man Who Could Fly	Bob & Milana Beamon	$18.95
The Missing Link	Charlyne Dickerson	$8.95
The Price of Love	Sinclair LeBeau	$8.95
The Smoking Life	Ilene Barth	$29.95
The Words of the Pitcher	Kei Swanson	$8.95
Three Wishes	Seressia Glass	$8.95
Through the Fire	Seressia Glass	$9.95
Ties That Bind	Kathleen Suzanne	$8.95
Tiger Woods	Libby Hughes	$5.95
Time is of the Essence	Angie Daniels	$9.95
Timeless Devotion	Bella McFarland	$9.95
Tomorrow's Promise	Leslie Esdaile	$8.95

Truly Inseparable	Wanda Y. Thomas	$8.95
Unbreak My Heart	Dar Tomlinson	$8.95
Uncommon Prayer	Kenneth Swanson	$9.95
Unconditional	A.C. Arthur	$9.95
Unconditional Love	Alicia Wiggins	$8.95
Under the Cherry Moon	Christal Jordan-Mims	$12.95
Unearthing Passions	Elaine Sims	$9.95
Until Death Do Us Part	Susan Paul	$8.95
Vows of Passion	Bella McFarland	$9.95
Wedding Gown	Dyanne Davis	$8.95
What's Under Benjamin's Bed	Sandra Schaffer	$8.95
When Dreams Float	Dorothy Elizabeth Love	$8.95
Whispers in the Night	Dorothy Elizabeth Love	$8.95
Whispers in the Sand	LaFlorya Gauthier	$10.95
Wild Ravens	Altonya Washington	$9.95
Yesterday Is Gone	Beverly Clark	$10.95
Yesterday's Dreams, Tomorrow's Promises	Reon Laudat	$8.95
Your Precious Love	Sinclair LeBeau	$8.95

Order Form

Mail to: Genesis Press, Inc.
P.O. Box 101
Columbus, MS 39703

Name _____
Address _____
City/State _____ Zip _____
Telephone _____

Ship to (if different from above)
Name _____
Address _____
City/State _____ Zip _____
Telephone _____

Credit Card Information
Credit Card # _____ ☐ Visa   ☐ Mastercard
Expiration Date (mm/yy) _____ ☐ AmEx ☐ Discover

Qty.	Author	Title	Price	Total

Use this order form, or call 1-888-INDIGO-1

Total for books	_____
Shipping and handling: $5 first two books, $1 each additional book	_____
Total S & H	_____
Total amount enclosed	_____

Mississippi residents add 7% sales tax